# SEVEN MINUTES
## IN *Candyland*

# SEVEN MINUTES IN Candyland

## Brian Wasson

Quill Tree Books

An Imprint of HarperCollinsPublishers

Quill Tree Books is an imprint of HarperCollins Publishers.

Seven Minutes in Candyland
Copyright © 2023 by Brian Wasson
Library of Congress Control Number: 2023934445
ISBN 978-0-06-326465-6

Typography by Corina Lupp
23 24 25 26 27  LBC  5 4 3 2 1
First Edition

# SEVEN MINUTES
## IN *Candyland*

# One

**I like to** think of myself as a jack-of-all-treats, master of none.

*Oh, you need Reese's?* Got you!

*Kit Kat?* Sure thing, fam.

*Starburst, hold the reds?* Yeah, bro, I can work it out.

*Big League Chew, Bubble Tape, and Fun Dip?* Nostalgia costs extra, but I got a guy.

About that last one. I don't really "got a guy." But I definitely got a system. And it all runs out of an obscure tech ed storage closet.

I scan to my right and left to see if anyone's around before using my key to go in. The good thing about the career and technical education (CTE) hallway is that it's not heavily trafficked. And the good thing about this closet is only three people in the whole school have a key. Mr. Perkins a couple doors down, the head maintenance guy, and me.

I flick the light switch, and somehow one sixty-watt bulb scatters away most of the darkness. It's a humid, cramped space. Tiered shelves rise against cinder block, making it seem like the walls are closing in. Hidden behind the rows of sound engineering and electrical equipment is a product that encroaches on the space like some invasive, sugary species: Scores of neatly organized bags of candy line two shelves. Chocolate and chewies on the top shelf of the far and left walls, and hard candies, classics, and off-brand on the bottom shelf of the right wall.

It's my candy stash. And I know dozens of bags of this sweet stuff may seem like a lot, but my cache actually pales in comparison to what student government's got in their closet just across the hall.

I head to the left wall, top row, and pull down a set of speakers and an outdated UV tech hub. My hand stretches into the upper dark spot where the light can't reach, rooting around till I find the four bags of candy I'm looking for. Then I take out sheets of stationery paper, blank greeting cards, and a couple pens from my bookbag.

I sit on an old wooden stool, my back against the near wall, the only unshelved one in the room. I set my bag beside me and remove my laptop, pulling up my email. Three orders already this morning. I take a pen and a piece of sky-blue stationery and start to write.

DEAR ROBYN,
    WE'VE BEEN THROUGH A SOUR PATCH LATELY, BUT ALWAYS KNOW YOU'RE STILL MY SWEET-HEART.
LOVE,
BRYAN

I tape a bag of Sour Patch Kids and a small box of Sweethearts to the card and toss it in my bookbag. "Next," I mumble. This time, I pull out beige stationery and a purple glitter pen.

GEMMA,
    I COULD'VE SEARCHED THE ENTIRE MILKY WAY AND NOT FOUND ANYONE AS LOVING AS YOU.
MY EVERYTHING,
JULES

Disbelief flashes across my face. "You've been going out, like, three weeks," I say. I doubt they'll last another two, to be honest. But I learned quickly that opinions are bad for business, so I keep my mouth shut.

Pull tape. Attach candy bar to paper. Toss it in my bag. Next.

TREVOR,
    YOU BIG DUM-DUM! I SAW YOU KISSING THAT SHADY BITCH SARAH BEHIND THE TENNIS COURTS TUESDAY . . .

My mouth goes wide as I read the rest, which is NSFS—not safe for school. "Dude, you cheated on Capri Morgan?" I say, incredulous. Along with his Dum-Dums, I decide to tape on a mini Butterfinger, too, because he truly let a good one slip away.

This all might look shady, but it's absolutely legit.

Last year, as student council's freshman class rep, I made candygrams the time-honored, traditional way. You know, kids pay a dollar, I deliver one piece of candy along with whatever school-appropriate message the purchaser wanted to give.

But I'm an ideas man, not a delivery man. And student government, if nothing else, is painfully rigid, insistent on a business model as unimaginative as the chocolate Kisses they sell for Valentine's Day.

So I struck out on my own this past fall; guerrilla marketing through social media, undercutting student council's markups with my discounts and sales, and broadening the candy selection. They're as big as I'm small. But the dinosaurs were big, too. I've already begun clawing at their bottom line just a few months after starting. By this time next year, they'll be the Blockbuster to my Netflix. Yeah, they're pissed about it, but nothing in the school's handbook says students can't be capitalists, too.

Mom and Dad sure are. I got the entrepreneurial bug from them. They turned a joint psychologist practice into a wildly popular couples therapy podcast and YouTube channel that's pulling in thousands of dollars a week in sponsored content. If only *Right the 'Ship* could steer their own marriage clear of the rocks. . . .

I breathe a heavy sigh, shrug the thought away, and focus on my short-term goal. My make-or-break, monthlong sprint. I check my phone for the date: Wednesday, January 14. The way things are going—seven dollars from first-period sales—chances of hitting my goal in time for Valentine's Day are pretty slim.

Before I leave, I do what I've recently come to call my Spider-Man walk. I climb the shelves and peek behind all the equipment for a glancing inventory check. *Let's see. I need one bag of Skittles and a bag of Dove Chocolates* . . . This used to take twenty minutes and more than a few precarious balancing acts to complete. Now? Well, I named it after Spider-Man for a reason.

I get down and jot the list in my palm when I startle at the slow creak of a door hinge.

*Shit!* I'm busted.

I wheel around, a look of wide-eyed horror spanning my face. I fully expect Principal Urman, the vice principals, and the three school resource officers to burst in, referral slips drawn. Technically I'm not trespassing, but who in their right mind wouldn't see me hoarding candy bags just across from the closet where stu-gov keeps its war chest and *not* assume I'm a thief?

But it's not the admins. No security guards, either. Instead, this girl spirits in with the same stealth I did, looking back to see if anyone's watching.

I stand there awestruck as she backpedals past the threshold, recentering her gaze on her phone as she walks under the light. Brown skin, rich and smooth. Black curls dizzily spiraling down and draping her shoulders like a shawl. The kind of eyes that say more with just a look than most research papers can offer up in their entirety.

I know her. It's Sterling Glistern. The girl I've been crushing on since sixth grade, when we both went on that science club field trip to Marine World. Her friends bailed on her to get funnel cakes right before the dolphin encounter, so we sat and talked a whole eighteen minutes while waiting for the show to begin.

She's a volleyballer. Dance squad captain. All-around cheerful, happy-go-lucky person.

So why are her cheeks tear-stained?

I don't know what to do, so I just stand there. She shuts the door with the greatest of care. As soon as the latch clicks, her sobs begin. Heavy sobs—the kind with intermittent snorts breaking up the heaves. She cups her palms to her face. I think about walking up to her and reassuringly touching her shoulder, but then I think better. Best approach this with the utmost caution.

I'm just standing there, trying to suss out the least intrusive way to announce myself when she first notices something. Her palms slowly split and lower as she takes in the side wall. She creeps over, curiosity and amazement enlivening her eyes. She moves a piece of equipment to the side. Then another, then another, like she's peeling back layers of a Reese's Cup wrapper. Her eyes liven to the newly discovered trove of treats.

She bends a black infinity curl around her index finger and studies the rows. She pops her gum like her jaw was made to eat things alive.

I open my mouth. My lips move, but no words actually come. It takes a moment to corral what little courage I have in these scenarios with impossibly pretty girls. Scenarios I never actually hoped for outside of my dreams. I keep my sentence short and sweet.

"Stu-gov doesn't carry Snickers, but I do."

She turns, sees me, and screams. I jump back, knocking into a shelf. A loud clank sounds out as microphones roll off and hit the floor.

"Jesus! You're gonna get me found out!" I say, putting a finger to my lips. "Why are you in here?"

Sterling slaps both hands against the ride of her jeans. "I was—" She doesn't finish her thought, just flips the question: "Wait, why are *you* here?"

"I, um—"

I can't answer, either. Her eyes move to my midsection. She relaxes a little, her face clouded with uncertainty.

"Were you, you know . . ."

"No!"

"Because I wouldn't have told anyone. I mean, I'm all for diverse and liberal forms of sexual expression. And you do you! Um, pun *totally* not intended, of course."

"Wha— *No!*" I repeat, my voice more defensive than I want it to be.

"Well, if not that, then what?" she asks, wiping the dampness from her eyes.

I still don't say, but it's not long before she figures out the obvious.

"Wait, I know you," she says. "You're the kid who went all rogue on student government. Kalvin, right? The Candyman."

"Candy *Guy*," I correct. Candy*man* is a horror flick about a

Black guy gutting various white girls with a prosthetic hook. So not exactly great for branding here in the South.

"Hold up," she says, "didn't we both go to . . ."

"Marine World," I finish. "Dolphin encounter." I'm smiling in spite of myself. She remembers me.

Sterling nods. "Good times." She then moves more equipment. On a hunch, she switches walls and shoves more stuff aside. When she's done, at least a couple dozen candy bags are fully exposed. She backs toward the light again. "So this is your stash?" she asks, twirling like she's just discovered Atlantis. "How'd you even get this setup?"

"You know Mr. Runkelow, the old AV teacher?" I ask. "He started letting me clean it out last year for extra credit. Moving stuff around. Hauling things to the dumpster. Making sure dust isn't getting in the machines. Pretty soon, I started doing it so much, he just gave me a key. Eventually he forgot he'd given it to me, and summer rolled around and he . . ."

"Retired," she says, nodding. Her lips curve down as a quiet acknowledgment of my lucky circumstance. "Wait. There's a new guy in AV. Mr. Perkins."

"Yeah."

"You're not afraid of him discovering your hideout?"

"He did, actually," I reply. "Last year. We have an understanding, though."

The look she gives is heavy with skepticism. Finally she comes out with "So basically . . . you bribed him to keep quiet."

I nod. Her eyes return to the candy. "Wow, people would kill to know this was here. But kinda risky setting up shop so close to stu-gov, am I right?"

"Had to. Not like I could get my hands on other closet keys. Plus, I kinda like the rivalry aspect."

"I bet. . . . So all this is yours?"

"Yeah," I say. "You're not gonna tell, are you?"

"Dude, I'm totally cool," she says, laughing. "Not even gonna extort you for candy or anything." Her eyes settle on a top row behind me. I look back. A corner of the Snickers bag peeks over the ledge. She holds up pinched fingers. "Well, maybe, like . . . a little extortion?"

I shrug. "Have at it."

She slinks over, her reach coming up well short despite standing on tiptoes. She looks back at me, donning a shy smile. "Could you?"

I walk over and cut in front of her, climbing a row and grabbing the bag. She brushes a lock of hair from her face as I hop down. I shake out three tiny pieces into her palm. "So I'm helping *you* extort *me* because you're too short to do it yourself?"

"I'm not short, I'm 'fun-sized,'" she protests, popping one in her mouth and heading for the door. "Thanks, Kalvin." She touches the door handle before turning back. "How'd you know I liked Snickers?"

"You were just staring at them," I answer.

"No. Before that." She points. "I was staring at *this* wall, and you said stu-gov didn't carry them."

"Oh. Yeah. You know the candygram you got last week?"

9

"Yeah?"

"I made it. Stu-gov can't sell stuff with nuts. It's a liability thing. Food allergies and such. But *I* can sell them. Chadwick Boston, your, um, boyfriend, got yours from me."

"Screw Chadwick," she mumbles, spitting out his name as if it were a rotted pecan.

"Wait. Was he the reason you snuck in here?" I ask.

She looks at me blankly for a moment, every trace of the smile she wore just seconds ago disappearing, and I tense up, thinking I've overstepped. If my cheeks could blush red, they'd be on fire right now. But she doesn't shut me down, so I add a "Trouble in paradise?" very quietly, cautiously, like I'm dipping a foot into a cold pool.

Slowly she wanders back to the center of the room. To my surprise, she actually answers. In a pointed, sincere way that makes me think she's been wanting to talk about this for a while now. "You could say that."

"Are we talking cloudy skies or thunder and lightning here?"

Her hands interlock at the back of her neck, lifting her abundance of curls. Her eyebrows go up, and she offers a laugh that's both sad and dry. "Try tornado watch."

I'm really starting to feel for her now. From what I can tell, Sterling has the perfect life. Good looks. Status. Top-flight college prospects. But obviously she doesn't seem to think so.

"And that's why you're avoiding him?" I ask.

She nods. "Yeah. It's like, I'm angry . . ." Her fists clench. "But I'm also afraid."

"Afraid?"

"Afraid I'll blow it."

I don't respond, and we exist for a long while in this humid, unsettled silence. Strikingly, another tear slips down as she looks off to the side, shying her red-rimmed eyes from me.

She sniffs and says, "My friends don't miss a chance to tell me how lucky I am to be with him. And I'm so not the jealous type, but lately I've just been getting this way."

Something she said piques my interest. I remember how my parents approach these situations on their podcasts. *Questions are like fishing rods*, my dad always says. *Just keep asking. Eventually you'll catch the truth.*

I head to the near wall and drag the stool toward her. She sits. In turn, I fit my butt awkwardly into the shelf space in front of her.

"So you've never been jealous over previous boyfriends?" I ask.

Wait. Am I really gonna implement my parents' advice right now? Yeah, I know they have degrees in this stuff and thousands of hours of experience. But they're so old. So *parental*.

"No," she answers.

She *answered*. Only one word. Two letters. But it's something.

I cast the rod out again. "How many boyfriends have you had?"

"Why?"

"Just trying to get a sample size," I say.

Sterling looks back up as she wipes the tear. I watch as she works the math in her head. "Five since middle school."

"And you've only been jealous of one?"

"Correct."

"*This* one?"

"Correct again." She sighs, impatience nudging into her voice.

"So what about *him* activates the jealousy in you?"

The questions spill out like apples from a tipped barrel. This is what my parents do, not me. *Who am I right now?*

I notice the barely there spark in her eyes as she gulps down the significance of my question.

Then, hesitantly, she offers, "I noticed he'd been growing distant lately. A little cagey. Maybe even a little avoidant. Then one day I was playing around and grabbed his phone and saw a text from a number I didn't recognize. I mean, it wasn't suggestive or anything, and he says it's nothing but . . ." Her words trail off as she eats her second Snickers.

"But you think there could be something? That it's within his character?"

"I just . . ." Silence swallows her words, so I fill in the void.

"What'd the text say?" I ask.

She gets out her phone and thumbs a couple buttons. "I forwarded it to myself . . ." Her words come out slow and heavy, like they'd been soaked in molasses and guilt. She shows me. The number isn't saved as a contact, which is weird when reading the friendly nature of the text. But the actual words are pretty innocuous: *Hey, thanks for talking. Feeling better now,* with a winking emoji tacked on at the end. But if it's bothering her, there must be an underlying reason.

I look up at her. "Sterling, do you trust Chadwick?"

"Of course," she's quick to answer.

Almost too quick, I think. Too defensive to be genuine. My parents would say it's easier to go around a defense than through it and *Why the hell am I still strategizing as if I'm my parents?*

But what else would I say to her, really? What advice could *I* give, other than theirs?

*Around the defense, not through it*, I think to myself.

I take a deep breath and I rephrase my last question: "Sterling, is Chadwick trust*worthy*?"

Her mouth opens immediately, but no words come.

"There is a difference," I add. "You're biased toward trusting him, because you don't want the conflict. But I'm not. So I want you to do something."

"And that is?"

"Pretend you're on a safari."

"What?" she asks, a short burst of laughter pushing out with the word.

I shake my head. "No, I'm serious. For the next week or so, just observe Chadwick, like any tourist would. Watch how he looks, acts, and carries himself around you. But try to keep your emotional distance. Okay?"

It's quiet for a beat, and then she lets out a long "hmm" as she chews over my words and the chocolate. In time, she comes out with "That's really good."

"Thank you."

She stops chewing. "I was talking about the candy."

"Oh, I . . ."

"I'm kidding!" she says, laughing, even though a new tear shines like a diamond at her cheek. "Your advice was wonderful."

She reaches for my hand, holding it in a reassuring way. Every bit of me wants to pull back at the shock of her touch. A popular junior girl, giving me the time of day, taking my advice to heart. If I could frame this moment, I would.

Then she hugs me tight before stepping back. Even beyond the tears, she looks happy again, eyes alight with new life. I wonder if my parents feel the same way I do right now, whenever someone writes to tell them how much their advice has changed their perspective. Whenever they do for other couples what they can't seem to do for themselves.

# Two

**I peek out** and exit first, and then beckon Sterling to come. The hallway's empty except for one freshman boy hunched at the water fountain. The liquid feathers his lips as he stares right at us through square-framed glasses.

"What? You've never seen two teens walk out of a storage closet before?" Sterling jokes.

He says nothing. We both burst out laughing, heading to class in opposite directions.

A few seconds later, the bell rings and I realize I've basically skipped third period talking to Sterling. Not what I'd intended, but honestly it doesn't matter. My third period is study hall, and my "teacher" barely knows my name. Ms. Finnegan definitely doesn't miss me.

Students filter out of classrooms. I pause, phone out in the middle of slow-flow traffic. I think of texting my friend Rod about what just happened when I see Sterling's best friend, Gianna Kyle, exiting class. She light-foots toward Sterling who's a few paces down the hallway, and they walk away. As I watch them, my crush on Sterling bears down like gravity. I don't feel like her equal anymore, the way I felt just seconds ago. It's like my foot's slipped a toehold and I've tumbled back into my correct social stratosphere.

Sterling turns back and flashes me a smile warm as sunlight. She holds just enough eye contact to make me feel like she'll actually remember I exist tomorrow. She and Gianna conspiratorially trade whispers as they walk with arms linked down the hallway.

I stand there, wanting to pull up Sterling's Instagram page and like every single picture, including the boring food-porn pics.

*Get a grip, dude.* I'm a mess right now. I close her page and shove my phone back into my pocket.

"I'm such a movie cliché," I say to myself.

"Not possible. You're Black. If you are a protagonist and Black, you are *by definition* not a cliché."

I shake my head as junior Dino James sidles up to me. "That's not true," I reply.

She nods. "It's most definitely true."

"Finn. *Star Wars*," I say.

"Side character," she answers.

"Monica Rambeau. *WandaVision*."

"Side character."

"Any Will Smith movie!" I shoot back.

"*Hitch*? *Bagger Vance*? *A*—fucking—*laddin*? Dude has a standing invitation to be some rich man's Magical Negro."

I could come back with *A*—fucking—*li*, but I don't. I'm sure she'd give me an itemized list of all the cinematic reasons I'm wrong about that one, too.

Geraldine "Dino" James is an expert at three things in life. Movies, video games, and knowing the exact whereabouts of her ex-girlfriend at any given time.

She's also my ride. We're down-the-street neighbors who never really hung out until we "found" each other online playing *ZombieWorld* a few years back, where her handle is @Melee-AttackBae. She's actually semi-famous as a gamer, placing in some tournaments and getting hundreds on her live streams. A novelty of sorts, she's the only Black girl gamer I've met in real life.

"So what's the move tonight?" I ask as we walk down the hallway.

"Battle royale in the new *ZombieWorld 3 Jurassic Era* mod."

I start walking sideways to face her. "So clear something up for me: Are the dinosaurs themselves zombies, or do you just have to fight both dinosaurs *and* zombies?"

"*Yes!*" she says, smiling giddily. "You in?"

"Naw, homework. Got a *Macbeth* test tomorrow in English."

"All right, fine," she says. I stop. She notices. "You're coming to lunch, right?"

"Yeah, I just gotta do a couple drop-offs after fourth."

Dino growls. "Okay, whatever, just don't be too late. Whenever you're not there, Rod tries to bait me into his philosophical debates."

"They aren't that bad," I reply.

The look she gives me is equal measures annoyance and thinking up exotic means of torture. "Last week, he ranted ten minutes about why there are so many types of tea when, according to him, they all taste like creek water."

"Okay, I won't be long."

She leaves, and I head to fourth, daydreaming my way through the period with Sterling as the leading lady. When class ends, I leave and cut right to make a couple drop-offs in the back courtyard. I give Gemma the regular candygram I made, which consists of one piece of candy and a note. It's one dollar. I hand Trevor the somewhat pricier special, which is three pieces and a note for $2.50.

I find Ashlynn Carter in her regular spot, sitting alone studying on the tennis court bleachers. I give her "the usual," her daily order of a mini Twix. On Friday, she'll give me two dollars, per our arrangement. Never a note with her. No pithy candy puns. Just sugar and a smile. Over the past few months, she's quietly become one of my favorite customers, probably because I can tell how much the candy brightens her day. It's so gratifying to bring a little bit of joy to someone's day.

As I head back to the courtyard, I mentally rerun the logistics of adding a third candy tier that includes an instrumental serenade as soon as I can convince Susie McNamara and her group to ditch their deal with stu-gov and play for me. She's the orchestra's principal flutist, who, for her senior project, created a woodwinds-only splinter quartet called No Strings Attached. She owes me a favor anyway, for hooking the group up with a few bags when they forgot to spring for refreshments ahead of their first show. But switching from stu-gov to me is a bridge too far, apparently. Everybody knows stu-gov's hands are dirty. Candy kickback schemes. PAYDAY to play. Barely anyone crosses them. Susie's no different. I get that, though. It's just business.

I walk the courtyard for about five minutes but don't see Robyn to deliver her candygram. However, several other people flag me down for purchase orders. Though most of my business is via email, I get several in-person buys every day. I don't mind it. It means business is good, after all. I can expect to hear either of two names when someone calls out to me. "Kal," which is fine. Or the unfortunate nickname the varsity soccer team bestowed upon me last year: "Shmelley," a derivative of my last name, Shmelton. Which is *not* fine. I grin and bear it, though, because as they say, the customer is always right. Even when they're wrong.

I go to lunch, and it's like most others. *Mostly.* Roderick Thomas is the first to notice the peculiarity as he and Dino sit at my table.

We're debating best Avenger spin-offs when Rod cranes his neck to look past my shoulder. "Yo, Gianna Kyle's been eyeing me kinda hard," he says.

I discreetly look over my shoulder, and there she is. She's at a long table with Sterling and some other junior elites. Sterling's beaming, though her cheeks are still glossy from the tears. I smile, too, happy I've helped turn her day around. I wonder what, if anything, she'll say when she confronts Chadwick. What he'll say back. How it'll go.

I turn back to my own table to see Roderick hesitantly raising his arm. He waves in such a way that makes each of his fingers seem like they've been devastated by arthritis.

"You sure she was looking at you?" I ask.

"Absolutely," he says, nodding. "Me and Gianna been playing this little cat-and-mouse game for a while now." He nudges Dino's shoulder. "Remember that time she literally bent down in front of me in the hallway?"

"She was picking up her pencil," Dino responds.

Roderick raises an eyebrow. "So we just gonna pretend squatting doesn't exist?"

Dino huffs, angling her body away from him. Crossing her arms, she says, "You're sexualizing her."

"No, I'm not."

"Women are not objects for men's pleasure. When will you guys get that?"

It's a wonder Roderick and Dino are friends at all. They couldn't be more opposite. A deadpanning, track-running gamer girl who's a die-hard feminist, and a loud-mouthed, Afroed, Biggie Smalls reincarnate who's a . . . *baby feminist? Feminist-in-training? Feminist if the light hits just right and you squint hard enough?*

Roderick's hands clasp as he leans in over Dino's turned shoulder. "*Geraldine.* I'm accurately recounting what had happened. I saw what I saw."

Dino's stare goes skyward. "Classic male-gaze behavior."

"I mean, I was *gazing*, but not in a creepy way. Kal, help me out here."

Both look at me as if I'm the jury at a trial. I know these two. They're nothing if not totally confident in the inerrancy of their own opinions. They won't let this go until somebody wins.

I throw a real sheepish look Rod's way: "I gotta say it was a little sexist."

His hands flail upward as he gives off an exaggerated sigh.

"Sorry, dude. You can't assume she's into you just because she—"

"What other possible reason could there be?" he interjects. "Why else would she be looking at me like I'm on the lunch menu?"

My mouth opens, but nothing comes out. I could come clean as to why Gianna and Sterling may be looking over here, but I keep thinking it's none of my business to tell. As much as Chadwick Boston comes off as a prick, I shouldn't be the one airing his dirty laundry. That's Sterling's decision.

"I'm just not convinced," I reply, glancing back at their table. This time, Gianna, Sterling, *and* several other girls are casting curious looks our way. Conversing and pointing and nodding like we're art at a museum.

"I'll prove it," Rod says. "Before the year's out, I'ma win Gigi's heart."

"Gigi?" I ask.

Roderick smiles. "Yeah, that'll be my pet name for her."

"She's not a dog, Roderick," Dino says. "And good luck going through Jordan Parris to get her."

"I will run through Jordan Parris like that tape they got at finish lines. What they call that, track star?" he asks Dino.

"Finish-line tape," she says.

"Yeah." He looks right at me. "*Finish-line tape*. Jordan can't handle me."

"I can't?"

Rod jumps at the voice coming from behind us, down the side of the table. I look up and startle, too. Jordan Parris stands there in all his six-foot-two soccer-phenom glory. Square jaw. Two sharp triangles for dimples. Brow furrowed into three perfectly straight lines. His whole face is like an angry work of fractal art. He's proof that what rich guys lack in personality, they can more than make up for in muscles and Ray-Bans and yacht club memberships.

Fellow junior Chadwick Boston stands right beside him. He's smaller and thinner than Jordan, but not by a lot. And he's got that frat-boy vibe. Khaki shorts. Button-down shirt. Cap bill curvature on par with the space-time continuum.

Roderick scrambles for a response, finally sputtering out with "*Michael* Jordan can't handle me."

"Yeah, yeah," Dino adds. "Rod's been working on his handles lately."

"That crossover, though," I add for good effect.

"Shut up," Jordan says. "I was right here. I know you were talking about me." He takes a step toward us and not-so-discreetly pushes Roderick's milk off the table, splattering it across Rod's new shoes. "Handle *that*."

Chadwick starts walking toward Sterling's table but

pauses when Jordan doesn't follow. Seems now *I've* captured his attention.

"Shmelley Shmelton. You played JV soccer this fall, right?" Jordan asks.

I nod, and he smirks.

"Well, if you ever hope to survive on varsity, maybe watch the company you keep."

When I don't say anything, he points a finger at me and clicks his tongue.

"Spring pickups start this week. Be there." He leaves.

Chadwick hesitates a beat, though. Like he's trying to awkwardly extract himself from a skirmish he never even wanted to begin. I catch the look in his eyes just before he turns. Something hovering above indifference but well short of remorse.

We watch as they head to the girls' table. Sterling stands up. Chadwick says some words. A part of me dies as Sterling eschews any confrontation and wraps him in a big hug.

Throughout the day, I notice I'm getting a few more whispers and sidelong stares from random people, but everything else is pretty normal. Dino drives me home as usual, and I walk into the sound of my parents' chipper voices laughing and bantering in a far-off room.

A year or two ago, hearing this would've delighted me. It'd be a positive sign, solid evidence the cold war consuming 274

Kerr Road was thawing. Today, I shrug the noise off with the same ease as I shrug the backpack from my shoulders.

It's cold, so I head to the living room to flick the switch for the fireplace. I look at the pictures adorning the mantel. Various iterations of three happy people. Happy together.

I pick up the picture of our family vacation in Hawaii, using my sleeve to wipe a smudge from the center of the glass. Then I just stare at it. It's perfect. We're all smiles as we stand at the restless lip of the Pacific. I'm sixteen years old now. The picture was taken when I was nine. It seems so long ago that we were like this. Hopeful. Close.

I'll never forget the half-day excursion trip we took to the tiny island of Lanai. We toured a majestic cliffside village lost to inescapable tendrils of time and progress. Kaunolu Village. The guide called it a pu'uhonua, or "place of refuge." It definitely was that day. Looking out in awe over the ocean, Mom and Dad couldn't help but comment on how at peace they felt. How sanguine they were about the future. The feeling stuck with me, even though it's been lost to them for a while now.

*If only I could get us back there. . . .*

My throat gets tight, and I put the picture back.

I consider heading to my room to bury my emotions in my pillow, but I decide not to. I take deep breaths to regain my composure. Then I head to the kitchen and make a PB&J. I start doing my precalculus homework at the kitchen table, making sure to be quiet as Mom and Dad record their show in the makeshift studio down the hall.

A few minutes in, I hear Deion and LaTonya Shmelton excitedly sign off with the tagline "Even in the roughest of seas, you can still right the 'ship!" Mere seconds later it's like someone presses the Mute button for the entire household.

Mom walks out first, her soft steps padding against the hardwood. She enters the kitchen holding a manila envelope in one hand. Her other hand drapes over her face as if she's wiping away her barely concealed exhaustion mottled with indifference. The red blouse she's wearing complements the deep brown of her skin. She sees me, winks, and bends down over me, lightly squeezing my cheeks as she presses her lips against my forehead.

"How are you?" she whispers.

Before I can answer, she's walking away again, heading out the opposite doorway.

Dad's next, his loud, deliberate footsteps heralding his arrival like a trumpeter before a king or rooster before the sun. He doesn't walk in the doorway so much as just marches through, straightening the red tie that pops out against his electric-blue suit.

"My son, Kalvin! Ah-*HA-HAAA!*" That's his signature laugh, which isn't so much of a laugh as a sound effect.

He's the talker in our family. And he's got this bombastic, Steve Harvey–ish way of storytelling where no matter what tale he spins, he always ends up being the star. Don't get me wrong, he's a great dad. But he's just not the most down-to-earth.

Their podcast was carefully crafted with an "opposites attract" motif in mind. The hard-charging giver of tough advice, and the spouse with wit as sharp as anything Cuisinart ever created right there to rein him in. They wisecrack and advise and speak openly of their own past conflicts, using them as "teachable moments" for tens of thousands of couples tuning in every Monday, Wednesday, and Friday. Their audience eats it up.

Well, *most* of their audience. Everyone except me. I stopped buying what they're selling years ago.

"What's going on, boy?" Dad asks. "How was school today?"

"Fine," I say, taking a bite of my sandwich. He narrows his eyes on me, and I think he's about to ask what I'm eating until he starts creeping closer. I stop chewing as he comes three inches from my face.

"Damn, boy, that acne flaring up again. Cheek looking like a crater on Mars. You know we just got that NASA rover up there, right? Pictures and video and errythang."

I lean away before answering: "Dad, it's been up there for years."

He waves my response away. Then brings a finger to my cheek, pressing it lightly against a bump. I lean away more as it throbs. "Ain't no matter," he says. "But we do need to get you some more cream. Looks like they starting to scar. You poppin' 'em?"

I swat his finger away. "No, I'm not popping them. Why would—"

"Good." He stands straight again. "You got my looks. Would hate to see you lose 'em at such a tender young age."

He heads to the fridge, taking out pieces of fruit one at a time and examining them like gemstones at a jewelry store. "You know your mom wanted a girl. Hairbows and earrangs and all that frilly stuff. But I saw that big-ass nose of yours on the 3D ultrasound and was like ah-*HA-HAAA!* My son!" He stomps a dress shoe on the hardwood for emphasis.

*My nose isn't that big.* I consider putting a hand to it but decide against drawing any more attention to my facial features. My eyes roll, but Dad doesn't catch it. He barely ever catches my and Mom's subtle signs of irritation. He's a terrific therapist, A-plus insight. But he's like a car mirror, too. His biggest blind spots are the ones closest to him.

Dad sits across from me at the table, Honeycrisp apple in hand. He takes a bite bigger than most apples—the juicy, crisp crunching and squishy chewing filling the next twenty seconds of dead air. He's eyeing me the entire time. It doesn't faze me, though. I'm used to it by now. His trademark *Let's get real* stare is a viral sensation, but he actually perfected it on me.

"What's up with you, boy? Girl problems?"

"No."

An eyebrow raises. "Guy problems?"

I shake my head. My problem is having to come home every day to the same low-level tension that's had this house in a chokehold for the past few years. But I don't tell him that. I just say, "School stuff."

"Stuff like what?"

"Stuff."

He nods and takes another loud bite, leaving my answer settling between us like dust.

Living with psychologists as parents, you pick up tricks of the trade. When people are around others, they'll do almost anything to avoid awkward, prolonged silences. It's a subconscious thing. So when their patients don't want to talk, psychologists use one simple trick to great effect: wait the silence out. Inevitably, words will come, perhaps first as halting small talk, but that'll gradually transform into thoughtful self-reflections as the patient gets more comfortable.

I've learned to expect this type of wordless manipulation. And I've learned to wait out the *wait*. I make a production of eating the rest of my sandwich as he watches me, licking strawberry jam from my fingers in the most carefree way possible.

After a while, Dad gives up. "Just remember, school ain't the only place to learn some thangs. A public education ain't worth nearly as much as a private revelation."

Footsteps sound out from a back hallway. It's Mom, her heels rising in volume with each step. She appears in the doorway, the same envelope pressed against her waist. She puts on a forced smile like it's a well-worn accessory. She pauses, waiting a beat before stepping into the room. She clears her throat and puts the envelope on the table in front of Dad.

"I just labeled it. Could you, um, handle it in the next week or so?" she asks.

Dad nods without looking up. "Sure."

"Good. Deion, Kalvin, want anything from the store?"

"I'm good."

"No, Mom."

She comes over and kisses my cheek, bending low. "Sorry about earlier. I was just in a rush." Then she rounds the table and squats beside Dad for a side-hug. He angles toward her, and they share a kiss that barely makes contact. She puts a hand to his shoulder as she stands.

I see their tired eyes and wonder what they could possibly be tired from.

"Good show today, Deion," she says, and I can tell she genuinely means it.

"Thanks," he responds. Staring back at his apple, he puts his own hand over hers. "You too."

And with that, she leaves.

Dad takes another bite of the apple, looking pensive, aloof, but mostly just tired. I know I could play the psychologist role, turning his question back on him. *So, Pops . . . what's up with you? Girl problems?*

But I don't because I'm not a therapist; I'm just a kid. A kid who doesn't exactly know the time or place something broke in his parents' twenty-year marriage, or if it'll ever be fixed. We sit in silence once again, and this time it's me staring at the envelope.

After a while, Dad leaves, taking the package with him. I head to my own room and pull a drawer-sized silver lockbox out from beneath my bed. I sold seven candygrams today. Would've had eight had Noah Leighton not demanded his money back after Jenny Innis threw hers in my face. Turns out, telling your boys you rounded third base when your girlfriend is the

29

ChasteLife youth leader isn't the best life decision. Whether or not Noah learned his lesson, I sure learned mine: institute a no-refunds policy.

So it's $11.50 total. I count it all out. One five, six ones, and two quarters. Not nearly enough to meet my goal by the Valentine's Day deadline. I log the money in with my grand total for the year, accounting for expenses: $9,073.

It's all here, in heaps of crumpled cash and so many quarters and nickels and dimes that my fingers now have that permanent metallic smell. It's not all candy money, of course. Much of it's the product of my Tiny Tots soccer refereeing job I've had for years, my ill-fated five-week stint at the Tastee Freez last summer, and various other random side hustles.

And I know hiding it under my bed is a bit childish, but I figured if I just kept socking money away into a bank account without ever spending, my parents would get all kinds of suspicious. So I just let them assume I blow it all on video games.

My fingers fumble around at the bottom of the lockbox, and I fish out a piece of blue notepad paper marked with one word and one number.

Messily Sharpied at the center is "Goal: $11,737."

"Way short," I say to myself.

The weight of the task tanks my mood. More than $2,600 left to go, a month to get there, and I'm *averaging* $12 per day.

I had it all planned out. I'd give them the money right before Valentine's Day and tell them it's for another Hawaii trip. They'd be over-the-moon excited, and we'd spend the weekend replaying our fondest memories of the last trip while planning the next.

Our pu'uhonua. Our "place of refuge." The place that saves us. The place that could save them.

I take one more long look at the money before shutting the box and heading to my desk for homework, knowing full well that I'm as far from my goal as I am from the destination.

# Three

**I spend an** admittedly obsessive amount of time the next two days scribbling Sterling's name in notebooks and on desktops, while analyzing our chance closet meeting and what she said about Chadwick. Could they really be on the verge of breaking up? Did Sterling actually take my advice to heart? Sure didn't seem like it, judging from lunch on Wednesday. The way she hugged him in the cafeteria, her anger misting away like sweat in a sauna. That scene is basically a nightmare. All it needs is a viper pit and a killer clown or two.

I get weirdly down about it, so I'm glad when Friday afternoon rolls around and Rod and I pile into Dino's back seat and we all take a trip to the mall. Lately it's become a ritual of sorts. Perfect weekend distraction. I don't have to be home. There's no pressure of school. I can just chill with friends.

Once we park, Dino immediately clears her throat and holds out her hand, reminding me of the only *imperfect* part of our Friday ritual. I hand her two Kit Kats. One for me and one for Rod. Along with a one candy per diem, we both pay her $5 in gas money every two weeks. Nowadays, Rod and I sit in the back seat because ever since Rod spilled Sprite on her dashboard, she's enforced a $2 upcharge for shotgun, or in Dino's words, "first class."

Our town's mall is the usual parade of brand-name stores. The rush of fountain water and shouts of children fill the cavernous main drag. We wander into the mall's epicenter, where Dino temporarily splits off from us. She has to go to the gaming store to pick up the new Diamond LE wireless headsets she pre-ordered last week. That leaves me and Rod near the food court.

I know it's a long shot a month out, but I even start asking a couple places if they're hiring. I'm desperate for a new revenue stream.

"Bruh, don't we have spring soccer drills coming up?" Rod asks. "How you gonna work after school *and* do that?"

"I'll figure it out," I say. It's a few seconds later before I process the implication in his question. I glare at him. He's busy looking at his phone. "What do you mean 'we'?"

"Oh yeah. I'm coming out for the team next year." He says it like he's cleaning his bedroom or taking the dog for a walk.

"But you don't— Why?" I ask.

"Moms said I need to start thinking about extracurriculars for college. So I decided to come out." Cramming the phone in his pocket, he says, "I'ma do theater this year, too."

"Do you even know the positions?"

He looks at me, his face suddenly animated, like he's sharing a secret only he knows. "Bro. *Goalkeeper!* I've been watching them on TV. All they do is just stand there. And I'm big anyway, so it'll be that much harder to shoot around me. Easy peasy."

He raises his hand to dap me up. When I don't move, he clicks his tongue, angling away.

"Aight, then." He ambles over to a bench that sits against a glass guardrail. I follow and settle beside him.

"Do you even know the first thing about soccer?" I ask.

"Of course! I've seen *Bend It Like Beckham.* And I had mad respect for that dude before, but now that I know he's a two-sports star?" Rod shakes his head in admiration as the word "legend" rolls from his tongue.

It takes me a whole ten seconds to figure out he's talking about Odell and not David.

I don't know whether I'm supposed to cheer him on or coordinate an intervention. Rod's walking right into a buzz saw, and not just because soccer's incredibly hard to pick up out of the blue.

"You do know coaches can't technically run spring drills because it's out of season, right?" I ask.

"So?"

"So the team captains run them . . ."

Rod squints, tilting his head at me, still not getting it.

"And Jordan's a team captain."

The varsity players have a nasty habit of treating routine scrimmages between them and underclassmen like monster-truck rallies. Blindsiding, leg whipping, and generally turning the "J-Fleas" into roadkill. Jordan's an especially egregious

34

offender, giving out dead legs and raspberries like suckers at Halloween.

Rod makes a soft *Ohhh* face with his lips, and the word quietly follows. A moment later, he shrugs and says, "I'll figure it out."

I nod. I actually admire his absolute and unyielding confidence in navigating situations he has zero experience with.

"Kalvin!"

I don't turn around at first, sure that nobody would be calling me here, but my name rings out again, this time with twice the urgency. I shift my body and look down over the railing to where the shout is coming from. A reed-thin blond girl is happily waving up at me. I don't even know her. I think her name is Keegan or Kieran or something. I wave back, and she scurries up the escalator and then hustles around the protective railing until she's standing right in front of me.

"Kalvin Shmelton, right? The Candyman."

"Candy *Guy*," I correct.

"Oh, okay. Hi, I'm Keegan."

"Hi, Keegan. What's your order?"

"Actually, I was hoping you could help me with something a little more personal. You know, since you're good at that and your parents are the best in the business."

*What is this girl talking about? And why on earth would she bring up my mom and dad?* I mean, I've heard kids talk about my parents' podcast whenever they have a clip that goes viral. So I know they're generally well-known throughout the school. But what do my parents have to do with me?

I narrow my eyes on her. "What exactly do you need help with?" I ask.

"Okay, so . . . this is between us, right?"

"Sure," I say.

Keegan looks at Rod, who says, "Sure."

She hurries to the food court to grab a chair, dragging it back and sitting right in front of me. "Okay, so . . . My boyfriend's really super into me, and I'm into him, too. And we're *great* together. We have fun, and we talk, and the sex is good. I mean, we haven't actually fully had sex yet, but we've done *other* stuff, and I've orgasmed, which is unfortunately not the case for most of my friends with boyfriends. But lately I've just been having these thoughts like I'm always missing out. And I've been noticing other guys, and they've been looking at me, too, and I wanna kinda be in an open relationship, but I'm afraid if I tell him, he'll absolutely take it wrong and dump me, and it'll get out, and everybody at school will call me a slut, and nobody will like me, and I'll never have another great relationship, and I'll have to transfer and—"

By the time I cut in with "Whoa, whoa, *whoa*!" she's already worked herself into an almost full-blown panic attack. Her face is flushed, and she's nearly out of breath, jittery as a seismograph during an earthquake, with words crashing together like whitecaps in a rocky river.

"I'm sorry," she spouts. The way she says it is like she's not only sorry that she's all keyed up but sorry that she exists, wasting air.

Right then, Dino returns from the gaming store. Her mouth gapes open, and she drops her bag when she sees me consoling Keegan. I try to ignore her.

"You don't have to be sorry," I tell Keegan. "Just . . ." I gently grab her wrists. "Do me a favor and close your eyes." She does as she's told, and I continue. "Do you experience a lot of anxiety?"

"Yes, why?" she snivels.

"Because what you're engaged in now is what we call 'catastrophic thinking,' which anxiety can bring on." *Whoa.* I catch myself in therapist mode. I feel like my parents are full-on possessing me right now. But honestly, I've got nothing else. And something about this advice *feels* right. I lean in and carry on: "I want you to try something for me. *Ground* your thoughts in the here and now."

"What do you mean?" she asks.

"What do you hear? Smell? Feel? Taste?"

She takes a hand away to wipe a tear before bringing it back to my palm. And then she describes her present. Kids laughing and a fountain gurgling. The warm, aromatic bread of Auntie Anne's. The smoothness of my hands. The weird-but-not-unpleasant aftertaste of Sbarro.

"Ol' greasy-ass pizza," Rod mumbles, but I'm quick to shush him. I feel my body getting squeezed against the rail as Rod moves toward me to make room for Dino.

Once the rise and fall of Keegan's shoulders steadies, I say, "Now open your eyes."

She does, inhaling deeply.

"Do you feel better?"

She thinks before answering. "Actually, yeah. You literally just cured me."

I shake my head. "I didn't *cure* anything. I just helped you stop a panic attack."

Right then, Keegan notices her audience has grown. "Hey, Dino," she says.

Dino leans forward. "Hi, Keegs. Look, girl, just keep shining. We've all had these feelings."

"You've considered polyamory, too?"

Dino blinks. "Oh. Shit. I thought this was about today's AP Lit quiz." She then looks at us, seeing the absolute disbelief in all our stares. She scrambles for a clarification, but I cut her off.

"Honestly, though," I say. "These panic attacks will come back if you don't tackle some root causes of your anxiety."

"How would I do that?"

"Therapy. You ever been?"

Keegan shakes her head. "How would that help?"

"First of all, a therapist would teach you to moderate your language."

She looks confused, and rightly so. Most people would think that'd mean not cursing.

I fill her in. "Like, for example, the words you used when you were describing your problem were kind of extreme. When you described possible outcomes, it was all *absolutely*, *never*, *everybody*, *nobody*, and *always*. See?"

Her head tilts upward as she replays her long, twisty Blue

Ridge Parkway of a lament. Slowly, she lowers her gaze to me again. "And that will fix me?"

"Keegan, you don't need *fixing*. But yes, it should help with the anxiety."

"Okay, so I go to therapy. What do I say to my boyfriend in the meantime?"

"Work on you first," I reply. "The rest tends to fall into place."

She wipes her cheeks and hugs me. Then she insists on buying me a late lunch. After two initial refusals, I give in. I get the sweet-and-sour chicken from Emperor Chinese.

When Keegan leaves, Rod takes and breaks open my fortune cookie. He squints at the strip of paper and asks, "Why're all these random people asking you for advice? 'You will die alone and poorly dressed'? *What?* Damn, these things getting gritty nowadays." He crumples the strip and eats the cookie.

I try to blow him off by saying "What people?" even though I know perfectly well what he's referring to. Since Wednesday, several students have come up to me wondering if I could help them with various personal issues, all at least somewhat related to the disparate stages of significant other*ship*: achieving, leaving, cleaving. Their problems seemed to have easy fixes to me. I could decipher through common sense and a dash of insight what they couldn't see through the fog of romance. The solutions to their problems came easy to me. It's the *why* that's been gnawing at me all this time. *Why are they asking me this stuff? Why now?*

It didn't matter. I refused to help them. Turned down all

requests. Would've turned down Keegan's if she hadn't cornered me on this bench. I'm not in the business of diving into people's personal lives, especially in the run-up to the emotionally fraught Valentine's season. *Candy* is my lane. All the money, none of the feelings.

When I won't give a straight answer despite Rod's prodding, he simply says, "Aight, then. Be that way."

Dino reaches past Rod and plucks a piece of chicken from my plate without asking. Again, without asking, she dips it into my sweet-and-sour sauce. She takes a bite, holding the uneaten part over her free hand as if it's a teacup saucer, and, mid-chew, opines on the situation: "You ever notice how cuffing season makes everyone deranged? Especially right before Valentine's Day?"

Rod nods, which is all the encouragement Dino needs to press on with her theory.

"Why people get together just because it's cold out and they don't wanna be alone during the holidays is beyond me. Like, it's okay to stay home alone. Get a hobby. This is *exactly* what RPGs were invented for."

"Speaking of games, how is it playing the *ZombieWorld 3* mod?" I ask Dino.

Her face scrunches, and she just huffs.

"That bad, huh?"

"Oh the *mod* is fine. It's just dumbass trolls again."

I've learned just by watching her streams that sexism and racism are basically an everyday part of what it's like being a Black girl gamer. It's amazing the horrible things people will say when they live across the country and can hide behind a handle instead of using their actual names. Even though she's one of the best *ZW3* players in the country, she doesn't get nearly the amount of respect that her white peers do. She's got thick skin, though. In fact, the only thing I'd ever seen truly get to her was her breakup.

Rosario Ortiz was Dino's everything, or so Dino thought. Turns out, when Rosie went to college, she'd decided a clean break from everything high school would be best for her. The "everything" included her girlfriend of two years. Reasonable, honestly, but tell that to the girl who got dumped.

"Has you-know-who been online lately?" Rod asks.

Rosie would often play just to pass the time with Dino. And Dino would record all of Rosie's investigative reports during the homeroom newscasts. They were cute like that.

Dino shakes her head. "Not since December, when I stood beside base camp and kept double-tapping her every time she regenerated."

We've been working on Dino not holding grudges.

"Maybe you should try to reconnect," I offer. "But *just* as friends," I'm quick to add.

"And relive my trauma? *Psshh.* No way."

"It's not trauma if she treated you well, which you admit she did."

"Way to be on my side, Kal," she says.

"I *am* on your side. I'm just saying you shouldn't needlessly burn bridges."

"But what if I *like* arson?" She pouts.

I *think* she's joking? With her, I can never truly tell. Intermittently, Dino has openly floated seven different revenge schemes, ranging from salting Rosie's parents' azalea garden to anonymously sending hot sauce–infused Edible Arrangements to her dorm. I guess letting feelings die down takes time, but I can't imagine this kind of attitude helps the process along.

I think about those last few months that Dino and Rosie were together. How Rod and I'd noticed they didn't seem as excited to see each other. How their convos sputtered and stalled like a car with worn-down spark plugs.

It's not like I don't like Rosie. She's fine. And even together they looked great, for a while, at least. But then I started to notice a listlessness settle onto their 'ship like an itchy blanket. Rosie, in particular, started to look uncomfortable, restless, and, worst of all, bored. As a result, she and Dino didn't kiss in public as much, their convos seemed more surface level, and they started doing old-couple things like burping in front of each other and watching HGTV together. That was toward the end of Rosie's senior year, and they actually lasted a couple more months after that. But honestly, everyone around them could tell their relationship had overstayed its welcome. Rod called them a *Transformers* couple. Cool and new at first but going irretrievably stale as the franchise wore on. It's a damn-near miracle those movies have lasted as long as they have. Same could be said for "Rosino."

"Just move on," Rod says. "Get with somebody else."

"I'm not falling victim to cuffing season," she replies.

Rod comes back with "But what if cuffing season falls victim to *you*?"

I'm not sure what that means, and I'm not sure Dino knows, either. But she doesn't reject his statement outright. Weirdly enough, it looks like she's giving it some thought.

Dino vultures a piece of chicken from me again. We people watch for a few minutes afterward as we finish my food.

"So what's new with you?" Rod asks me.

"It's been a pretty interesting week, actually," I respond. I feel like I should offer something to the convo. Not too much, but I can't be totally tight-lipped about this. Hesitantly, I offer up, "You'll never guess who came into the closet."

"Gianna?"

"Close."

He stares me down. "Sterling?"

I nod. I'm knocked off-balance as Rod bear-hugs me, so much so that we spill onto the floor, making quite the scene. But he doesn't care.

"BRO! She's your forever crush! When you gonna ask her out?"

"Dude, I can't. She's still with Chadwick Boston."

Rod makes a stank face. "Boat Shoes Chadwick?!" He gets off me, lowering his hand to help me up, as well. I stand with him. "Dude don't even deserve the name 'Chadwick.' It should've been retired years ago after . . ." Rod can't even bring himself to say his name. He simply bows his head and traces a cross at his chest, whispering, "God rest his soul."

"They've been dating for years now. It's not like she's just gonna break up with him."

"She will when she gets to know the real Kalvin."

I look askance and breathe heavy at his words. *The real Kalvin?* The one whose brain goes AWOL whenever he's within a five-foot radius of a hot girl? The one who's so inept at relationships that he can't even fix the most significant one in his life—his parents'? They're counting on me, and I'm counting chump change.

The real Kalvin doesn't sound all that enthralling to me.

"I'm declaring it right now!" Rod says. "You and Sterling together at next month's ball!"

The ball. The school puts it on every year around Valentine's Day. This year's theme is Knights and Knaves, a nod to both medieval chivalry and strained attempts at alliteration.

Rod leans in for his next words, as if they're A-level top secret: "You know a couple days back when Gianna was peeping me?"

I nod.

"I also noticed Sterling looking at you."

Not exactly new news, considering both Sterling *and* Gianna were looking at me and me alone. But it is kind of enlivening to know that someone thinks you've got a chance. If only that someone was me.

"Dude, I've got no shot," I say, almost plaintively. "Why're you trying to hype me up like this?"

"What is a best friend if not a glorified hype man?" he replies. "And besides, me and Gianna need y'all to be together if we're gonna double date. Wait, no, triple date!" he adds, looking at Dino. She rolls her eyes as she rises from the bench.

"And how do you expect to win her over, Rod?" I ask, glad to get the attention off me. I feel a bit sheepish, too. I can't muster the same hype for him that he has for me. Envisioning him winning over Gianna is like envisioning a trip to the Andromeda galaxy. Awe-inspiring, mind-blowing, not gonna happen.

"I'ma use my charm" is all he says.

"That's not a plan. That's an aspiration. And besides, Gianna's hot."

"And?"

"And you're like . . . pre-hot." *Nice save, Kal.* "Do you have an actual plan?"

I even wonder whether questions like this are just egging him on. Prodding him to take on an unwinnable task.

Rod fans the question away as if he were shooing a gnat. "I'll wing it."

I bend past Rod to make eye contact with Dino. "Thoughts on Rod's 'plan'?" I ask.

Her reaction surprises me. "Plans are overrated."

He grins. "Royal Ball's in one month. Plenty of time for each of us to get a date. Will you join me on my noble quest?"

She huffs, and I think she's about to rebuff him, but she simply raises a hand, smiling wide. "I will join you."

"Get hype!" he says. "Up top!"

They high-five and look at me. I can't pinpoint what makes me reluctantly agree. Peer pressure? Faint hope? An itching desire to change the subject? Whatever it is, I find myself indulging in the what-ifs of next month. Particularly, *What if this works?*

I had one goal for the next thirty days: saving my parents' marriage. Somehow, Rod and Dino have convinced me to go for two. I'll admit this one's more interesting, but I'd say it's more daunting as well. As we walk toward the exit, they come up with date ideas and debate 'ship names, as if our couplings are a foregone conclusion. I just listen in awe, wondering what exactly I'm missing.

# Four

**Monday's not a** school day because it's the MLK "Day of Service" holiday. Every year the school gives us the opportunity to complete various volunteer tasks to get service-learning hours we need to graduate. Since Dino's a junior and we're just sophomores, it's more serious for her. So at her prodding, Rod and I decide to attend.

The school football stadium is just as alive with activity as the landscape around it is alive with fresh blooms courtesy of an unseasonably warm midwinter. Two of the first people I see are Chadwick and Jordan, pulling up weeds along the near bank of the stadium. My shoulders slump. Even on my off days, I've gotta deal with them.

It gets better, though. As I jog farther down the sloping brick path to the field, I spot Sterling and Gianna with some girlfriends. They're at the west end digging a row of holes for planting shade trees.

And then it gets confounding. Rod stands between a set of goalposts, in a black T-shirt and jean shorts, looking like he moseyed here straight from class. It's warm but not *that* warm.

As I get closer, I can even see a bright-red hair pick in his 'fro. I walk to the track and notice what's in his hand: a set of dandelion weeds. They haven't begun cutting grass this early, so the field's pocked with them, especially near the goal. One by one, he brings each to his lips and softly blows, gifting the feathery seeds to the gentle breeze.

I sign in by the home-side field gate at the fifty-yard line and then walk out to meet him. When I get there, I ask, "Why're you on the field?"

"Figured I'd get used to being in the goal since I'll be playing soon," he mutters. Then he blows another dandelion. "Plus I can practice my vocals."

"Vocals for what?" I ask.

"*Hamilton* auditions."

I'm about to ask *Where'd this come from?* until I remember Rod did say something about doing theater a couple days ago. Instead, another question comes to mind.

"You can sing?"

Rod drops his fistful of dandelions. "Bro, I just got first pew in my church choir last year. If you'd stop being a heathen for one hour and accept my invite to Greater Praise Missionary Baptist, you'd know that by now."

Skepticism crowds my expression as I give him the once-over. He looks like he's telling the truth, so instead of grilling him, I just drop it.

Rod motions to his left. "Hey, what you think about River Schaeffer? For Dino," he asks.

River's leaning against the gate beside the visitors' bench holding two fistfuls of weeds. She's the type of person who, instead of throwing them away, would take them home and mash them up with pestle and mortar to make an herbal medicine or the best spice blend you've ever tasted. She tends to be in her own world a lot, so I'd never really considered her. But she is gorgeous and easygoing. *Maybe?*

Dino jogs out to meet us. "Fellas, what's the move? Litter pickup by the creek, hedge trimming along the gate?"

I look back at Rod. "Let's find out."

He and I fake like we're clueless about the simplest tasks for the day and head toward River with Dino in tow. River's one of the environmental club's student supervisors for the day, which is a great *in* to get her and Dino talking. As we approach, River's ever-present grin grows to a full-blown, teeth-shimmering smile.

The hug she gives me is longer and tighter than my grandmother ever would've dared. She deeply inhales the scent of my shirt collar before letting go. She does the exact same to Rod.

"Fellas," she says smoothly. "Your energy is strong today. I'm glad for it. You'll need it to carry out your husbandry of our grand Mother this morning." She waves a hand across her body like she's presenting a spread at Thanksgiving. Then she points toward the opposite end of the field. "But should your chi happen to get depleted, there are Fig Newtons and Zebra Cakes by the water cooler at the home gate."

I glance at Dino, who's thoroughly amused. *Not the best start.*

River steps to her next, letting the weeds fall and taking Dino's hand like a palm reader. My gaze travels toward Sterling in the distance. She's busy shoveling, but Gianna's broken away from their group and is jogging this way. I hear River say, "Dino James. Gamer girl. Your soul speaks through your hands."

"Oh yeah? What's it say?" Dino asks. Laughter bubbles just beneath the surface of her question.

"That you were born for both toil and leisure, the twin domains of the deity Mbaba Mwana Waresa. Your hands till fields of knowledge with nothing but a pencil and a TI-83. But they also craft whole worlds of pixels, just like the beloved Zulu goddess made her own palace of rainbows."

"My hands say all that?"

"Yes," River answers. "Our hands are the most informative part of our body. Your hands are wise, Dino James. And cute, too."

At this, I turn back, wondering how close Dino is to bursting out laughing. But she's . . . *not*. Far from it. She's staring right into River's eyes. An absolute lapdog. Enthralled, soaking up every word like it's a ray of sun.

I look at Rod, who's confused as ever. He can't help himself but to ask what we're both thinking: "Are you like . . . a mystic?"

Not breaking eye contact with Dino, River says, "'To label me is to negate me.' Kierkegaard. Well, roughly paraphrased."

"You've studied Søren Kierkegaard?" Dino asks, her voice an octave higher than usual.

River releases Dino's hand. "I'm a student of the world and of truth. I seek it out, wherever it may be."

50

It's right then that I see something spark in Dino's brain. She's stumbled upon that same *Maybe?* I came across just minutes earlier. She looks at me. I raise an eyebrow. She turns back to River.

"Hey, River. Would you like to maybe get coffee sometime? Just to, you know, talk existentialism? Kierkegaard, Sartre, Camus?"

River smiles. "I love KSC. I would love that."

Rod and I watch as they slip out of the gate and head toward the bleachers. Dino pulls out her phone. "What's your number, so I don't forget?" she asks.

"I don't have a phone. The 5G interferes with my astral projecting."

"So what, like people send a raven to contact you?"

"Oh, I have Gmail."

I spend the next few seconds balancing my joy that Dino may have been the first to achieve our Valentine's ball goal with my nascent concern that River may be a cult leader.

Gianna approaches us, breaking up my thoughts. She points toward the track. "Hey, you guys know where River's going?"

"Just to the bleachers," I say. "Why? You need something?"

"A few of us soccer girls were gonna take a break and wanted to play a quick game of World Cup. We need a key to the field-house to get a ball, though."

I shrug. "You could ask her. I'm Kalvin, by the way."

"I know," she says. She brushes a wave of auburn hair from her face before sticking out her own hand. We shake.

She knows. I do my best to bury my smile. Sterling's been talking about me.

It's no wonder Rod likes Gianna. She's gorgeous, an absolute sunflower. And everybody says her personality is just as radiant. Which makes it a mystery how she and Jordan ended up together.

"Do girls' tryouts start this month?" I ask.

"Next," she says. "But we're doing conditioning beforehand. Do you play?"

I nod. "JV this past fall."

Rod clears his throat, and I realize what should've been obvious. This moment is tailor-made for an introduction. "My friend here plays, too," I add, not sure whether that's technically true.

Gianna turns and studies him. Someone yells out, "Never mind, Gianna! Casey has one in her car!"

But she doesn't break her stare. She just says, "Hey, you look kinda familiar."

He nods. "Yeah. Fifth-period class change. B wing. We got a class across from each other. I'm Rod, by the way."

"Oh yeah." They shake. "Which position?" she asks.

"Goalkeeper."

"Cool! Me too! I'm second string on varsity! Are you a strictly in-the-box type or more of a sweeper keeper?"

"Oh, I'm a sweeper. Vacuumer. I take out the trash, too. Whatever Moms needs."

The look I shoot Rod has to be on the level of the survivors who watched the *Titanic* sink. Lines crowd Gianna's brow. Rod notices our stares and opens his mouth, but only an *Uhh* spills out.

When I think things can't get any more awkwardly silent, Gianna gives off one of the most dramatic gasps I've ever witnessed. Then she bursts into a fit of giggles. The hand-to-mouth, leaning-back type. Slowly, Rod's embarrassment thaws. His smile peeks out like a groundhog in winter.

"You are soooo funny!" Gianna giggles.

My mouth drops open. *Wow.*

"Hey, you wanna help me move the goal? I could use a strong man like you." She's tugging at his wrist before he can even answer. As they're walking down the field, Rod looks back and shrugs. I give one right back to him.

That leaves me alone, looking at Sterling across the field. Somehow, I doubt my efforts will be as fruitful as Rod's or Dino's, but I guess I have to try. It's either that or stand here alone in a field looking stupid.

Thankfully I don't have to do this alone. Halfway into my walk toward Sterling, Dino rushes back onto the field and catches up with me. She tells me about her plans with River in her usual dry, understated way, but I can tell she's hiding some level of giddiness by the way she sucks in her cheeks as she talks. The more I learn about their chat, the more I'm convinced River is more Jane Fonda than Jim Jones—eccentric rather than apocalyptic. This reassures me, and by the time we reach Sterling and the tree planters I'm unreservedly happy for my friend.

Sterling drives her shovel into the ground and rests a foot on the blade. Even though it's January, she's in green shorts and a white tank top pricked with mulch. There's a dull glow on her brow she wipes away with a dirt-caked arm, and, somehow, she's just as beautiful messy as she is all dolled up.

"Hi, guys!" she says. "Dino, love your hair."

Dino touches a hand to the top of two thick, braided pigtails: "Awww, thanks, Sterl Girl! And your curls . . . poppin' like Rice Krispies, as always."

"Thanks! Shovels are along the outer fence if you wanna grab some."

We go over. Dino grabs one, but I grab two in case Rod comes back to us. When we return, we get right back to digging, the three of us going at it without talking for the first minute or two. I can't tell if it's good that I'm not saying anything stupid or bad that I'm not saying anything at all. Out of nowhere, Sterling forces my hand.

She stops and straightens herself, back arching so that her chest pops out. But more in a stretchy way than a flirty way. Then she looks right at me. "Kalvin, old buddy, old pal. You wouldn't happen to have any Snickers in those pockets, would ya?"

I stop digging and shrug. "Nope. Fresh out."

"Come on, dude. Don't tell me you don't have a stash that you're just munching on all day."

"I actually never get high on my own supply."

She laughs, and I do a praise dance on the inside. Who knew

watching *Scarface* with Dino last year would turn out to be one of my best life decisions?

"Okay, Walter White," Sterling responds.

Smoothing my imaginary collar, I come back with "I kinda like to think of myself as more Stringer Bell."

"You're in a suburban high school, not inner-city Baltimore," Dino mutters. "Plus, Idris looks way better."

I glance back, and she's still shoveling. Rod jogs over, having left Gianna and crew to their game. He's smiling. I can tell that in his mind, at least, the conversation went well. He grabs his shovel and starts on a hole.

I turn back and flinch because Sterling's moved in much closer now.

"No, no. Wait, Dino," she says. "Idris Elba, huh . . ." Her eyebrows lift as she puts her hand to my chin and tilts my face at odd angles like a doctor would at a checkup. After her impromptu exam, she nods approvingly. "I can kinda see it. In the eyes. The nose, a little." She backs away again.

I let out a breath.

"Either way, though, you're a badass kingpin, so you can't go wrong."

"True," I say, going back to shoveling.

"If I ran a million-dollar candy ring, I'd stash some everywhere," she says. "Lockers. Teachers' drawers. Gym floorboards. Places I'd just completely forget about, and then one day, months later, I'd just happen to come across them, and be like 'Oh, there's candy'!"

"You sound like you've thought about this a little too much."

"Or maybe you haven't thought about it enough," she replies. "You can't tell me you wouldn't do something spectacular if you had that much money, no inhibitions, and no limits. Dino, what would you do?"

"Stalk Rihanna," she says without breaking from her shoveling.

Sterling cranes her neck. "Rod?"

"Same."

Then she looks back at me. "Your turn, Kal."

I stop. Think about it. Then I say, "I would go to Hawaii."

"Ahhh. Okay. Maui, Oahu, or the Big Island?" she asks.

I shake my head. "I'd go to Lanai."

Thought lines river across her brow as she studies my face again. But not like the previous time. More seriously, like I'm more complex. It's as if I've just gained a third dimension in her eyes. "Have you been there?" she asks.

"Yeah. With my parents once, a few years back."

"What's there to do there?"

*Rekindle lost love? Reignite the dying embers of a marriage gone cold?*

"Read. Walk around. Watch the ocean."

"Come on. There's gotta be more to it than that," she says, her tone almost pleading. It's there that I notice she's actually interested in what I have to say beyond just my advice. She's interested in me. Where I've been. Where I'm going. It's like she senses there's more to me than what I'm allowing myself to give.

56

Maybe it's me succumbing to the whole crush dynamic, but she seems like the kind of person I could open up to.

I stake the blade of my shovel into the ground and rest a forearm against the grip. Then I tell her about the Shipwreck Beach and the rugged-earth Garden of the Gods. The way the dirt roads and pure-blue skies above make it seem like the island itself is nature's last and loveliest secret.

Then I speak wistfully of Kaunolu Village, the pu'uhonua, the ancient cliffside refuge. I leave my parents out of it, though, because a refuge is just that—something that protects from the outside world, her included. She listens to it all, the whole time biting her bottom lip like she's chewing on a thought.

Once I finish my ode, I can't help but notice how much more relaxed I am around her than just minutes ago. Heart rate settled and slow. Smiles quick and unreserved. My gaze meeting hers like an equal, coming and going as it pleases.

"Sounds magical," she says. "Like an absolutely wonderful escape."

"It is."

She lets out a long sigh. "Wish I could escape some things right about now." She tries to disguise her glance toward the group of guys across the field, but I catch it. I don't even have to look to know who she sees.

"Speaking of which, how'd the thing that we talked about go?" I ask.

"It kinda didn't," she mumbles. "We'll talk later."

I don't push it. Too many more questions and Dino and Rod

will pick up something. Plus, I don't think it's something she wants to talk about right now. We go back to shoveling, a contented silence wrapping around us with the breeze.

I glance to my side, and Rod's going back and forth from shoveling to pretending the shovel's a twirling baton; throwing it up, misjudging the catch, and inevitably jumping out of the way to dodge catastrophic injury. I look toward Sterling again.

Randomly, I ask, "You know what else Lanai used to be famous for?"

"What?"

"The whole island used to be a pineapple plantation."

She touches a hand to her lips. "Oh my God, that place really is magical!"

"I knew you'd be interested in that."

"Wait. *How* did you know that?"

"Yearbook last year. You listed pineapple as your favorite fruit."

"So you know I like Snickers. You know I like pineapples. What else do you know about me, Kal Shmelton?"

Immediately I regret saying it. My skin gets an icky, Peeping Tom–ish twinge, except instead of looking through girls' windows, I'm memorizing their dietary preferences.

Her neck tilts and her face contorts as she leaves me twisting in the wind for a response. Desperate, I come out with "I know you suck at shoveling."

She gasps. "Seriously?"

"Seriously," I say, nodding. "You've been at that same hole for, what, twenty minutes, and it's still just half a foot deep."

She crouches, studying the hole she's created. "You liar. It's soooo much deeper than half a foot."

"That can't be more than seven inches."

Sterling sticks her arm in. "It's at least a foot. Come look."

I go over to her, squatting beside her shovel. My neck cranes far enough that my head eclipses the hole. "Sterling, there's no way that's—"

I barely notice the motion of Sterling's arm, and by the time I register the fact that I've been tricked, it's far too late. My back feels like it's being hit with a spray of shower water. I spring up, and dirt cascades from my shirt.

"You just threw dirt on me!"

"Because you deserved it." She laughs.

I grab a handful of mulch and toss it, making sure to aim below her head.

"Hey!" she says, her face mangled in mock outrage.

"Hey yourself!"

I lurch back as she grabs and throws another handful, aiming right at my new sneakers. As she turns to run, I grab more mulch and fling it wildly, hitting her neck and back.

"Punk!" she yells, fingers gliding through the back of her neck. "You got dirt in my kitchen."

*Huh?* "I've never even been in your house," I say.

Sterling turns, mouth wide open. "Kalvin . . ."

From behind me, Dino audibly groans and says, "Oh my God, you are *such* an only child."

"What?" I ask.

Sterling smiles wide as I've ever seen despite her faux attempt at anger: "Kalvin. A *kitchen* is the back of a Black girl's hair."

Earnestly I ask, "Why do they call it a 'kitchen'?"

"I dunno, because 'basement' is too gauche? Could you please help me, though?"

She turns, lifting her back curls, and I instinctively glide toward her. For a good minute, I carefully pluck brown wood chips from her hair, tensing every time my fingers graze her neck. If she's uncomfortable with me this close, she doesn't let on. I might as well be a jeweler clipping on a necklace. At this moment, there's no place I'd rather be. Not even Hawaii.

"What's going on here?"

We both turn and see Chadwick stalking toward us. Jordan's right behind him. Sterling steps away from me, shaking out her curls.

"Kalvin's doing penance for messing up my hair."

Words leave my lips, halting and awkward. "I was, um, just . . . getting out some wood chips I got in her hair."

Chadwick looks both confused and annoyed as his eyes flit from Sterling to me, but he says nothing. However, Jordan is suddenly a bona fide chatterbox, directing most of his questions toward Rod. Rod stops shoveling, stands straight, and looks off in the distance as Jordan snakes an arm around his shoulder.

"My man Roderick. *Buddy.* Pal. How you been, man?"

"Good," Rod mumbles.

"Good to see you up off the couch, out volunteering on this fine day. You getting a *handle* on this whole shoveling thing?"

"Yep."

I turn to face the two. Dino stops digging, knifing her shovel into her hole. She doesn't look up, but I can tell she's listening. And by the way her jawline's moving, I can tell she's angry.

To my side, I hear Chadwick whispering "Can we talk a sec?" but Sterling lightly swats his hand away, having taken on a new interest in the conversation before us. She inches up to where she's beside me as Jordan's badgering persists.

Jordan sticks a hand out. "Well, I just wanted to say no hard feelings about lunch the other day, bro. What better time to reconcile than in the spirit of MLK?"

Everybody can see it. The trap Jordan's just laid. But just as well, we see Rod has no choice but to spring it. If he refuses to shake, Jordan gets to lay claim to being the "bigger man."

Rod hesitantly reaches out, sealing his fate in the process. Jordan simply pushes with one arm and pulls with the other. Rod stumbles and falls over his hole.

As Rod struggles to get upright, Jordan points, the anger in his voice no longer papered over by false sincerity. "Don't think you actually need that shovel, bro. Your *mouth* dug the hole you're in now."

Before I can react, Sterling's gone from my side, marching up to Jordan's face. Dino falls right in beside her.

"You stupid *asshole!*" Sterling shouts.

Dino follows up with "Lay off, you jerk!"

"He started it!" Jordan protests, holding up his hands as he looks dead at Sterling. He doesn't even so much as nod in my or Dino's direction. It's like he thinks he only needs to justify his actions to those in his social circle.

"Are you in elementary school?" Sterling asks.

"Sterl, this guy literally said he was gonna try to come after Gianna."

I look toward the far goal. Gianna's stopped playing and has peeled off from the soccer girls. She's looking this way but is far out of earshot.

"And maybe her leaving your ass would teach you how not to be a douche," Sterling says.

As big as Jordan is, Sterling's literally backing him down.

"Oh, so you're coming at me for defending my girlfriend's honor?" he asks.

Sterling shakes her head. "Don't try to pull that shit on me! Gianna's honor doesn't need defending."

I hear Chadwick's voice behind me: "Sterling."

She either doesn't hear or willfully ignores him. I watch as Jordan's backpedal edges him just feet from another hole.

"I can't defend my own girlfriend?" Jordan asks as he points toward Gianna, who's jogging over by now.

At this, Sterling cackles. "I think you know *very little* about what Gianna thinks about you as a boyfriend."

Jordan's walk slows just inches from the edge. I bounce on my toes, ready to witness the catastrophe. Folding his arms, he asks, "What's that supposed to mean?" His voice is quieter now that Gianna's closer, but still very insistent.

"Wouldn't you like to know."

"*Tell me*. Did she say something?" he demands, freezing, his heels at the precipice.

"Whoa, buddy. You wouldn't wanna intrude on the sanctity of conversations between girlfriends, would ya?"

"Sterling!" Chadwick yells.

"*What?*" she snaps back, her body half twisting so she can see him.

"Could you calm down, please?" he asks softly.

Sterling makes a face like she's just bitten into the bitterest, most sour lemon ever. I sneer back at Chadwick, not even trying to hide my disgust. Why would you undercut your girlfriend like that?

It's too late. The momentum's gone. Jordan's hands flail skyward as he walks away. He doesn't fall in. Not even so much as a slip. "I'm not dealing with this anymore," he says.

Between Jordan's escape and Sterling's spat with her boyfriend, my blood is set to boil. Surprisingly, Gianna comes to Sterling's side, not Jordan's, asking what's going on. Sterling glares at Jordan but bites her tongue. "Nothing, girl. I'll tell ya later."

I look around. A few people at different volunteer stations are watching, but our little fracas seems to have slipped by unnoticed for most. Even the two overseeing teachers are just standing at the home-side gate, looking at their phones.

I'm too wired not to do anything, so I start marching, tracking behind Jordan's steps. I have no idea what I would or possibly could do when I confront him, but I know I'll sure as hell die trying to make things right. Figuratively. Maybe even literally, as solid as Jordan is.

My sight, blurred by anger, locks on to his profile. The closer I get, the more rage I feel. Rage for Rod. Rage that Jordan didn't get what he deserves. Rage at everything that isn't right and just about the world. But I don't get to him to mete out justice. Someone else beats me to it. I see a shovel in the corner of my eye. Then a person: Rod.

He raises it to eye level, and I yell "NOOOO!" while lunging for him.

I don't immediately process that Rod's not looking to assault Jordan, just to embarrass him. Jordan turns right in time to see Rod turn over the blade above Jordan's head. Dirt and mulch landslide down his face, neck, and back.

"Shit!" Jordan yells.

I glance around again, and now the whole stadium's looking. Gianna's hands cover her mouth.

Dino says, "Oh my God," and Sterling goes, "Wow."

Rod hesitates at first, half smiling, half shocked. Not sure if he should celebrate or run. Jordan shakes the dirt from his head and spends a few seconds just blinking it away. Once he's blinked enough to get his bearings, he spins, looking for Rod.

*Run!*

Rod starts barreling toward me. Past me.

Jordan takes off after him, yelling "Come back here!"

He doesn't get far, courtesy of one discreet, wildly impulsive move I make. A two-inch relocation of my foot. Jordan face-plants, and I hear laughter sprout like weeds in all directions around me.

Jordan staggers up and stares me down with this rabid look in his eyes. I stop laughing. I think I'm done for until a voice rings out from the midfield gate.

"Hey! What's going on?" It's Mr. Pollard, the gym teacher.

I look at Jordan, who's still staring, still breathing hard. But his fists slowly unclench. He turns and storms away, brushing the sleeves of his shirt to a chorus of quiet giggles. Like a doting puppy, Chadwick follows. When they're almost at the gate, Gianna finally detaches herself from Sterling and jogs after her boyfriend.

That afternoon, Dino drives me and Rod to the dessert shop on our way home. There, we treat him to a chocolate shake and strawberry surprise cupcake to celebrate. We even jokingly make a toast.

"Eat, drink, and be merry, for tomorrow we die."

If I know Jordan, he'll make sure of that.

# Five

**Surprisingly, days go** by where Jordan doesn't murder either me or Rod. Sure, the times we make contact in the cafeteria, I can almost see steam rising from his scalp, but he never acts on it. In fact, up until Thursday, the week's kind of boring and uneventful. And even Thursday, most of the morning is perfectly perfunctory.

Until third period.

I do the same routine as last week, heading to the closet to fulfill a couple candy orders, hoping for no surprises. Instead, I get three: Gianna Kyle, Avery Ashley, and Garrison Charles.

They're crowded around the entrance to the storage closet when I get there, each carrying bags of Starbursts and expectant smiles.

"We heard you liked candy," Avery says. She's the first to rush out at me, shoving a bag into my chest. I bumble and almost drop it, totally flustered by the moment.

"What is this?" I ask.

"Starbursts," Garrison says. "But Avery's bag is open because she really likes the pinks."

Avery gasps. "Don't act like you didn't get an orange."

"No, I mean why are you here?" I ask.

Gianna steps up, meekly sliding between them and me. In that disarming, aw-shucks sort of way, she says, "Sterling kinda told us you give really good relationship advice, and we wanted to see for ourselves."

*Sterling.* A spiderweb of connections begins to build in my mind, all leading back to her. It suddenly makes sense now why Keegan randomly approached me at the mall. Because it wasn't random.

"We'll pay," Garrison blurts out, pointing to the candy.

Nope. Nuh-uh. No way in hell. Too many things could go sideways. "I've got enough candy," I reply.

"What, you want, like, *money*?" Avery asks. The way she says it, her question blunt with each word tightly wrapped in a sharp Southern accent, I think she's giving me attitude. So I give it right back.

"Yeah, like, *money*."

She blinks, taken aback, and I immediately regret my response. Not only are they the most popular juniors in school. They're also friends with Sterling. Avery raises a finger, and I think she's about to jam it in my face, but instead she pivots, pointing at Garrison. "Do you have cash?"

Garrison makes a face. "Ewww."

Avery turns to me. "Do you Cash App or Venmo?"

"Do I *what*?"

Avery's confused that I'm confused. She opens her mouth,

and I can tell she's about to enunciate the question like I'm some tourist when Gianna jumps in.

"Don't mind them; I got cash," she says, pulling three crisp bills from her clutch. "Will tens work?"

I just stand there, stunned. They think I'm good at this, and maybe I am. What's for certain, though, is that they're willing to pay me to find out. This could be what puts me over the top for Hawaii.

I don't know what to say. "I don't—"

"Not for the whole period. What did you do with Sterling last week, like six or seven minutes?" Gianna asks.

I feel the money brush my fingertips, and it feels great, like power and success and confidence.

It feels like a goal that was barely a dream becoming a touch more real.

"Yeah . . . ," I say hesitantly. Then, much more self-assuredly, "*Yeah*. Sure."

"Great!" Avery jumps up and down, doing a high-pitched squeal-clap. "Yay, I'll start."

She doesn't even wait for me to lead her in; she just grabs my wrists and drags me.

It takes exactly twenty-six minutes to get through all three. Three seven-minute sessions, a couple minutes of transition time in between them, and the couple minutes it takes to exchange contact info, because any good therapist needs to be reachable in case of a client crisis.

For Avery's session, we talk about how her on-again, off-again relationship with Brady True has morphed into an unhealthy codependency, and game-plan how to start setting some clear boundaries. I've learned from my parents that therapy isn't a one-hit deal, so I know to "schedule out" for future sessions. It's a win-win. Consistency for the client. Guaranteed money for me. I put Avery down for the following three Tuesdays.

For the next session, Garrison readily admits to having trust issues with his boyfriend, Greg Peterson. Diving into his history, I can tell it primarily stems from his mother leaving his father when Garrison was young, creating within him a subconscious fear of abandonment. Garrison isn't totally sold, though, which I'm okay with. Learning from Mom and Dad, I know therapy is more a waiting game than anything. We still agree to schedule the following two Fridays.

Whereas Garrison's a skeptic, Gianna's more of what therapists would call a "pleaser." She wants to please and thus has a difficult time saying no. It's what has her worrying about her boyfriend Jordan Parris's feelings more than her very justified concerns about his need to run the relationship.

"The word 'no' is a muscle," I tell her as she leans against a chocolate shelf. "You've got to start using it, or it'll always be weak."

"But it's hard," she protests, mockingly banging her head against a post.

"Just like working out is hard *at first*. But the more you do it, the easier it gets. Like this." I walk up to her, swiping the Baby Ruth she's holding from her hand. "Only one freebie per visit. I already gave you a Ghirardelli Square."

I know I should be charging for everything, but I'm too nice. Always been that way. I was hit-or-miss with elementary school honor roll, but my Citizenship Award game was elite. Kindness isn't just a switch I can flick to turn off.

A smile almost breaks to the surface of her pouty face. "How do I even start, though? I just know Jordan will ask me to his parents' lake house for their anniversary next month, and if I go it's gonna be so weird, and I'll be resentful because we'll be missing the ball, but I'm honestly terrified I'll wuss out and go along with it."

Gently, I grab her elbows, willing her eyes to meet mine. "Okay, just remember this simple trick. If you feel too weak to say no in the moment, just say, 'Let me think about it for a while.' That buys you two important things: time and space."

Fireworks go off in her eyes. She bear-hugs me so tight she bruises a rib. "You are a goddamn *saint*, Kal Shmelton! I could literally kiss you right now."

While I would gladly accept in most circumstances, I think the bro code would consider any kind of kiss from your boy's crush a class-five violation.

I say, "I'll settle for scheduling a follow-up."

The rest of the day comes like a hurricane. Eight more people approach me with referrals from Keegan, Gianna, and Avery alone. Apparently Sterling told all of them sometime last week, and then they went and told Brianna Partridge's crew, who went and blabbed to the cross-country girls, who somehow spilled the deets to the Mercedes Mafia, which is weird because the two groups don't even talk. Even some random number texts me during sixth period today, saying they go to Forsyth High, a county over, and asks, Do you do virtual appts??? followed by an upside-down smiley-face emoji.

I text back: Sry. Don't do out-of-network.

And they're not even coming exclusively for relationship stuff. Folks are wanting to get help with stress over school and advice on family issues, too. You name it. All willing to pay $10 per seven-minute session.

I'd made $72 in candy sales since last Thursday. It was an uptick from my average, which is expected in the midst of cuffing season. But Valentine's Day is just twenty-three days away, and I'm more than $2,000 short. Having these rich kids pay $10 a pop could fill that gap.

I feel like I'm walking on air by the time the final bell rings. The walk to my locker feels more like a glide, and I keep thinking about how having that money could change everything. How Hawaii is a heartbeat rather than a world away. It's all I can do not to yell triumphantly and hoist my AP US History book like a trophy or spike it like a football.

The feeling doesn't last long, though. My locker slams shut, and I barely avoid getting my head caught.

I stare at the skinny arm that slammed it. It's Maddie Trout. I see the taunt in her eyes, her tongue sliding around her lips like she's looking at prey. Even with her wispy black bob, she still looks menacing. My veins strain against my neck at the sight of her.

"What?" I ask.

"I know what you're up to," she says, hands crossing over her chest.

"I'm not up to anything."

"So you're not giving dumb-ass therapy advice to gullible teens?" she asks.

I shake my head. "Why would I do that? I'm not a therapist."

"And you're also not allowed to sell candy independent of a school club, but being an unethical troglodyte didn't stop you before, so why would it now?"

Maddie's the student body vice president and the person in charge of their candy fundraising. The person with the most to lose with my candy business as competition. But it's not just that. Since last year, well before my biz even existed, I've been getting Chernobyl-level bad energy from her. The genesis for her hatred is about as clear to me as a storm cloud. I don't care, though. She's a spoiled, rich brat. The type who'd purchase a globe and think they owned the world. Her mom's a big-time tech exec, Dad's some hotshot lawyer, and they treat Maddie like she's the Next Big Thing. To me, she's No Big Deal. But apparently, for some reason, she thinks I'm a Big Problem.

"Maddie, I don't know what you're talking about." I make sure to smile through my denial. Digging a hand into my pocket,

I take out a stick of my ICE BREAKERS gum. I tuck it into her palm. "I think you should *chill out* a bit."

"I have a source saying you're doing your little sessions in the tech ed closet. Is the candy there, too? Some ungodly orgy with you, Piaget, and Pop Rocks going on?"

Maddie's friends with Garrison, and she also succeeded Rosie, Dino's ex, as the primary investigative journalist and anchor for the weekly student homeroom newscast. Maddie has a nose for finding things out. It's no surprise she's aware I'm doing therapy. But I know acting dumb will drive her up a wall.

"Your source is wrong," I tell her.

She stamps her foot. "Kalvin Shmelton, I hereby demand you stop selling candy right now!"

"Or what?"

"Or . . . or . . . I'll tell!"

I almost laugh in Maddie's face. What could she possibly say? *I heard this rumor that a boy was giving his peers advice on relationships and life?* Even if the admins did take her seriously, what could they possibly do? Give me a week's detention?

Smirking, I respond, "Just for that threat, I'm gonna lower my prices again to cut into your bottom line. You can call it a Tic Tax."

I spin around her and walk away, quietly wincing at my atrocious wordplay. *Tic Tax, Kal? Ugh.* Should've left that one in the drafts. Maddie grunts, and I hear her footsteps trailing me, chasing me down. She brushes up against my side.

"Okay, that candy pun didn't even make sense, Kalvin. A tax isn't a price cut. It's a fee levied by the government to—"

"*Maddie*," I interrupt. "Go away."

"Only if you stop selling."

"And if I don't?"

"Then once I get solid proof, I'll go to admins and get *both* your little endeavors down!"

"On what pretext?" I ask.

"GCHS code of conduct, article five, subsection two-a: 'Unapproved soliciting or sales of contraband shall incur a penalty of no less than a five-day suspension.'"

*Suspension?* I stop at that, as hallway traffic continues around us. *Jesus.* Detentions and write-ups are one thing, but colleges aren't in the habit of overlooking suspensions.

"I'm warning you," she adds. "Don't mess with me again, Kalvin."

I square up to her, annoyance and confusion scrawled all over my brow. "*Again?* Maddie, I didn't mess with you the *first* time! But you've had it out for me since last year, for God knows what reason."

"Don't you play dumb!"

"I'm not *playing* at all, Maddie. Now back off."

I leave her standing there in a huff.

When I get to the end of the hall, I cut left down a hallway and hurry through the courtyard to make my way to the C wing. Maddie's words have my nerves on high alert now. I cannot get caught. But I also can't stop. This is my revenue stream, after all. It's my parents' marriage, too.

I discreetly open the closet and do a quick inventory of candy I need from the store. *One bag of Reese's. More Skittles. York Peppermint Patties.*

I hear a knock at the door. It's soft and unintrusive, not authoritative like an admin, so I ignore it. I pull the money I earned that day out of my wallet to count. And then I hear the knocking again.

"I have business hours," I mumble. "And a life."

I know I should be grinding nonstop to get to my goal, but between the chem test first period and an in-class English essay, I'm fried. I get back to tidying up a bit, thinking about how I could make this space more presentable. Maybe some decorations would liven it up. Definitely an actual chair to go along with the stool. A coffee table and throw pillow, maybe? Whatever, I'll figure it out.

Even though I'm exhausted, I decide to get a head start on tomorrow by prepping some more preorders.

Purple stationery. Red Sharpie:


DEAR CAYLEN,
    YOU ARE MY RIESEN D'ÊTRE.
YOURS,
AMELIE


Red stationery. Purple Sharpie:

BARRY,

    WHAT DO YOU GET WHEN YOU PUT TWO BIG,
SUPERSWEET NERDS TOGETHER? . . . US.
LOVE,
LIONEL

The knock comes once more, this time much louder. I watch the door. *Mr. Perkins? No, wouldn't be him.* He's usually speeding out of the parking lot along with the students after final bell. Besides, he has his own key.

I tense up when I realize who else might want to catch me here. *Maddie.* I get up and storm to the door, pushing it open and totally ready to go off, when I see Sterling.

"Hi, can I come in?" she asks.

It's a miracle that I can even sputter out a "Sure" the way my brain just turned off. And it's not until she wryly smiles, glancing to my feet and back up, that I realize I'm still blocking the door. I move out of the way, and she enters.

I watch as she circles the room, repositioning a few pieces of equipment to expose hidden candy bags. She marvels at what she sees and wonders about all she *doesn't* see.

"Would you say there are, like, ten thousand pieces total in here or twenty?" she asks.

I'm thinking, *What?* But I answer, "Ten thousand?"

She nods. "Do you ever think of what it'd feel like to bury yourself in candy like kids do with sand at the beach?"

*No, can't say I have. I tend to think normal things.* "Um, why're you asking me this?"

She lets out a half laugh as her gaze centers on me. "Sorry, it's just the kinds of things my dumb brain thinks about."

I'm both fascinated and unsettled by this. Fascinated because I've never thought of candy as anything beyond its practical utility. Eat. Feel good. Crash. Eat some more. Unsettled because why would she call herself dumb?

"You're not dumb," I reply.

She just kind of shrugs. "Sure," she says in a manner that's much less sure than the word itself. Then she takes two steps toward me.

"So our last meeting here started a bit inauspiciously, so can we try again?" She holds out her hand. "Hi," she says.

"Hi. I'm Kalvin."

A smirk edges into her smile. "Yeah. I know."

We shake, and it's like a wellspring of joy bubbles up from somewhere deep within me. To think that she actually sought me out. I try to think of a pithy comeback, but all I can come up with is "That makes two of us."

She squints. "You know your own name?"

"No, I meant I know—"

"Dude." She laughs. "I'm just kidding!"

Now, her smile is all sparkly teeth and joie de vivre, and it's like the sun during an eclipse: I just can't stop staring at it.

Sterling's eyes travel again, settling after a while on some random spot on the back shelf. "A place this cool needs a name." It's more of a declaration than a suggestion, the way she says it. "You got a marker?"

I pull out a black Sharpie.

"Tape?"

I conjure that, too. She takes both and heads to the far end of the closet, ripping a strip of cardboard off a box in a bottom corner. She lays it flat on the back shelf and writes. When she's done, she tapes the sign on a row that's as high as her forehead. It reads:


CANDYLAND
POP. 1
MAYOR KALVIN SHMELTON


"Candyland, huh?" I ask.

Sterling nods, admiring her own creativity as I cautiously walk up beside her. "Population you." She turns to face me, shoving the Sharpie in my face like it's a microphone. "Tell me, Mayor Shmelton: Does it get lonely being the only?" she says.

"Not really. It's kind of a nice break from things."

"Things like what?" she asks.

I think of school. My parents. My social life.

"Everything," I say.

I can tell she wasn't expecting that answer, because her lips shut, sucking in between her teeth. She turns from me. Whatever retort she had locked and loaded is lost to the universe.

To restart the conversation, I risk a question: "So your thing with Chadwick? You said we'd talk later."

She shakes her head and sighs. She runs a hand atop the shelf filled with bags of suckers, her fingertips gathering the dust. She stares at her fingers before placing them to her lips. One quick exhalation and a cloud of dust mites mushrooms before her eyes. Watching the spectacle, she says, "Honestly, I . . . I just flaked out."

I hear the remorse in her voice. The quiet ache for a second chance. The reaching desperation to recover a fumbled opportunity.

"Sorry to hear that," I respond.

Her shoulders rise and fall as she chirps "It's fine" in a tone that's a complete 180 from before. It's as if her emotions were a bookbag she'd just shrugged off. She whips back around to face me, giving me a slow, appraising look. "So to recap. You have a candy conglomerate that's dueling sword to sword with Big Bad Stu-Gov, and you're hiding it right across the hall?"

"I wouldn't say 'dueling.' More like nipping at their heels."

"I genuinely am impressed, though," she says. "Badassery off the charts. Honestly, I'm kinda jealous of you."

The words make me blink. I wasn't expecting to hear that from Sterling Glistern of all people. "You have no need to be jealous of anything," I say.

She shrugs again, twisting away from me with the ease of a feather in the wind. "So I was wondering if you could help me out," she says. The statement hangs in the air like a question.

"Sure," I reply.

"Wait, it's ten dollars, right? Should I pay now or later? Oh my God, inadvertent candy joke," she says, smiling.

I wave it off. "It's Now *and* Later, actually. And don't bother. It's free for you." I'd feel some type of way requiring my crush to pay to see me. "After all the referrals I've gotten through you, you might as well be a business partner."

Sterling holds her hand out. "If I'm a partner, then I'm damn sure getting my fifty percent."

I take her hand and shake it. "I owe you a debt of gratitude."

She makes a sulky face but doesn't respond. I wedge myself onto a shelf directly across from her. "What do you need?" I ask.

She sighs as she sits down on the stool. Blowing a wisp of hair from her face, she says, "I need Chadwick to fall in love with me."

"Chadwick?" I ask, the word coming out mousy.

*The guy you seemed like you were about to tear the head off of, all Black Widow–like? That guy?*

"Yeah. Remember? My boyfriend."

"Mm-hmm," I manage to croak out, too scared to try for another actual word.

"Okay, good. Honestly, even though I flaked out, maybe that's a good thing. Maybe we could salvage what's left of us and turn it into something special. I mean, if I only think about the good parts about him . . ."

"His good parts?"

"Yeah. He's kind to me. Intelligent. Driven." She turns my way, eyelids pinched, as she asks, "A catch, right?"

I'm not sure if she actually wants me to answer, so I don't. I just say, "That's quite a change."

"True. But no relationship is perfect, am I right? And I guess I just think . . . maybe we're still worth a shot. Maybe it's something we can grow into."

"So you wanna make him fall in love with you somehow, like in the movies?"

"Well, maybe not *fall*. Just rekindle or something. You know what I'm saying?" She spies my hesitance and says, "What am I even saying? Of course you don't."

She gets up to leave, but I hold out my hand.

"*Wait.*"

She pauses.

"A doctor doesn't have to be injured in order to know how to do surgery."

"Okay, then, Kalvin," she says, crossing her arms as she sits again. "Tell me what you know about rekindling romances." There's an undercurrent of cynicism in her tone, like she knows the idea of me understanding her situation is as far-fetched as geolocating the end of a rainbow.

"I've heard my parents give advice on it all the time."

"Talk is cheap," she fires back. "What do your parents do?"

"Do for what?" I ask.

"To keep the romance burning."

Her question sets me back. Therapists talk about clients'

lives, not the other way around. Besides, how would I look if I told the truth? My parents do nothing. They stand by and let their kid do the heavy lifting.

After several false starts, I sputter out with, "They make sure to sit together and talk every day."

*Technically true. They have a podcast, after all.*

I turn away from her to gulp down my nerves. When I sit back up, Sterling watches me curiously as she grasps for any insight she can pull down from the slippery platitude I just offered her. Luckily, she doesn't ask a follow-up.

"I just need something," she says. "Something big to bring back the romance. And I feel if he just falls hard for me, he won't step out, and I won't be so jealous, and maybe we can salvage something. I dunno."

She thwacks a hand against her forehead like she knows it's a stupid idea. I don't say anything, but I agree with the hand. It *is* stupid. An irrational frustration wells up in my chest. Questions sprout like pikes in my brain, and I want to jab her with each to puncture and kill this idea of hers.

*How could a high school student possibly think they love somebody? Why would you even* want *to? Do we truly even know what love is?*

My mom once said on her and my dad's podcast that to really love someone, you had to know them through all four seasons. She was speaking literally and figuratively. She meant you need to experience someone over a long period of time—at least a full year—to make sure they don't bait-and-switch you. But additionally, you need to witness how that person experiences both ups and downs—all "seasons" of life.

I want to throw Mom's advice in Sterling's face.

"Do you think I'm being foolish?" she asks.

"No," I murmur, sinking back, my shoulder blades pressing against a shelf. I can tell the meekness in my answer is discouraging to her. It's like a light goes out in her eyes. She does this thing where her mouth shifts right as her gaze takes a downturn.

"Sometimes I think I'm a little off," she admits. "Most times, actually."

And there she goes again. Putting herself down like that. It's like she wants to believe it. I want to shake her by the shoulders and say, *You're Sterling freaking Glistern! Perfection personified. The most resplendent girl to ever walk these halls. How could you possibly think so lowly of yourself?*

"You're looking at me the way my dad does sometimes," she says, a sad little laugh trailing her admission. "Every time I come up with another of my stupid ideas."

"What's another idea you've had?" I ask.

"Well, there was the time in kindergarten when I tried to fly off our rooftop with a jerry-rigged industrial fan and kite sails as wings. When I was nine, I built a backyard trebuchet to fling empty paint cans at my annoying neighbor. Oh, and who could forget the Great Laundry Room Hazmat Incident in seventh grade?"

Although I'm infinitely curious, I refrain from asking for

details. I've got the sense she'd rather not relive it. Instead, I simply say, "Sounds like a future NASA scientist."

"Figures. My parents always said I was a bit of a space cadet."

"Did they encourage your experimentation?" I ask.

"Not when there's a three-thousand-dollar cleanup bill on the back end."

"But still . . ."

She shakes her head. Then she asks, "Did your parents encourage your childhood schemes?"

"Yes," I say right away. It's so quick to come out because it didn't require any thought. As long as I was safe and not hurting anybody, they let me plan and plot to my heart's desire. They don't know about my candy biz or the therapy, but I imagine they'd be mildly amused by the situation, at worst, if not totally delighted.

I'm kind of getting an idea why she's so quick to call herself dumb. When the ones closest to you aren't telling you you're smart, what else are you supposed to think?

"What's it like to have perfect parents?" she mumbles.

*I wouldn't know.* I'm not sure if her question is rhetorical or real, but in either case I wouldn't answer. Something tells me talking about them might help her relate, but the thought of it unsettles me. Truth be told, *Sterling* unsettles me. Not in a creepy way, but her questions and prods for info always seem to knock me off my guard.

"Parents are parents," I say.

Sterling nods, but in a noticeably solemn way. It's like she's affirming my answer but also confirming her childhood experience was much different from mine.

I crouch, willing her eyes to meet mine. "You were a kid then and a teenager now," I tell her. "You have every right to feel and do off-the-wall things."

She raises an eyebrow. "So you'll help me do this one really insane thing?"

*Um, no.*

There's no way in *hell* I'd help my forever crush lock it up with some preppy jerk face. But how to say no without sounding like a total asshole? I could play the "ethics" card. We're just talking now, as friends. And a trusted friend can *absolutely* hate on a relationship they feel is bad for the other person. But the minute she becomes a client, it's a different story. It'd be way out of bounds for a therapist to finagle with a client's personal life. Inserting myself into Sterling's love life would ensnare me in all sorts of problematic situations. Plus, I *like* this girl. There's no way I could be objective, or even all that helpful. Major conflict of interest.

I don the most sheepish smile I can muster and say, "I'm not actually in the matchmaker business."

"Ugh . . . Well, okay." She stands. Pats me on the shoulder. Turns to leave. "Appreciate you listening."

She's all the way through the exit when a random thought sneaks up on me and puts me in a chokehold. Helping her will keep her talking to me. If I lose that, I lose Sterling. I would be an *idiot* to let her go.

And what if a little relationship demo work is what she needs? I could be her Mr. Fix-It, tinkering and toggling and tweaking as much as necessary. But maybe instead of a teeny, tiny hex wrench I—*Oops!*—use a hammer.

The ethics of it all materialize before me like a ghost I can't shake. I dash right through it and grab her hand before she leaves.

She spins around.

"I've reconsidered. I think maybe I can help."

Help her.

Help myself.

Sounds pretty ethical to me.

# Six

**I'd had my** doubts, but the new *ZombieWorld 3 Jurassic* mod is pretty cool. I'm playing as a Utahraptor armed with an M16 military-grade rifle, hunting down zombie Cro-Magnon men and necromancing Neanderthals. Dino's leveled up already to a Spinosaurus, which comes equipped with a Stinger rocket launcher and munitions capabilities. We've managed to kettle the allied Darkseeker Army and Necromorph cultists into their abandoned factory base—don't ask me how a factory made its way into the Late Cretaceous period—and are planting explosives around the perimeter.

Dino's her best gamer girl self when unburdened by the pressures of live streaming. Don't get me wrong, she's good when folks are watching, but the way she executes trench raids when the spotlight's off is just poetry in motion.

I push my headphone mic closer to my lips after wiring a brick of C-4. "You think we've put down enough?" I ask.

"Yeah. I laid down extra at the load-bearing wall, so we should be good."

"How far away should we be when it blows?"

"The dried-out riverbed by the dune is probably good."

Dino's answer gives rise to a question I'd been meaning to ask: "How did your coffee date with River go?"

She doesn't answer right off, and I frown, thinking it didn't go well. But after a beat of silence passes, she speaks up. I can hear the sheepishness in her voice when she asks, "Which one?"

I gasp. "*Seriously?* Two dates? It's been three days!"

"I *know*," she says. "It wasn't planned. It just sort of happened."

"*What* happened?"

"So, it started out a little weird with the tantric handshake in the middle of Starbucks, but she turned out to be really down-to-earth. We literally talked from six till closing."

I smile wide at the news, peppering her with questions as I guide my Utahraptor to the bombed-out substation that feeds into the factory, jumping and navigating around the live wires as I hunt for zombie Cro-Magnon stragglers. Dino tells me about the ease of their conversations on existentialism and sexuality and favorite teen rom-coms, and how even the silences in between chatter were soft and comfy and buoyed by starry gazes. About how they shared a crumb cake slice at the table before closing and a hug and kiss at Dino's door as the night ended.

Honestly, this news rivals the developments between me and Sterling this week. Dino and River may or may not work out, but at least Rosie's in the rearview. And that's great for everyone involved.

"And all that was Tuesday?" I ask.

"Yeah, and Wednesday was even better. She took me to the arts center downtown for this poetry reading. And she actually read—from Anne *Freaking* Sexton!"

I remember the name. We'd read two poems from her freshman year when studying feminist literature.

"Which poem?" I ask as I watch Dino's Spinosaurus emerge from the shadow of the factory. She heads left toward the smokestacks.

"'Her Kind.' It's like my favorite." Unprompted, she even recites a verse, her voice all feelings and vibes:

> *I have gone out, a possessed witch,*
> *haunting the black air, braver at night;*
> *dreaming evil, I have done my hitch*
> *over the plain houses, light by light:*
> *lonely thing, twelve-fingered, out of mind.*
> *A woman like that is not a woman, quite.*
> *I have been her kind . . .*

Dino snaps her fingers when she stops, but my brain can't get past *Twelve-fingered?* Scrunching my face, I quietly ask, "This is supposed to be feminist?"

"Yeah."

"Why would she compare herself to a witch, then?"

"She's, like, a bad witch. Not accepted by society."

"Why doesn't she wanna be a good witch, like Glinda?" I ask.

"Because that's what the world wants her to be. Polite. Docile. She wants to be something different. Besides, well-behaved witches rarely make history."

"Oh," I say.

And then she says to herself more than anyone else: "You gotta love the Anne Sexton rep. Even her name's cool AF: *Sexton*. It's like, if a surname could also be a pickup line. Can't get more YOLO than that."

"Sure can't."

"Yeah, I can just imagine her and Shakespeare talking in the afterlife and him being all 'What's in a name?' and her coming back with 'Bodily autonomy, bitch.'"

I exit the substation and gaze at the pixelated sun in the distance, tinged with purple and low-slung over the desert plain. "It's getting late," I say. "We should blow it soon before the Vampiraptors come down from the caves."

"True dat," she replies. "Lemme just do one last perimeter check."

Despite my misgivings, I say nothing. She's the expert, after all. I run to and climb a thatched guard tower to keep watch.

"Kalvin," Dad calls out. "Come get ya food! I ain't cook this meal and set out the good plates just to watch your dinner get cold. Ah-*HA-HAAA!*"

I cover my mic and yell back, "Just a minute, Dad!" Then, speaking in a low voice, I say, "Okay, Dino, we gotta blow this thing. What's your position?"

She doesn't respond. "Dino?"

Again, more silence. I get all panicky, remembering the pack of rabid Chupacabras near the oasis I failed to round up and kill.

"Shit," I breathe, scrambling down from the tower. I sling my gun over my back and unsheathe my bowie knife so I can run faster. I sidle up to the factory wall and slink around the corner as I hear a scream. The Necromorphs begin their chants, and the sound of zombies furiously raking their nails against the inner wall plays loud in my headphones.

Cautiously I skulk toward the next corner. When I get there, I close my eyes.

*You can do this, Kal.* I open them and count down. "Three, two, one . . ."

I jump the corner and slash desert air with my knife before I can process what I'm seeing. It's Dino's Spinosaurus, in no danger whatsoever. On the contrary, she's pointing her rocket launcher right at the head of a dinosaur much smaller than her.

"Dino, please!" it pleads.

It's then I notice the gamer handles along the side rail. Mine, @MeleeAttackBae and now . . . @ThePrettiestRose?

"Rosie?" I squeak out. "What are you doing here?"

"Exactly," Dino growls. Her dinosaur backs her ex's into a wall.

Rosie's dinosaur is a Nomingia, which looks like a cross

between an ostrich and a lizard. It's one of the beginner-level dinosaurs, equipped only with a revolver, which Rosie's managed to drop. A cloud of sand mushrooms into the air as Dino kicks Rosie's gun away.

"I just wanted to talk," Rosie says, "and, and, and you didn't respond to my text, and I saw you online and figured this was the best way to just come talk to you."

"By breaking into my game?"

"I'm still on your invite list."

I shake my head, getting an image of a long-suffering wife putting a nightly candle at her windowsill just in case her philandering, absentee husband decides to return. *Jesus, Dino.*

"Well, consider yourself uninvited," she huffs.

I holster my knife and walk up to Dino's Spinosaurus, touching its shoulder. "Dino, drop the rocket launcher."

After a long pause, the Spinosaurus takes the launcher from its shoulders and sets it on the ground. Its comically tiny arms cross as one of its massive feet begin impatiently tapping against the sand.

"Thank you," Rosie says. "Now can we talk?"

I swear just then Dino's Spinosaurus rolls its eyes. "What's there to talk about?" she asks.

"About *us*," Rosie says. "You know, there wasn't really ever any closure."

"Yeah, because you broke up with me like a day before you went off—"

"And I'm soooo sorry about that. That was stupid."

My Utahraptor waves as it creeps out from between them. "I'm gonna check out for a while to eat dinner," I say, but neither respond. They're too wrapped up in their own drama. I scurry up a sand dune. Looking back, I see them aimlessly walking toward the glow at the horizon.

Seeing two dinosaurs walk off into the sunset would normally be a heartwarming sight, but I get a queasy feeling watching them. I'm about 99 percent certain they're better off apart. Yeah, they looked great together. But their problems ran deeper than surface level. Like waxing a car instead of working on the engine. A patchwork of grand gestures meant to reflect the sheen of contentment rather than the reality of stagnation. And somehow, for a long while that worked for them. Or at least they'd managed to convince themselves that it did.

I remember one day last year, sometime in May, when Dino opened her locker to scores of long-stemmed roses. Rosie stood off a ways beaming as passersby oohed and aahed. Dino calmly stepped back, smiling the company smile, doing her best to look happier than she was. Doing her best to breathe, in fact. Anybody who knows Dino knows she's highly allergic to most perennials. Apparently, Rosie did not.

I rip off my headphones and hurry to the kitchen. Dad's sitting at the table, the pendant light washing down on him like he's being interviewed in one of those police procedural shows.

"Where's Mom?" I ask, to which he mutters something incomprehensible while stuffing his mouth with mashed potatoes.

I take a bite of my own, chasing the food with a gulp of red Kool-Aid.

"How was your day, son?" Dad asks between chews.

"Pretty good. Got a B on my calc test."

He genuinely smiles, reaching over to touch my shoulder. "My boy. That's that new math, huh?"

I don't answer.

"Gettin' smart there, ain't ya. Not like them dumbass cousins of yours." He leans in closer to me. "You know they smokin' weed, right?"

"Dad, weed is legal in basically half the country. You know that, right?"

"Alls I know is it's illegal in *all* my damn house," he responds. The *ah-HA-HAAA* that trails his words is much more muted than usual, like he's phoning it in. Dad takes a bite of his pork, and I do the same. Then he washes it down with water. Dabbing the corners of his lips with a napkin, he says, "Valentine's coming up soon."

"I know," I say.

"You know one of the best surprises your mom ever had was when I took her to Greece for Valentine's way back when."

"You took Mom to Greece?" I ask.

"Greece. Sicily. Monaco. All around the Mediterranean. Been wanting to get back there ever since."

"Why haven't I seen those pictures?"

Dad shrugs. "Lost the film. Err'body ain't have those fancy

iPhones ya'll got nowadays. And the only clouds we knew about had water coming out of 'em."

"Must've been nice," I mumble.

"Sure was," he replies, and for a moment I notice this contented look in his eyes, like he's watching a highlight reel. "We really did love traveling, your mom and me." He clears his throat and narrows his eyes back on me. "So, got that special someone? I know y'all have a ball in a few weeks."

I shake my head. "Nope. Nobody."

"Well, you ask anybody?"

I hate where this is headed. Each question, although well intended, has the psychological effect of shrinking me down until I'm a puddle of teen angst and embarrassment.

"Not yet," I mutter.

"What's stoppin' you? You handsome. And you know me and Mom would pay? And your cousins Ray-Ray and Treyquan got that limousine they bought for that side hustle they doing?"

I squint at him. "The same ones you said smoked weed?"

"Come on, boy. You gotta see the good in folks," he replies.

I'm not the one who just dragged my own kin for smoking a plant, but I digress. The line of questioning does give me a chance to change the conversation, so I take it.

"Why don't you ever do fancy stuff like that with Mom anymore?" I ask. "Dances? Limos? Stuff like that."

I can tell that just the act of asking the question pains him on some skin-deep-but-still-non-superficial level. It's the pin-prick of reality. An acknowledgment that their relationship has, in fact, indelibly changed.

He makes a face I can't quite discern as his eyes find a spot on the wall behind my shoulder. "Life, I guess. Thangs come up, get in the way."

The answer coils around me like a python. It's that same, suffocatingly guilty feeling that's nagged me for years now. The biggest "thing" that's come up in their marriage is me. I read somewhere a few years back that one of the biggest reasons parents divorce is issues involving kids. And it fits. Children are a time suck, an energy suck, and a resource suck. Plus, I butt heads with my parents a lot, and it's only gotten more frequent the older I've gotten.

I'm not saying I'm totally to blame. All married couples endure conflict, after all. But maintaining a marriage and a successful business and a family would be a labor of love for anybody. I guess with me around, they slowly have begun to figure the payout for all that work just isn't worth it.

It's easy to imagine what a Kalvinless life would be like. There's no doubt that they'd be dancing the night away or taking extravagant Euro jaunts if I weren't here. The spark might still be there if my very presence wasn't always here to smother it.

And I've seen the pictures to prove it. They went to Tokyo one anniversary. South Africa for a Christmas holiday. Australia just because.

The pictures of breathtaking places stopped right about the

time I took my first breath. It was like that chapter of the family photo album ended, usurped by another, more humbling one. A chapter in which I played the protagonist.

*Or, maybe the villain?*

That one trip we took to Hawaii was my only taste of the pleasures and feelings they'd long since jettisoned for domestic life. If I could just get back there . . . If *we* could just get back there, maybe they'd realize life didn't have to be an *either/or* choice. Maybe it could be *both/and*.

I spent the day fixing relationships. I can fix this. I *need* to fix this. I just need the chance.

Most of dinner pokes along with aimless talk and stretches of silence as long as dark country roads. But I know something's up because Dad's eyes keep flitting left when he thinks I'm not looking. I know two things from this: Mom must be out on the porch, and the question about him and Mom must've hit a sore spot.

As we get nearer to emptying our plates, I see him become visibly restless, shifting in his seat. I know he's annoyed Mom didn't show for dinner. But it's more than that.

"Pork loin's a little tough," he says out of nowhere.

*Is this a trap?* "Yeah," I respond tentatively. "A little."

He rests his fork beside his plate. Then he gets up, once again dabbing his blue cloth napkin to both sides of his lips. He tosses it onto his plate and walks away, muttering something that sounds like "So's life."

I take just a few more minutes to finish my own food.

Then I collect both our plates and carry them into the kitchen, rinsing them and placing them into the dishwasher before heading back to my room. When I get there, it's nighttime in the *ZombieWorld* desert. I look out from the dune, but Dino and Rosie are nowhere to be found, so I leave my room again, heading to the back porch.

On my way there, I detour to the mantel, clutching the picture of Hawaii, both hope and fear twisting around me as I run my thumbs down the frame. I hope to God I can pull this off. I fear I won't.

As I'm putting it down, I spot something else. Tucked behind another picture is a manila envelope. The same one Mom gave to Dad and said to take care of. He must've laid it here and just forgotten. He didn't even seal it. I scan the room before grabbing it. I study the label.

"Walcott, Walcott, and Brown?" I whisper. It's a law firm. But not their business firm. A new one. *Did they switch?*

Every instinct says to open it. My heart jumps at the thought of it, and I get all trembly with each whiff I catch of the paper. It could answer so many questions. But it could also shoulder me with so many new and unpleasant realities, none of which I'm ready to deal with.

I can't bring myself to do it. I tuck it back into the space.

I head to the porch, opening the back door and looking right toward the rocking chairs. I don't see her. She coughs, and I look the other way. I see her leaning over the railing as if the night's ever so gently trying to pull her away from us. As I come close, drifts of cigarette smoke filter into my nostrils. Smoking was a habit she'd kicked ten years ago. We'd had a party to celebrate and everything.

I stand beside her. We stare out past the shimmering pond, and out to the pines that knife into the horizon. Crickets chirp incessantly, and armies of candle flies swarm the lights posted at each side of the balcony.

Dad doesn't care for the porch or the backyard ripped from a Yellowstone tour pamphlet, or those quiet moments marked just as indelibly by what you *don't* say as by what you do. When I was much younger, I'd often wonder how they could be so opposite yet exist so well together. I don't wonder anymore because it's obvious they can't.

I point to the cigarette she's dangling over the rail. "You're . . . again?"

She looks at me, a day-weary smile barely propping up her cheeks. "I'm taking a vacation from quitting," she says.

The word "vacation" brings back memories and emotions ill-fitting to the moment. Dinner together. Talking together. Just being together.

"How was your day?" she asks.

I think about the highlights. Meeting with Sterling. Scheduling clients. "Good," I answer. "Yours?"

She nods. "Your father and I had a good show." She takes a drag of the cigarette.

"What was it about?" I ask.

"Self-love."

"What's that got to do with relationships?"

"In order to truly love your partner, you've got to love yourself."

I guess that makes sense. Nobody wants an Eeyore moping around all day giving off woe-is-me energy. But I do wonder how that simple calculation misses the mark when it comes to my parents' marriage. From what I know, they have cloud levels of self-esteem, and I'm sure their fans would say the same. But as for loving each other?

So as not to seem brash, I broach the subject of their love in a roundabout way. "When did you first fall in love with Dad?"

Her face tightens a bit, a vague suspicion of the intent of my question lingering at her lips and brow, but after a moment it relaxes. Her eyes narrow on the distance as if she's just spotted a memory. As she gazes, I see her profile. Lustrous skin on the dark side of chocolate. Long black hair streaked with strands of gray that catch faint light like tinsel. The beginnings of wrinkles living at the corners of her eyes. She's aging, but in the graceful way of a swan or butterfly.

"I believe it was the second time he proposed," she says.

"*Second?*"

She laughs. "Your father was very eager to get on with this thing called life."

I'd heard about the proposal. The candlelight dinner and evening balloon ride over the countryside. Mom would always joke that she had to say yes because "How the hell else was I supposed to get down?" But I never knew that it wasn't the only proposal. Or that she didn't love him until then.

I bend my upper body over the rail to try to meet her eyes. "Why'd you say yes if the love was so new?" I ask.

Her head turns my way. Her grin is wide and full of wonderment at her inquisitive child. "You're surprised?"

"Well, yeah. With your 'know 'em through all seasons' talk, just seems a little . . ." *Hypocritical?* "Suspicious."

"Well, actually, Kalvin, the love was there well before that night."

"I don't understand," I say. "You just said—"

"You asked about *falling* in love. The feeling. Which, you're right, I hadn't experienced yet. But I'd made the decision to love him a long time before that."

"What's more important, then? The feeling or the decision?" I ask.

She's silent for a long moment. Her stare detaches from me and casts back out to the pines. Mine follows.

"I suppose I'd say the decision. Your father, the feeling. God knows what's right."

*God knows what's right.* I doubt she's ever answered a call-in with that line.

My parents seem to be, at that moment, standing on opposite sides of the same mirror, seeing only their perception of what's right, never seeing the other. Maybe that's why they're struggling now. After all, how can love be sustained if the two sides can't agree on its basic utility?

It strikes me that they can't see things as clearly as I do right now. They're so entangled in their emotions, they can't tease out how a breakup would destroy the other person. Rip apart the family, even. And besides that, their careers are premised on a happy marriage. If that vision crumbles, we can kiss our finances goodbye.

I nod and mumble, "Only God knows."

But I'm not answering her question. I'm answering mine.

With new resolve, I say good night and head inside. On my way back to my room, I head to the mantel and snatch the envelope. The same hope and fear is still there, but a new feeling threads in: determination. I have to know exactly what problem I'm facing if I'm gonna be the one to solve it.

# Seven

**Dino comes down** with the flu on Sunday, so Rod and I catch rides from Mom till the next Friday. Not much goes on aside from more referrals, less candy sales, and no Jordan, thank God. Apparently he came down with the same bug that knocked Dino out of commission, so he wasn't around for soccer drills.

The money count stands at $9,395, so some progress. But not nearly enough seeing as how it's fifteen days until Valentine's Day.

When our triumvirate finally does get back together, Dino is strangely silent on the car ride to school. Nothing about River. Not a mention. And when I prod her about last week's rendezvous with Rosie, she's cagey about giving any real answers. So I'm glad when Roderick dives into the back seat with me, all excited, if only because he breaks up the silence. I regret that sentiment the second he opens his mouth.

He shoves a crumpled sheet of paper in my face: "Okay, so I've been thinking about my *Hamilton* audition and really wanted to give 'em something creative. You know, mega brain.

So I was thinking, *What's the show's main focus?* Culture, history. Culture . . . *and history.* So last night I made a mash-up of that song by King George—you know, 'You'll Be Back'—and the nineties rap megahit 'Back That Azz Up' by Juvenile."

I catch Dino's face in the rearview. You'd think she'd just seen a ghost. Or bigfoot. Or a ghost chasing bigfoot. She stays quiet, though.

I take the paper and make a big show of studying the lyrics, chin-stroking, pensively nodding and everything. Then I hand it back to him, along with a palatable reply: "It's a head turner, all right. You know, maybe you should workshop this with the theater teacher?"

Roderick sinks into his seat, obviously hoping for a more positive reception. His gaze drifts to the window as he says, "Aight, bet."

I feel a marrow-deep need to offer some sort of consolation, so I say, "For what it's worth, I think you'd have a natural stage presence."

I hear Rod's hands clasp together as he turns back from the window to me. "That's what I've been telling folks! And when Gianna sees me up there, it's a wrap."

"Jordan didn't scare you away, huh?" I ask.

"Negro, *please.* He won't touch me after how I got him."

I don't share the same confidence, but I don't want to argue.

He spends the next four minutes describing the "research" he's been doing this past week to prepare for auditions, which mainly consists of watching YouTube clips of Broadway shows like *Dear Evan Hansen* and August Wilson's *Fences*, for which he's quick to point out that "Now, I'm not a Denzel hater, but his performance fell flat for me."

Dino makes the mistake of asking, "Which part in *Hamilton* are you going out for?"

Rod looks at her like she's lost it. "Easy. Aaron Burr. Handsome, like me. Misunderstood antihero, like me. Plus, dude was a badass and a trailblazer."

"Sure was," I say.

"*First. Black. VP. In US history!*" Rod says, sounding out each word. "And brotha was just walking around challenging folks to duels while slavery was still goin' on? *Psshhh*, my boy Burr had that colonial swag."

"Wait," Dino says. The car rolls to a stop and her neck goes full ostrich as she strains to get a good look at Rod. "You think Aaron Burr was . . . *Black*?"

"Black as LaKeith Stanfield in a frock coat," Rod quips.

"*Nooo*," she says. "He wasn't Black."

"I saw what I saw, Dino."

"You did not see that," she replies.

"You got Disney Plus?" he asks.

Calmly, she says, "I have Disney Plus. Please don't say . . ."

"Stream *Hamilton* on Disney Plus!"

Dino looks dead at me. "Kalvin."

I shrug, thinking about the surprise "gas tax" hike she foisted on me two months ago. "Aaron Burr was a lot of things to a lot of people. Who can say?"

"*Shut up!*" Dino yells. The look she gives me is shot through with curses and ill wishes and obscure, evil magic.

They spend another two minutes arguing the merits of using a TV conglomerate with a mouse as its figurehead as a historical reference point. When we park at school, Dino shouts "Out!" to the both of us.

Dino usually gets to school about twenty minutes early. Not many students are there by that time, so I use it to restock. Today, I'm reupping on Dove Chocolates and LIFE SAVERS. The first surprise I get is that the Candyland closet door is unlocked. My breath catches. I turn the handle and get the second surprise when the door creaks open. I jump at the sight of a silhouette standing in the dark like some spectral figure in a horror movie.

The shadow slowly raises a hand, and I don't know whether to tackle it or run. Instinctively I flick the light switch and the figure comes to life.

"Mr. Perkins?" I say, my words coming in ragged gasps. The hand he'd raised—the one I thought was reaching out to drag me down to hell—is merely holding an open Crunch bar. Smiling, he takes a huge bite.

Mr. Perkins in the light is unequivocally *not* scary. The prototypical dude-bro white guy with a permanent five-o'clock shadow and hair that arches at the front like one of those wavy car-lot inflatables caught in a windstorm. The type of teacher who wants his students to like him. Which is fine and all, but Perkins seems to never have gotten the memo that he still has to, like, *be* a teacher.

"Wow, you were so scared," he says, chewing through a hearty laugh.

"What are you doing here?" I ask.

"Collecting my due, man!" It's only then that I notice the bags of Peanut M&M'S and miniature Kit Kats tucked underneath his right arm. *Jesus.* I forgot. As a trade-off for his discretion, Mr. Perkins gets two bags of his choosing every month. Usually, though, he has the decency not to ambush me.

I close the door behind me, shaking my head, wondering how a guy with a college degree could be so immature. "Could you have at least warned me?" I ask.

"Where's the fun in that? *Oh.* Speaking of not fun. Where's the Blow Pops, man? They're my favorite."

He slaps my shoulder as I walk past mumbling, "They're discontinued."

They were my least profitable candy, precisely *because* they were his favorite. Back when I stocked them, whole bags of the things would mysteriously disappear every week. When I finally confronted Mr. Perkins about it, he swore up and down—lying blue tongue and all—that he didn't know what I was talking about.

"You could bring them back seasonally. You know, like how McDonald's does the Shamrock Shake?"

*Or maybe you could pay? Because you have a salary.*

Instead of saying that, I shrug and say, "I'll think about it."

I snap to attention as he claps and says "Great!" while backing toward the door. He puts his hand to the handle. "By the way, just a forewarning but all utility and storage locks are being changed in the next few weeks."

"Why?" I say.

"Because somebody anonymously tipped off the admins that kids were getting unauthorized access."

*Maddie*, I think. Definitely sounds like a move she'd make.

"But don't worry," Perkins says. "I got you. When they do, I'll dupe my key and give it to you. Know why?"

My back is to him, so my eyes roll freely as I ask, "Why?"

"Because I like you."

*Because I give you candy.*

I wait to hear the door shut before letting out an exaggerated *ugh*. He's so insufferable sometimes. I can't get too aggravated, though. The locks info was a solid tip. He's effectively running a protection racket, but honestly, it's protecting me.

By the time third period rolls around, I'm upbeat again. Perkins is long gone from my memory. And even though I've only gotten two candy orders, I'm totally booked for therapy. Garrison's my first, and though he'll never admit it, he really seems to be embracing therapy. I have an intake with a girl named Reese, and that opens the door to a world of candy puns I've been wanting to try out.

But I'm particularly pumped because today I have the first straight guy on my caseload, John "Tater Tot" Stevens. There's an unfortunate stigma that leads to cis guys thinking therapy is for weaklings, so I'm glad he's breaking the mold, willingly seeking out help because his girlfriend says he's been putting up emotional walls. When it's his time, his session slogs by. It was a tough seven minutes, but I think we're closing in on a breakthrough.

I send him out with a "You did good today, Tater."

"Thanks, Kal," he says.

I pat his back. "And remember: Your *best* ability is your *avail*ability. You can't be there for her if you're not totally there."

He nods as I wave and shut the door.

I think about how rewarding this work has been so far. Candy is temporary, but making yourself into a better person has ramifications that can last well beyond our adolescent years. I get the opportunity to shape students' lives. Who wouldn't be fulfilled by that?

I coast off that giddy feeling until noon, right before the lunch bell.

I hear the usual sounds that buzz through the classroom pre-dismissal. Zippers unzipping. Books sliding across desks and into bookbags. Students waltzing right over the invisible boundary between "class talk" and idle cross talk.

And then comes that perfectly annoying newscast jingle presaging the most perfectly annoying girl in my world. I look up at the mounted TV and see Maddie.

The school tucks homeroom into fourth periods on Fridays, figuring it to be the least intrusive time since they know no learning is actually happening right before the lunchtime bell, anyway. So during this ten-minute sprint to lunch, we get a weekly recap, any pertinent announcements for next week, and a "Gregg County Special Report" from our honors journalism class. Topics have ranged from *Why does the cafeteria always smell like cardboard?* to *Who rearranged the school signage out front from "Welcome Back" to "We Blame Cock"?* The feminist society was singled out as the probable culprit in that prank, very unfairly in my opinion.

The journalism class is good, so there's some really slick production, camerawork, and editing by behind-the-scenes folks. But it's inevitably Maddie in the anchor chair. She's not actually in the anchor chair today, though, nor is she behind her news desk. She's in a regular swivel chair, legs tilted like they're in italics, hands folded at the lap of her pencil skirt.

She does her usual introduction, and I'm about to shrug her off when the camera pans to two students sitting across from her. I stop zipping my bookbag and zone in because one of them, Kayleigh Davis, sits across from *me*. In Candyland. She's a client.

"Welcome, Kayleigh. Welcome, Todd," Maddie says, gesturing both to the girl and her boyfriend as she greets them. Then she turns directly to the camera, trading her tight-lipped smile for her signature robotic stare. "There is a new epidemic going around the school these days. A scourge sweeping our hallowed hallways like a virus. It's called 'wellness.' It's been discovered by our expert investigative team—led by me—that Gregg County students have recently begun drifting away from generally accepted resources of knowledge such as WebMD, Instagram, and Reddit's 'Am I the Asshole?' thread, in search of more personal ways to grow themselves and their relationships."

Maddie squints ever so slightly as the camera zooms in.

"Oh, sure. Our students are paying the price for quote, unquote personal growth . . . but what are we actually getting in return?"

My heart starts beating against my chest. The chatter around me is white noise. *I'm about to be exposed. But why?* Kayleigh's always told me I'm the highlight of her day. And she's been one of my most responsive clients, implementing my advice and faithfully completing the homework activities. *Why would she put me out like this?*

Maddie begins the interview with some background on the couple: "So you two have been going out for a super-long time. Since elementary school, correct?"

The couple nod along as Maddie goes through a laundry list of milestones she has written down in a notepad.

"You guys got together at a meet-cute by the monkey bars near the four square court, right? And it says here, Kayleigh, you were there for Todd's bar mitzvah. By the way, a belated mazel tov, Todd. Congratulations."

"Thank you."

"Todd, you attended Kayleigh's grandad's funeral in ninth grade," Maddie continues, "and Kayleigh, when Todd broke his arm during wrestling last year, you spent the whole night in the hospital waiting room?"

"Yeah," Kayleigh says, nodding again.

"And even bigger, during one special, chilly evening in late September of last year, you two lost your virginity to each other."

The class collectively gasps. Kayleigh's eyes flash with confusion. "Wait, we didn't tell you that."

"It was on the Gregg County High Confidential gossip app," Maddie replies.

Todd raises his palms. "How'd you even know it was cold out?"

Maddie shakes her head. "Doesn't even matter. However, what *does* matter is that as of Wednesday, you guys are officially *ex*-boyfriend and -girlfriend."

*What?* When I saw her Tuesday, she never even mentioned this! We just talked about ways she could grow personally. I don't even think Todd came up.

Kayleigh and Todd both tentatively nod, lightly touching hands as they do.

For all her woodenness in person, Maddie certainly does have a way with those she interviews. As she looks from her notepad back to the couple, her face softens until every laugh and worry line now whispers notes of sympathy. She reaches out and barely touches Kayleigh's kneecap.

*Wow, she's really good at this.*

"So what happened?" Maddie asks.

Kayleigh glances at Todd as if she's silently asking permission to expose their most personal secrets. He nods, and she looks back at Maddie. "Well, I had been going to therapy . . ."

"*Therapy!*" Maddie flings her notepad to the floor.

The sound silences the class. Everybody's captivated. I sink

112

low in my desk. I feel like getting swallowed by a sinkhole and being consumed by Earth's molten core would be thousands of times more preferable to what will come next. Maddie's gonna paint me as a fraud in front of the entire school.

"*Therapy* broke you up," Maddie reiterates.

Kayleigh scrambles for a response. "Well, yeah, but—"

"And who exactly is your so-called therapist?"

"I'm not really comfortable reveal—"

"Kayleigh, please," Maddie says. "Don't let others fall victim to what happened to you two."

Kayleigh shakes her head. "It's not like that. It's just—"

"Well, if you won't tell, *I will.* I consider it a public service to expose the truth for all."

I'm praying for the lunch bell. Hoping to jet out for the main office to pick up my transfer application. Wishing the teleport had been invented so I could just beam myself to my new school.

Maddie looks directly into the camera, eyes now burning through the lens. "The so-called therapist, a.k.a. person responsible for this catastrophe, walks among us in these very hallways. He has a locker beside you. He eats lunch in your cafeteria. He drinks from your fountain, probably backwashing. We've seen him. We know him. And now we can hate him. This person is—"

"KALVIN SHMELTON IS A MIRACLE WORKER!"

The camera quickly pans from Maddie to Kayleigh, who's now out of her seat, looking all kinds of pressed to get her side of the story out.

"Kalvin helped Todd and me see what we couldn't for all these years. That sometimes growth has to happen alone. That breakups aren't always bad news. And that every relationship doesn't have to have a fairy-tale ending. And that's okay!"

Kayleigh steps closer. Everybody's looking at the TV, and risking lightning-quick glances toward me lest they miss the drama unfolding live on-screen.

Out of frame, Maddie sputters, "But you were *crushed* by the breakup!"

"For like a day!" Kayleigh says. "But honestly, it was a long time coming. Better to rip off the Band-Aid quick, am I right? And Todd and I talked afterward, and we're still friends, but we really do think our next journey can't be together. The lessons I learned from Kalvin eventually helped us both see that."

"*Hey!*"

I don't see Maddie's face, but the widened camera angle catches her hand frantically waving. "You can't just come on my show and do that!"

Some stagehand off-camera yells, "It's not your damn show, Mads!"

She ignores it. "You promised you'd help me expose the truth about who broke you up!" she continues.

"I promised to talk *about* our breakup. And that was the truth." Kayleigh redirects her attention from Maddie back to the camera. Her face fills the frame as she takes two steps closer for her final appeal: "Look, it's winter. It's dark out. It's the holiday season. Life hurts for a lot of people right now. So whether it's with Kalvin, a counselor, or a professional, get help if you need it. Seriously."

In a cinematic flare made for Hollywood, a tear streams from her right eye. She glances back at Todd before returning to the camera.

"And sometimes the best relationship status is 'single.'"

Kayleigh grabs her phone from her pocket, almost fumbling it as she swipes and touches the screen until we all see the Spotify logo. She presses the screen again and the melody to Ariana Grande's "thank u, next" starts playing. With Ariana's words comes Kayleigh's voice.

It's somehow fitting that Kayleigh's not a good singer. Pitchy. Prone to unneeded runs. Weirdly veering into falsetto when alto would do just fine. Because that's how people and relationships are: strained and imperfect, but full of heart.

*Todd taught me love*
*Todd taught me patience*
*And Todd taught me pain*
*Now, I'm so amazing*

Judging from the look of the class, we all wish he'd taught her some voice modulation, too. But it's cool. Todd looks pretty sick right now, but I admire him. We all do. And that goes double for Kayleigh. To go through a breakup while remaining friends takes a lot of maturity.

Maddie signals the camera operator to cut the feed as

Kayleigh shoehorns the lyrics into one of those dances you see white girls do on TikTok. By the chorus, most of the class is either singing or lip-synching along.

The bell rings and the class storms out the doorway, marauding for the cafeteria. When I leave, Dino's standing out front in the hallway. The whole walk she coos mom things like "Are you sure you're okay?" and "It didn't come to stay, it came to pass," and "I will rain down bloody vengeance upon her if it's the last thing I do!"

Okay, so not all mom things, but I appreciate the passion.

Anyway, it's weird explaining that I don't feel all that embarrassed anymore, judging from my classmates' reactions. I received several pats on the back as the bell rang, two finger guns, and a "Great job, boss" from Rikki Pilson. And Ashlynn Carter, who barely ever says anything, quietly asked if I could fit her in sometime. It's like they all heard Kayleigh and Todd's breakup story and recognized the good I was doing, even if *good* didn't necessarily look all that good at first blush. I'm relieved, honestly. In all her flame throwing and truth uncovering, Maddie neglected to mention I get paid for therapy, which might have really landed me in hot water.

However, this new reality doesn't dissuade either me or Dino from being mad at Maddie. She was totally out of pocket for the stunt she pulled. She's usually composed for those things, but Kayleigh's defense of me had Maddie looking absolutely unprofessional. Dino, Rod, and I scan the cafeteria the entire period looking to confront her, but she doesn't show up at lunch. Even though I'm mad at her, a big part of me wants her to come so I can laugh in her face, too.

Without her to distract us, the convo inevitably centers back on me.

"So, Kalvin," Dino says. "Therapy. Wanna elaborate?"

I'm about to start explaining when Rod shushes me. He glares at me and whispers, "Bro, Hippo!"

Dino asks, "What are you talki—"

"Dino, keep your voice down," he says. Lowering his own voice, he adds, "Kal gotta keep that Hippo Law or he could get in big trouble."

"It's HIPAA," I correct. "HIPAA law."

Rod looks confused for a moment but then nods. "Good, 'cause y'all doctors had me wondering, naming laws after safari animals."

Dino looks directly at Rod, her words as authoritative as a teacher giving detention: "Kalvin's not a doctor. Therefore, he doesn't have to follow HIPAA. But he *should* be keeping his friends in the loop about these things. Don't you wanna know why he didn't tell us?"

"All I want to know is what the profits are for," Rod replies. "You getting a car or something?"

I take a bite of my cafeteria lasagna so I can think through an answer. I feel sheepish for not telling them sooner. The weird thing is, I don't really even know why I didn't. They'd be totally chill about it, although Dino might raise her ride price seeing as

117

how I have another stream of income. In retrospect, I'm glad the cat's out of the bag. Maddie, for all her bad points, spared me the awkwardness of having to defend not revealing to them my secret endeavor when it first started. Now they're set to defend my secret endeavor against her.

My answer is as uninsightful as it is short. "Nope. No car."

"This why all those folks was coming up to you asking for advice?" Rod says.

"Yeah."

"This got anything to do with your parents?" Dino asks.

"Why would that be?" I ask, my voice rising.

She eyes me suspiciously. "Because you're a therapist. And your parents are therapists."

The sheepish "Could be" I give, married with a shrug, is hint enough that this definitely *is* about my parents, and that it goes a lot deeper than them being therapists. These are the only two people I've ever told about my parents' issues. They know everything's not sun and rainbows at 274 Kerr Road. But they also know not to prod. I've made it clear over the past few months that my parents' marital woes are mine alone to help fix.

So we all just slide to the next subject like understanding friends would do. It's not until sixth period that I have to explain my business endeavors again.

I walk in the doorway to my honors Italian II class and see Maddie. We're doing a "gallery walk" of poster board stations with different Italian landmarks we have to describe using Italian adjectives. She's at "the Colosseum" with a few others. She writes spaziosa ("spacious") in looping red letters beside it before popping on the cap to her marker and setting her eyes on me. Her lips are straight as a pencil, but I see the scowl in her eyes. I give her a wicked smile I hope burns right into her soul.

"Signor Shmelton, unisciti a un gruppo per favore," Mrs. Rossi says from her desk. I march right over and grab the pen from Maddie's hand.

"Good looking out," I say to her. "Thanks to your little stunt, I'm booked solid for the next week. Couldn't have come up with a better advertisement if I'd tried."

I scribble vuoto ("empty") beside the picture and jam the marker shut again.

Maddie huffs. "Cut the crap, you shameless rake! We both know you're only getting business because of who your parents are."

I shrug. "Actually, I'm getting business because I'm a capitalist," I respond. "I saw an opportunity, and I capitalized."

"You're a *thief* is what you are!"

My body tenses at the word. Maddie and the group take off for the next famous site, the historic Tiber River. I march right along with her.

"You're really never gonna get over me taking on your monopoly, are you?" I ask.

"Candy is *my* thing, Kalvin. Besides, if you had to cheat to do it, why should I get over it?" she says. "Our sales *sucked* last year because of you. And you're screwing with them again." She swipes the marker from me and writes Ombreggiato!, which translates to "shady."

Her eyes land on me with this settled, rock-hard perma-stare. In fact, if her eyes were lasers, I'd be a smoking mound of ash right now. I'm really getting to her. And honestly, I'm feeling really good about it.

I swipe the marker back, basically stabbing my word onto the poster: SQUALLIDO ("DIRTY").

I turn to her again, getting in her face and whisper-shouting to her as our group members write their adjectives: "For the last time, I have no idea what you're talking about! I did absolutely nothing to you last year. Hell, I barely even knew you!"

"So if *you* didn't start the rumor that our Blow Pops were pre-licked, then who did?"

I'm speechless only because I literally can't answer. I vaguely remember some funny business going on with stu-gov candygram sales last year, but I didn't have a girlfriend or a candy business, so what did I care?

After a few seconds of silence, Maddie stamps her foot and asks, "How can you live with yourself?"

"Silenzio, per favore, Signorina Trout."

Red in the cheeks, Maddie looks at our teacher. "Scusa, Signora Rossi!"

Maddie turns and jets to the next poster, me in lockstep, bending my lips to her ear: "All I needed to do is be a better business person than you. I didn't need to start any rumor."

"And yet conveniently, you're the only person who benefits from it," she whispers. "I bet this was in your long-range plans. Start a nasty rumor. Move in on my turf while we're vulnerable.

Slash prices to win market share. *Cheat* your way to the top." She stops in front of the Leaning Tower of Pisa, snatching the marker from a group mate. After she's done, Storto!!! ("Crooked!!!") fills half the poster in broad, looping letters.

"Look! I don't know where that rumor came from," I answer. "But I do know your obsession with me is misplaced."

"I'm obsessed?" she says, her voice rising again in spite of herself.

"Signorina Trout!" Rossi admonishes. We ignore her.

"*Yes!*" I say. The word comes in loud and low, like a freight train. I take the marker. I fill the other half of the poster board with Instabile! ("Unstable!").

Our whole group looks at us like we've gone off the deep end. Maddie jerks the marker back. Breaking away from us, she marches directly across the classroom to the abandoned city of Pompeii, reduced to ashes after the eruption of Mount Vesuvius. She elbows the group that's already there out of the way.

Looking straight at me, she pronounces: "When the time's right and I've got iron-clad proof of what you're up to, this is exactly what your *new* little endeavor will be!"

Under the protestations of the teacher, she writes, Distrutto ("Ruined").

# Eight

**The next week,** a sense of dread settles in my gut like a heavy meal. Maddie's been quiet these past few days, but a quiet Maddie is probably a dangerous one. And she's not the only scorned classmate waiting in the wings to exact their revenge. There's no way Jordan's forgotten what Rod and I did to him on the field. Not the kind of enemies you want to have at school.

Plus, there's the contents of Mom and Dad's envelope. When I went back and took it off the mantel last week, I spirited it to my room with every intention of reading what was inside. But I chickened out. Just lay there staring at it for hours. I even held it up to the light like a total goofball, seeing if I could glean clues. It's only a few pages from what I can tell, as light as a conversation at a coffee shop. Still, it had been weighing on me all weekend.

I've been carrying it in my bookbag every day. I just can't summon the courage to open it. I head into the Candyland closet and take it out of my bookbag. Then I sit down on the floor, holding it up to the light again. I see the faintest outlines of paragraphs but not much else. After just seconds, I stop, sighing as I smack the envelope across my head. *Why can't I open it? Just rip the damn Band-Aid off, Kal!*

But I don't, again. I flick my wrist hard, tossing the envelope, listening as papers flutter out and slide against concrete, a few even slipping under the shelving. Someone knocks at the door. Zoe Mortgenson. I forget, she's always early. I spring up, gather all the scattered papers I see, not even sure if I got them all. I want to read them so badly, but not like this. Not among company. It takes every bit of my will to stuff them in my backpack. I dust myself off and welcome her in for her appointment.

In spite of the feeling of helplessness that consumes me, I power through my initial four sessions. I'm surprised at how rewarding they are. Turns out, Tater Stevens told his football buddies about how good of a session he'd had, so after Zoe, it's Rodrigo Velasquez, Bernard "Bam Bam" Nicks, and Dontrell "D-Train" Fredericks.

The most interesting part is Rodrigo and Dontrell weren't even here for relationship problems. Rodrigo's been experiencing anxiety over his junior year workload, and Dontrell wanted pointers on how to get emotionally closer to his mom after her recent health scare.

Never in a million years would I have believed I'd be helping the Gregg County High offensive line work on coping with stress and communicating their feelings. Now, if someone would just help them with picking up blitzes, they'd be unstoppable.

When Dontrell leaves, all the anxious emotions rush back to me. I only get this feeling before big soccer matches. I press my back against the door as my heartbeat goes into overdrive. Sterling's my next client, and she'll be here any minute. Just thinking about seeing her again comes bundled with all the nerves of prom or homecoming. I can't totally rule out doing something stupid like offering her a corsage.

I spend the next few minutes thinking over what I'll say to her. Is it ethical to compliment a client's outfit or tell her she smells nice? To tell her you had a dream about her last night? Even if it was completely innocent and fully clothed?

I get out my phone to text. But *who*? Dino? I don't exactly trust the interpersonal skills of a girl who once idly mused about bleaching her ex's lawn. Rod? There's no way I'd trust him to give me girl advice.

*Mom or Dad?* They're too busy dealing with their own mess. A mess that doesn't exactly inspire confidence that they can help my situation.

It's just me. I have to figure it out myself. I pace to the center of the room, hoping that slapping my cheeks will knock some sense into me. Maybe even a witty line or two.

I practice. Wide smile. Back straight. Shoulders pinned back.

"Sterling, *sup*? You're looking quite sterling today."

*No, stupid.* I smack my face again, this time from sheer disgust. *Okay, try again.*

Wider smile. Back straight. Shoulders slightly more relaxed, less uptight.

"*Yo.* Sterling. Peeped you in the parking lot this morning. Still got that WAP, I see. White-ass Prius."

*Am I trying to get slapped?* I shut my eyes tight and bump my head against a shelf. *Okay. One more time.*

Slowly, I backpedal away from the shelf. Smile so wide it hurts. Posture straight. Chest out.

"Wow, you're actually here. I knew 'Cleopatra' was on my client list but never truly thought she'd show up. I must've been in denial."

"How'd you know my middle name?"

I jump and nearly trip over the stool. I clutch my heart as I turn. Sterling's right there, quietly closing the door she'd just slipped through. She looks at me, a vague sense of suspicion creasing her brow.

"You've been looking at my files or something?" she asks.

"No, I just—"

She meanders closer to me, arms crossed. "Breaking into the counselor's office? Checking my psych logs before our appointment?"

"I'm sorry, I just—"

"Did you read the one about the body?" she asks, staring right at me.

"Excuse me?" I ask, my voice squeaking like a bath toy.

She holds her stare for an impossibly long time before it finally breaks. "Dude, I'm just fucking with you," she chuckles. "My middle name's Haley."

I give off this awkward laugh to mask the fact that my nerves were kinda on edge after that *body* comment. Eventually I say, "That's a pretty name. I mean, Sterling's pretty too."

She closes the distance between us, doing a slow twirl around me on her way to the right shelf. She walks her fingers past bags of candy. "Do I look more like a Sterling or a Haley?"

"Both are a little . . ."

"Country club–ish?" she asks.

I nod. "Maybe something more down-to-earth would suit you. Like Mildred? Or Dolores, maybe?"

She glances back at me, meeting my nod with her own. "I'm gonna politely pretend to agree while ignoring what you just said."

"Ignoring your therapist already," I reply. "Not a great start for you."

"Calling me Mildred. Not a great start for *you*."

"Fine, then, *Sterling*. How'd you even get that name, by the way? If it's so . . . country club–ish?"

"I'll let you figure that one out," she cryptically answers.

With those words, she turns and winks. I tighten up. I literally stop breathing for a couple seconds. Even in the dim lighting, she's radiant. Like she's her own light. A mysterious solar flare bursting out from the ether, filling the entire room with beauty.

"You okay?" she asks.

I snap to.

"'Cause you looked like you were just spacing."

"Yeah, just going over some mental notes for our session."

I motion to the stool, and she sits. Dispensing with the witty rapport, I start with a simple "How's it going, Sterling?"

She smiles at the question. "Good, actually. Et vous?"

"I'm good," I say. "Ramping up the biz."

"Oh, candy sales, that's right. Just a couple weeks before Valentine's Day."

"Actually, therapy. Candy sales are kind of flat, to be honest."

In fact, they aren't anywhere near the level I need to hit my goal. Candy sales before holidays are always like that first hill on a roller coaster. Up and up and up until the big day, followed by a steep drop-off. Unfortunately I'm not getting that Valentine's bump I was expecting. It's Wednesday, February 4, ten days till my deadline. I'm at $9,633, more than $2,100 short of my goal. I've had to take some drastic measures to even get to where I am at the moment. I've instituted an on-call help line that's $1 per text, $1.50 if the text comes during evening hours. I'm testing the waters on after-school sessions, which seem to be catching on with the sports and band crowds and has really helped me up my cash intake these past few days. And I started a referral rewards program that nobody uses because since I refuse to give away the brand-name candies, the "reward" is those cheap candies in the strawberry wrappers you get from old people on Halloween.

But my most unpopular move by far is a "no more freebies" policy. A free piece of candy was something everybody looked forward to. Cassie Marx would close her eyes and just sigh at the first bite of her usual Twizzlers. Henry Chen would hold Lindor truffles in his palm like stress balls all session. And I could see the sparkle in Gianna's eyes as she'd take her precious time choosing between Baby Ruth and Ghirardelli.

The freebie was one of life's little joys. The grandparent slipping you a $5 bill and a wink at the end of a visit. The barista putting an extra shot of espresso into your white mocha. Now it's gone, a decision that hurt even me. I hate to be a Scrooge about it, but it's a cold world.

"Aww, I'm sorry," Sterling coos sympathetically. "Do you know the reason sales are off?" I shake my head. "You know what I think? I think you're such an extraordinary therapist that couples are less reliant on shallow gestures like candygrams and more into creating deeper, more sustainable relationships."

"I think I've only been doing this for a few weeks."

"A week is an eternity in high school time. It's like, seven whole days!"

"You sure it's not eight?" I ask.

"You sure it's not eight?" she whines right back to me.

I lean on the shelf ahead of her. "So, tell me. How did you spend your eternity of a week?"

"The usual. Homework. Hung out. I did order new heels for the ball."

"Nothing with Chadwick?"

She shakes her head, trading her sulk for a more even-keeled expression, but I can tell the question was deflating.

"So . . . how are you and Chadwick?" I ask.

"Um . . . not great."

*Excellent!*

"What happened?" I ask, biting the inside of my cheeks to make sure I don't start smiling.

"We got into a fight. Long story short, I tried to drag him on a date with me, but all he wanted was to play video games and chill at his house."

"So you felt rejected?" I ask.

"Rejected. Angry. Disappointed. You name it."

"What brought about these feelings?"

"He turned down mini golf."

My face must be betraying my confusion, because she clarifies: "Our very first date was mini golf. I guess I tried to re-create it."

"Why don't you re-create it for me?" I reply.

"Sure," she says, begrudgingly at first. But then, as she's speaking, she gets this curious look, centered around a soft smile. It's as if she's laundering a lighter mood through a distant memory: "First, he was a perfect gentleman and brought me a flower. Then when we first got to the Fun Park, he gave me all the tickets he won from Hot Shot so I could win this cute stuffed bear. On go-karts, he'd literally spin himself out to avoid hitting me. Even after I hit him like twelve times because I felt like being an asshole. And even on the mini golf course, he was such a sweetheart, too. We were tied at the final windmill and I double-bogeyed, so he threw his ball in the pond so I'd win."

I suck in my cheeks at the thought of Chadwick being anything aside from a pretentious jerk. Seeing her smiling makes me angry, too. Mom always said that good memories can anchor good people to bad significant others. *Is this what's happening now? Is Sterling being dragged back into a better time, before all the distrust and drama?* I have to think of something that'll squash this.

"Did you plan the evening?" I ask.

"Yeah. I'm pretty much always the ideas person with us. We've done mini golf, goat yoga, wine and dine. Although we had to do the nonalcoholic option, of course. All my ideas, though."

"And you're okay with that?" I ask.

Her smile disappears. She looks as if she'd never even considered the possibility of an alternative. "Why wouldn't I be?" she finally says.

"Seems like it'd take a lot of mental energy to do all the planning."

"Not all of it. He handles the big stuff. You know, Valentine's Day. Dances. My birthday."

"So to clarify: he handles the holidays that traditionally revolve around the man courting the woman and leaves the little stuff to you."

Sterling's body draws in on itself, like she's huddling to protect herself from the cold. "I wouldn't say *little* stuff. Just . . . stuff."

"Doesn't matter. For example . . ."

I grab a bag of candy corn, ripping it open. It's my second-to-last bag, and I'm okay with spoiling it, because honestly candy corn tastes like wax and despair and we're all better off without it.

I take out a piece. "This is *stuff*," I say. I drop it onto the floor.

"Okay?"

She watches as I turn the bag over, spilling its contents onto the floor. It goes everywhere. Some slide under the shelves. Some skitter toward her feet. Many others scatter to crevices that'll be an absolute bitch to clean later. When all the candy has rattled and rolled to a stop, I say, "Little stuff adds up."

I sink back as far as the shelf space will allow me and don the self-satisfied smile of a professor who's just guided a student to an aha! moment.

But there is no aha! moment. In fact, gravity seems to drag down her whole disposition.

"It's not totally like that," she says. She sounds defeated, like my little thought experiment came barbed with razor wire that cut right through her red-ribboned delusion. I feel really bad all of a sudden. Amazingly bad.

"I'm sorry," I say, and I truly mean it.

"It just feels like he's on the horizon nowadays. No matter how fast I run or how hard I swim, I still can't reach him."

"Maybe he doesn't want to be reached," I reply.

Sterling looks me dead-on in a way that's jarring and sets me on edge. "Kalvin," she says. "Whatever's going on with him right now, this *isn't* him. He's not the same guy I fell in love with. And I want that guy back. I am determined to get him back."

The word "determined" smacks me like a mallet in one of those old Bugs Bunny cartoons. She's set on seeing this through, no matter how hopeless it seems to the objective observer. But again, people tend to think more rationally outside of love than in it. If I'm gonna land this plane where I want it, I can't just go blindly barging into the cockpit of Sterling's brain. Better to be a calm, clear-eyed air traffic controller.

"I know you're not matchmaking, but do you have any advice for me personally?" she asks. "I'm literally sleepless with anxiety."

"Just think it through," I say.

Sterling nods, obviously disappointed I'm not giving anything more specific, but kind enough not to show it. She's about to get up when another thought hits her. A mischievous smile forms. "Are you taking anybody to the ball?"

The question catches me off guard. I hadn't really thought of taking anyone. In fact, the only girl I've been thinking about this past "eternity" is sitting four feet away from me, completely unaware of my infatuation with her.

I shake my head. "I'm more of a 'sit home and play video games' person than a ball person."

"You can be both," she responds. "Kalvin. I can totally set you up with someone. Please let me."

Despite me shaking my head, she indulges her matchmaker fantasy.

"You and Keisha Illan would look gorgeous together. Or there's Tiffany Tyler if you can stand to go out with a freshman. Or even maybe Lauren Meyerson. Actually, lemme check on that to see if she'll be in town that weekend. . . . So that's, like, two and a possible."

"My dating life is not some spades game," I protest.

"But I can help you win at both," she says.

At this, I perk up. "You play spades?"

"Glistern family tradition. Cookouts, Kool-Aid, and spades has always been the move."

Sometime during the last century, it was decreed that spades was the Official Black Card Game. It's basically a rite of passage in our community.

"Maybe we could team up sometime," she says.

"Maybe."

"In all honesty, it would be nice, though. Being able to share that with someone."

"Spades?" I ask.

"Not just spades. *Black* things."

I nod. I know exactly what she's talking about. Gregg County High is about 5 percent minority, if that. As Sterling would say: it gets lonely being the only. Nobody to share cultural jokes with or commiserate over near-constant microaggressions. When Black people here do link up, it's a wonderful thing. It's like reuniting with a best cousin from childhood. We smile harder, laugh louder, and say goodbye just a smidge later than we should.

"You're right," I say. "There's not enough *Black* things here. And definitely not enough Black people to share them with."

"I'm glad I found you, then," she says, and I get a little dizzy on the inside. Her mischievous expression returns. It's impossibly cute the way the right side of her smile twists upward as the left side of her bottom lip curls inward. "I have a thing. It's . . . at a country club. This weekend."

I nod. "Ah. Country club. Figures."

"Yes. I, Sterling Haley Glistern, have a *thing* at a *country club*. Long story short, my parents are members, and I go from time to time because the food is good and they'll mercilessly nag me if I don't."

"What's this gotta do with me?" I ask.

"They're having a teen mixer this Sunday. It's open invite. You can be my Black friend."

"You *are* the Black friend, Sterling."

"Okay, then. You can be the Black friend's Black friend, then."

"Can Rod and Dino come? You know, the Black friend's Black friend's Black friends?"

"Sure, why not?" she answers. "We can have a whole token-Negro, Russian-nesting-doll situation."

"I don't know," I answer, rethinking the whole thing. Not really feeling like running into Chadwick or Jordan. "I'd be a third wheel, with your boyfriend there and all."

"Oh, he'll be out of town on Sunday. So you coming will be so much less lonely for me," she pleads. "And I can introduce you to some girls I know."

The only girl I want to know is Sterling, and she's right here, one-on-one in a freaking hallway closet with me. This is every high school boy's dream scenario. So how can this conversation be going so sideways?

"Please, Kalvin," she says, trading her smile for a look more befitting a lost puppy dog. "I'm begging you to come. As a personal favor. *My brotha*."

I can't help but laugh at the last two words. "Guilting me over our shared Blackness."

"By any means necessary," she quips, crossing an *X* over her chest with her arms.

"I don't think that's what Malcolm was getting at." I chuckle. "But I'll go."

She squeals and happy claps, looking like a kid at Christmas. And even though she's obviously still simping over Chadwick, for the moment I feel like I'm the most important person in her world. It's a great feeling, too.

"Think of this as an appetizer for the main course, the ball," she says.

I shake my head but don't actually say no this time. Maybe she's wearing me down.

"Okay, so . . . ," I say. "Since you're so excited about it, what would be your dream ball?"

"Easy. Me and Chadwick. Beautiful dress. Royal theme, so we're good there. That symphony-type music they do in the historical fiction shows. Oh, and lots of desserts and candy."

Chadwick. It's a fight not to roll my eyes. I mutter, "Sounds cool."

"Just cool?"

I paper over my mood with a smile. "Sounds *great*," I correct. Then I grasp at any idle strand of a topic that would change the subject. I clap, and she perks up.

"Best candy, based on vibes alone," I say.

She opens her mouth, but when I add, "And don't say Snickers," it shuts again.

Her gaze goes skyward as she brings a hand to her face, stroking her chin over invisible things. Finally she looks back at me, smiling. "Almond Joy. *Boom.*"

"Why?" I ask.

"Duh. It's got almonds. It's joyful. Could you ask for anything better?"

"Aight, aight, I get it," I say, nodding. "That's gonna be my new nickname for you, by the way."

"Why?" she asks.

"Chocolate. Joyful. Rough around the edges."

She gasps in mock anger. "You jerk!" To emphasize the gesture, she even kicks my leg. But the laugh weaving through her words gives away the game. We catch each other's eyes again. We're both grinning at the prospect of a genuine connection, a nascent friendship.

# Nine

**The rest of** the week goes mostly as planned except for a surprise visitor to Candyland on Friday: River. I'm seeing out Raveena Chopra when I open the door and River's just standing there. Not River the astral-projecting, philosophizing free spirit of a girl. Just River, the girl. Miffed. Upset. Casting wildly about for answers. It's actually kind of disconcerting how "down-to-earth" she is.

"Can I come in?" she asks.

Though I usually don't take walk-ins, it's a no-brainer to wave her in. Since Dino hasn't said much about them, I'm curious to hear how things are going. However, as I catch the hint of distress playing hide-and-seek in her tired gray eyes, I know this won't be a celebratory update. I offer her a mini Snickers, which she politely refuses.

"So what's up with you and Dino?" I ask.

She sits on the stool, placing both hands neatly in her lap. Her words are quiet, emptied of the confidence she had on the field two weeks ago: "I was hoping you could tell me."

*What?* That doesn't make any sense. I remember Dino raving

about River. Their conversations. Their kiss. Everything about them seemed to click into place. I even remember thinking she could finally be the girl who'd replace . . .

Rosie.

What did she and Dino talk about when they met up in *ZW3*?

I narrow my eyes on River. "When's the last time y'all talked?"

"We emailed back and forth a few times this past weekend. After, um, after our last date, we'd tentatively said we'd meet up again but didn't commit to a time. When I brought it up in the hallway a couple days ago, she just, um, kinda avoided the subject." She sputters through her sentences in a completely stilted, un-River-like way. I can tell she's flustered, her tone pinballing between annoyed and dispirited. It's like she doesn't know how to be properly angry—or anything other than at peace with the world.

I'm so irritated with Dino right now. She'll regret it if River slips from her radar. I can't let that happen. I scramble for any kind of excuse. "You know she had the flu, right?" I say.

"But that was *last* week. And you can email with the flu. It just doesn't make sense."

It makes perfect sense, actually. I just can't let River know why.

River stands, looking around and uncomfortably running her hands down her thighs—doing these things just because she doesn't know what else to do.

"I know you all have privacy rules, but can you tell me anything about what's going on?" she asks.

It's my loyalty to Dino that keeps me from answering, but I don't like it. Each shake of my head feels like I'm betraying a friend, even though I barely know River. Dino should be enduring these questions, not me. And I'm definitely gonna tell her as much when I see her this afternoon. Probably some other choice words, too.

"I can't," I say, and she nods to reality.

She hands me $10. We say our goodbyes. But the unspoken words between us are as low and loud as the creaking shut of a heavy door: *It's over*. I get a pit-of-my-stomach feeling as I look at the money in my hand. For what she paid, I could've given her resolution. But instead, I gave her a dead end. For the first time, I feel like I betrayed someone's trust.

*I had to do it, though. I need to get this done for my parents.* That's what I tell myself, at least.

I stew for the rest of the day. When the final bell rings, I get my chance to confront Dino. Rod's prerehearsal is today in the school auditorium. Prior to auditions, the theater teacher is allowing a couple weeks of open rehearsals for those interested in practicing. Rod's been begging me and Dino to come to one of these, so we decided on today. I have to wait around after school until it starts. I head to the courtyard to chill but see the dreary weather matches my mood, so I go back inside. I walk to the CTE hallway but stop when I see some guy in blue coveralls at the Candyland door. I get nervous when I hear the hum of the drill he's aiming at the handle. When he leaves, I cautiously approach, fearing the worst. I pull the handle. It doesn't budge. I'm locked out.

"Need a little help?"

I look right, and two doors down it's Mr. Perkins peeking out of his room. He's got this glassy look that you'd expect to see in a hookah bar, not a school. He steps out and approaches me, unlocking the closet door.

"Thanks," I say, stepping in. He follows, to my surprise. I watch him as he roams the perimeter of the closet, moving equipment to scour the shelves for my stash. "You . . . need something?" I ask.

"My fee" is all he says.

"Fee?! I already paid you your two bags."

He pulls down a jumbo bag of Starbursts. He turns toward me, his eyebrows arching. "Come on, bro. I thought we were cool like that. A dynamic duo. Timon and Pumbaa. Aladdin and Genie. Mirabel and Bruno. Except you can be Bruno because you're the one always sneaking around in dark places."

He rips open the bag and pops an orange Starburst into his mouth. I slap my hands against my waist.

"This is extortion!" I say.

"It's business, man," he responds. "You should know that more than anybody. Simple supply and demand. I supply the key. I demand compensation. Besides, who you gonna tell? A teacher?" His laugh comes out in a short burst. As he walks past me to leave, he slaps my shoulder.

At the threshold, he pauses. "Oh. Almost forgot." He jams a hand in his pocket, and I hear the jingle of metal. Out comes a handful of silver keys. He plucks out two and says, "I'm pretty sure these are yours but test out *both*. If one doesn't work, let me know."

I have no idea how he knows because they all look identical to me. But I take them. We both step outside. I close the door and try the first key to his grumbling chorus of "Admins got me handing these out for the whole hallway, like I'm king of CTE or something. They don't pay me like a king, that's for damn sure."

I look over my shoulder at him.

"What? Never heard a teacher curse before?"

"No," I reply.

"Well, I guess both of us have secrets to keep, then." He winks and turns.

I open the door and pull out the first key when I hear, "Yo, Mad dog."

I wheel around, and Maddie's standing in the hallway, arms crossed, foot tapping, surely having been locked out as well. Perkins is sauntering toward her, but she's glaring right at me. She huffs when we make eye contact.

"It's Maddie, actually," she says.

"Yeah, whatever. Listen, I got stu-gov's keys. . . ."

I slink back into the closet and shut the door behind me. The last thing I want to do is endure Maddie's harangues about my ethical shortcomings. I'm in there just a few seconds when I realize maybe it isn't the best idea to be in here when I know Maddie's just across the hall. If she hightails it to the principal's office to set up an impromptu sting operation, I'm a sitting duck. So I sneak back out and head into the first open and empty classroom I come across a few doors down. I sit at a desk and whip out my laptop to do what I've been avoiding the last two weeks. I have to cut costs on the Hawaii trip.

The triage is necessary because I can't make up almost $2,100 in a total of five school days. I've tried everything to boost my income, but I'm at a piddly $9,789. Haven't even broken the $10,000 mark.

Plane tickets are pretty much set, so I don't even look at that. The one big expense I *can* change is lodging once we get there. It's a seven-day trip total. I'm planning on us staying three nights in Honolulu before heading off for a three-day sojourn to the nearby island of Lanai. Then it's one more night in Oahu before heading back home.

For a while I've had my heart set on beachfront stays at the Shallows Resort Hotel chain. They're all over the state and bill themselves as "A Paradise in Paradise." Their online reviews and pictures are outstanding. It's the cost that's a punch to the gut. I swallow hard as I click off the page and google "Cheap Hotels Hawaii." I settle on Oahu Econo Lodge. It's three miles from Waikiki Beach, but it lists under amenities free Wi-Fi, basic cable, and "complimentary OJ, coffee, and bagels before 9:00 a.m., but only if Tony's working the front desk because he's the early riser."

*Okay, weird.* But it saves me $650, so it'll have to do. I copy the page URL and email it to myself to reserve later.

Okay, so the goal is now down to $11,087. Better but not great.

Next is the big romantic dinner. Obviously my parents will be paying for most of the food once we get there, but I did want to treat them to a special meal as sort of a highlight. Their favorite place is that high-end steakhouse, Ruth's Chris. Dinners routinely run into the hundreds of dollars. I hate to do this, but it's gotta go. I search for restaurants in the area, filtering by price, and soon enough find Ruth's Deli. Judging by pictures, it's a hole-in-the-wall spot nestled between a Sheetz and an Auto-Zone. The reviews basically say if you can get past the faint smell of diesel, the ambience is pretty good.

*Umm, mildly unappealing.*

But their aloha burger looks delicious. I think about it. Maybe we get our orders to-go and just eat outside Ruth's Chris. Boom. $250 back in my pocket. I nod to myself and copy the page URL.

Next is travel to Lanai. Although it'd be perfect jet-setting with Island Air, I can't justify the cost. Back to Google, I go. It's a close call between Mahalo Mike's Copter Experience and Big Jim's Trawlers and Tours, but I go with Big Jim due to him having slightly fewer OSHA violations. It's a little more expensive, but safety's a big thing for me, and I can't compromise on that.

So that saves $300. I make a couple more minor changes like substituting an authentic luau for quiet, candlelit meditation and reflection on the beach. When all is said and done, the total cost is down to $10,466. I smile at the number. I'm back in the game, baby.

To boost my mood even more, I'm walking toward the

theater when I hear footsteps hustling behind me. I turn and see Tater Stevens with a big smile on his face. He's holding a huge, hand-drawn poster. He slows to a stop when he reaches me.

"Hey, Tater," I say.

"Sup, Kal," he says, his country drawl stretching the two syllables into soliloquy territory.

"How's the girlfriend?"

"Great. Gonna give this to her. You know, like a ball proposal."

He holds up the poster. It's a picture of a guy wearing those skimpy wrestler trunks standing sentinel outside a jail cell. *Okay, that's weird.* Apparently, he's watching over an anthropomorphized heart as it grips the bars. The text below reads "You've got my love on lock."

I'm beaming. It's absolutely astounding how much he's opening up. Although I know it'll make me late, I stay the extra minute or two as he brags over the drawing.

"And you see the heart's behind bars," he says, pointing. "Because it represents my love. . . ."

"I see," I say, touching the edges. "And I like that it's framed by flowers. And you've got the Rock as the prison warden there. She a big fan of his?"

"That's Cupid, Kal."

I look closer. "Oh. . . . Okay, well. Regardless, I'm proud of you." I pat his shoulder. He does the same, the force of his hand nearly sending me into a locker.

Although the new calculations and the run-in with Tater

put me in a good mood, I mask it because I'm still supposed to be mad at Dino. I don't mention River when I meet her out front near the ticket booth. She and I head upstairs to the balcony level, which is empty besides us. We find spots up front toward the middle and let the velvet theater seats swallow our bodies as we watch the stage below. Eight people are onstage. It's mostly kids from the theater classes passing each other along the front apron as they wind their way through various monologues and musical numbers. Rod, however, is alone over to the side. He's pulling up the toe of his shoe for quad stretches like he's about to run laps. Once he's done with that, he does the side-to-side torso twists and a couple shallow lunges.

I lean right, looking beyond my feet perched against the rail of the mezzanine balcony to study him. Then I lean toward Dino. "What's he doing?"

She lifts the bill of her Yankees ball cap and sits up a bit to look. Shrugging, she says, "I dunno. Being Rod, I guess."

The bill goes back down. She reaches into the buttered popcorn bag resting on the chair arm between us, grabbing a fistful and shoving it into her mouth.

Since I'm not a huge fan of candy, I have resorted to stashing other snacks in the tech closet, like several bags of buttered Pop Secret. Sometime back, I witnessed the janitor chuck an old microwave from the remodeled teacher's lounge into a dumpster. I fished it out and smuggled it in the closet.

I take a few pieces to eat as well, wiping the oil from my fingers onto the velvet chair. We've downed about two-thirds already, my share mostly stress-eating over the contents of my parents' envelope. I get fuller and queasier thinking about it. Although I've yet to open it, I have a hunch it's bad news. I mean, how often does anyone get an envelope with good news? College acceptance? Checks? Party invites? Those are all online now. The US Postal Service carries bills, junk mail, and sorrow. But if I can score this Hawaii trip, whatever bad thing is in the envelope won't matter.

Mr. Lipton clears his throat, and the participating students fall in line at center stage. Rod's in the middle, leaning every which way and introducing himself to everyone whose hand he can grab and shake. His voice carries even to the upper rows.

"Hi, I'm Roderick. I'll be your Aaron Burr for the evening. Oh, you're goin' out for Lafayette? The French dude? Voulez-vous coucher avec moi? That's an old French proverb, by the way."

Dino groans. The guy whose hand he just shook sidesteps away from him, eyeing Rod curiously but saying nothing.

Everybody exits the stage, and Lipton explains that one person will get up at a time to "rehearse" either lines from the play or creative interpretations of scenes. Afterward, onlookers will be free to give constructive criticism.

Dino sits and starts picking at corn kernels in her teeth as a small guy with long hair and glasses does a passable Alexander Hamilton. The downstairs folks start their critiques. The boy smiles politely at most but seems to take Rod's to heart. He chokes the mic and nods intently as Rod says, "Bro, you gotta ride that beat like it's Paul Revere's horse."

Mr. Lipton nods, too.

I grab some more popcorn and check my phone. I wonder what I'm checking it for, really. I'm not expecting any calls or texts, and I rarely get email orders after school hours. Maybe I'm hoping to see something from Sterling, but that's impossible because we never exchanged numbers. *What would I even say to her?*

Another therapy request from the random Forsyth number. I ignore it.

Dino begins checking her phone, and I look back at the stage as first Riley Morgan and then some other girl go up. Neither are that good, so instead of listening to the criticisms, I begin thinking of how I can talk to Dino about the Thing that happened last week during our *ZW3* rendezvous. Finally I just come right out with it.

"So," I say. "Wanna talk about what happened between you and Rosie?"

She gets squirrelly all of a sudden, shifting in her seat but never looking up at me. "Not really," she says, an answer as short as I'm sure she wants this conversation to be. But good friends don't let evasions just slide by.

I follow up with "What about what happened between you and River?"

Dino pauses. Her eyes flit toward me in a deer-in-headlights sort of way.

"She came by today. Asking about why you ghosted her. I told her it could've been the flu, but that wasn't right, was it?"

Her eyes hit the floor. She stays silent, so I fill in the blank space.

"Kinda odd how your new crush is feeling left out right after your old one randomly comes back into the picture."

"Rosie and I—just went for a walk," Dino responds.

"In a desert?"

She doesn't respond, so I press the issue.

"Did she say anything I should know?"

Her body stills again, thumbs no longer swiping the phone screen. Suddenly, she slaps the phone to her lap. Crossing her arms, she says, "If I tell you, will you promise not to bug me about it?"

"Sure."

Before speaking, she looks around the mezzanine, as if making sure nobody else hears her secret. "Rosie said maybe we were too hasty to break up. That we should reconsider."

*Jesus.* This isn't good. And not because Rosie isn't a good person. She *is*. But I don't want my friend getting caught up with someone so wishy-washy. River's possibly the spaciest person I've ever met, but even she seems more grounded than Rosie. She's nice, caring, consistent. That's what Dino needs. *Not* Rosie. Dino's coping mechanisms are not the best, and some of them are in fact illegal in the state of North Carolina. Another letdown might send her over the edge. She can't stand real-life roller coasters, and I honestly doubt she'd fare much better on the emotional ones.

We hear clapping from below, so we clap, too. Dino cups

her hands at her mouth and yells "You go, Glen Coco!" for good measure.

As I watch and wait for the noise to die down, I notice a sliver of light wash over the seats beneath me. A door quietly latches shut and a girl walks down the aisle. I can't see a face, only red hair made dark and damp with rain, but I know it's Gianna. She scurries into a seat several rows behind everyone else.

*Huh. Is she here for Rod?*

Can't be. I shake off the thought.

I'm still processing Gianna's presence when I hesitantly ask Dino, "What'd you say to Rosie?"

"I said . . . I'll think about it."

That means eventually she'll give in. Rosie's a charmer, and Dino's thoroughly charmed. I imagine what I'd say to my clients right about now, but no words fit the moment. Mom and Dad always said therapists *never* should counsel people they know. I can see why now. When you do, you take sides. You root for things to happen and things not to happen. And you get invested in preferred outcomes rather than personal growth.

I stop looking at Gianna and glance toward Dino as another performer gets up. Seeing Dino, kind of pitiful and hopeful at the same time, somehow zaps most of the anger out of me. I nod, taking great pains not to show any negative emotion. "Well, if you need me, I'm here to support."

"Thanks," she says.

"It's what friends do."

"And you know I'm here for you, too, right?"

"What for?" I ask.

"Your parental situation. It's still a thing, right?"

A very big thing. One I've never really talked to anyone about in depth. The only reason Dino knows is because she's seen them interact before. She's felt the chill that settles over Shmelton family dinner like an evening fog, when their most probing questions involve passing side dishes and asking about my day.

I've lived for years through their cold war, so long that I've gotten used to it. Steeled my emotions to the iciness. I wouldn't say it's a comfortable situation by any means but tolerable—like people who can stand to wear short sleeves in thirty-degree weather.

"It's not a thing," I lie.

"So they're cool now?"

I don't answer.

"Kalvin, just because they're not openly fighting doesn't mean—"

"It's not a thing because I've got a plan," I say, my voice firm.

She shifts in her seat to face me, nearly knocking over the popcorn bag as she rests a forearm on the divider.

"And you think your plan is gonna swoop in to save your parents' marriage . . ." The way she says it is almost teasing. Like she's opened the door to the future and is just waiting for me to enter and see what she already knows.

"Yeah," I answer. That one-word response hides the

annoyance I feel at her right now. There's a reason I don't talk about my family's issues. Because other people don't know my family. Dino has no idea how we work. Why this plan will work.

She nods pensively. "I'm interested in seeing how it all shakes out."

After I pulled my punches on the Rosie thing, this is how she comes at me? The annoyance metastasizes into an anger that tightens in my chest, but I keep an even keel. Gazing out to the stage, I say, "And what's your plan for when Rosie dumps you again?"

It's a low blow, and I see her in my periphery sinking back into her seat. She folds her arms again as her body draws tight. The soft glow of the theater sheds light not only on her face but her mood as well. Embarrassment. Shame. Indignation.

I think that's the end of our conversation until she springs up about a minute later, snatching her jacket and walking away. Halfway down the row, she turns back, storming toward me and bending low to get in my face.

"Here to support, huh?" she spits. "I'd hate to see what you do to your enemies."

With that, she leaves for good. I rise to give chase but pause once the music strikes up. I look out over the railing as Rod gets up from his seat and runs toward the stage's side curtain. He swoops low to pick up a tricorn hat and swaggers toward the microphone at center. All this time, the strings intro to Juvenile's "Back That Azz Up" rises in volume. And then come the lyrics:

> *We don't like the tax on tea, yeah,*
> *We want it free, yeah*
> *King George across the sea, yeah,*
> *Let us be, yeah*

Even more oddly, of all the cheers I hear, Gianna's cheering the hardest.

# Ten

**It's raining now.** Started right when I left the theater. I feel like the gods are angry at me. I mean, why not? Everybody else is.

Not only is Dino mad at me. Now Rod's mad, too, because Dino was our ride. He stands beside me under the theater's front awning as I watch sheets of water pour down right in front of us. He's side-eyeing me, not making the slightest effort to disguise it.

"Bro, has your mom texted back yet?" he asks.

"Not yet," I say, crossing my arms to guard against the cold. Two cars pull up. We watch as two theater kids jog out with coats over their heads. The cars drive off, red taillights disappearing into the watery distance.

Rod huffs, turning and meandering back toward the entrance. I watch him as he takes the orange pick from his hair and moves toward his reflection in the windowed wall. He busies himself shaping up his 'fro for about a minute before that gets tedious. He then stabs the pick back into his 'fro and marches back to my side. "Man, what you even say to her?"

"I was just talking about Rosie."

"You know that's a sore spot," he says.

I've long known it was, but somehow Rod saying it sinks me deeper into a pit of guilt. My reaction to Dino's skepticism of my plan was to rip off her biggest emotional scab. I shouldn't have done that. No friend should. Even Rod, who's not exactly known for his sensitivity, wouldn't have tread the ground I stomped all over.

"Well, what should I do?" I ask. The question itself leaves a weird taste in my mouth. I guess these past few days, I've been so used to giving advice that I'm forgetting how to get it.

"Apologize, dummy," Rod says.

It's good advice. Probably the best advice, if I'm being honest. But if I apologize, it'll make it seem like I was wrong, which I absolutely wasn't. Rosie is bad for Dino, and Dino needs to know that. A quick apology might make the learning process harder.

"Maybe," I say.

Rod grumbles something, but I can't understand it.

Another car pulls up. Two more kids burst out of the front doors and pile in. The car creates a wake of water as it speeds off, leaving us to the sounds of water pelting rooftops and songbirds singing in the rain.

"Why don't you just make her a special candygram? Except make it like a bouquet or something."

I look at Rod, wondering when exactly he became the *friend whisperer*. He's talking about Dino, but I'm thinking

Sterling. Maybe I could give her one to cheer her up. She'd probably love it. It's not like Chadwick would ever do anything like that for her.

"That's actually a really good idea, Rod."

"Oh, I know. They just come naturally most times. Kinda felt for a while like I should charge for them. Like, give a dollar, get a tidbit of life knowledge from yours truly. Sort of like what you do, but quicker. Therapy for the person on the go." He holds out his hands like he's propping up a theater marquee. "I'd call 'em 'Rodibles.' Like *edibles*, except instead of feeding you drugs, I feed you little bits of wisdom."

"I . . . actually like that," I admit. "That's amazingly catchy."

"I know."

Rod pulls his pick out again as another car approaches. A blue Tesla.

"Somebody got money," Rod mumbles.

The car's passenger-side window lowers, a hand reaching across from the driver's seat to wave.

"Kalvin, Rod, need a ride?"

I crouch and see Gianna.

"Hey," I say. "Yeah, we'll take one."

We get in, Rod in the back and me riding shotgun. Gianna's tying her damp hair back into a ponytail. No wonder Rod likes her. Aside from Gianna being smart and super considerate, I'm again struck by how gorgeous she is. A quiet and polished beauty. Speaking of gorgeous, I'm just now realizing how nice this car is. I look around. Wow. I touch the seats and console. I even run a hand across the dashboard before realizing how weird that must look and jerk it back. But Gianna's cool about it.

"Nice, huh?" she says. "I thought the whole electric car thing was just a gimmick when Dad got his five years ago, but after my sister got one for her birthday, I was sold. Guess you could say we're a Tesla family."

*Tesla family?*

"Hold up, you Tesla Gang, too?" Rod asks.

Gianna glances at the rearview. "Ride or die," she responds, returning her eyes to the road.

I look back at him and make a *What tha hell?* face. He can't even drive. Rod just shrugs.

Gianna glances at me and says, "I would show you everything the interface can do, which is like a *zillion* things, but I'm, you know . . . driving. Safety first."

Rod points and says, "Hey, as the saying goes: hands at ten and two so you don't kill your crew."

A laugh slips out of me. I'm thinking, *What?* But Gianna giggles, too.

"Rod, you are an absolute *riot!*" she says.

I stop laughing. Glancing back, I see him raising an eyebrow as he mouths the word "Rodible."

I give Gianna our addresses.

"Okay, great," she says. "I just need to make a quick stop at the country club to pay my tennis instructor. It's on the way. That okay, guys?"

My eyes go wide. I'd mentally prepared myself for a country club visit later this weekend. Not right now. "Yep."

She eyes the rearview: "That okay with you, Rod?"

"Ten-four," he says. "Or should I say 'ten-two'?"

She laughs again. "Oh, you're so funny!"

My eyes roll so hard they may as well be dice.

"By the way, I saw your performance at the rehearsal today." She gives a chef's kiss to the rearview. "C'est magnifique! I never knew you acted!"

"A damn fool," I say under my breath.

Rod ignores me. "I've been known to break a leg or two here and there."

"That's awesome! Who're you going out for?"

"Aaron Burr," he says.

Maybe it's just the asshole in me that can't resist the urge to mock, because I blurt out, "First Black VP." I smirk at my own joke.

Gianna doesn't get it. She just looks at me confused, and it gets quiet. My face craters.

I hear a *tsk*ing sound from behind me, and then Rod's tut-tutting voice. "Open a history book, Kal," he says. "Dude's white."

It's silent for a moment before Gianna gets the conversation back on track.

"That's so cool, Rod. I'm a total theater nerd myself," Gianna says. "I would've been up there if I wasn't so exhausted from soccer workouts right before."

I feel a buzz at my hip and get out my phone. It's Rod: Yo, Dino was right, man. I looked it up. I feel like crawling in the back seat and choking him.

"You going out for *Hamilton*, too?" Rod asks. I can hear the smile in his voice.

"Wouldn't miss it. Actually, Lipton said I'm a shoo-in for one of the Schuyler sisters, but keep that on the down-low. In all seriousness, though, I did have one slight critique for your rap."

"Like what?" he asks.

"It was a bit surfacey," she answers. "Like you were manufacturing your emotions and intensity. Have you ever heard of method acting or the Meisner technique?"

I glance back at Rod, and he looks just as confused as I am. Where's she getting all this?

"No," Rod mumbles.

"Oh, it's where—"

A text interrupts whatever she was about to say. Without thinking, I glance at the phone on her console. The screen's lit up with Jordan's name. Her words trail off as she reaches down and clicks a button to make it go dark. Instantly, her whole mood changes. She accelerates faster, hits the turns harder. Her lower lip curls into her mouth like she's chewing on a thought.

"How's your . . . predicament, by the way?" I ask.

"Same shit, different day."

"Oh?"

"Yeah," she sighs more than says. "Can't really talk about it right now, Jor—JP's kinda being an asshole about me exercising my no muscle. We'll talk next time we meet, though."

I hear Rod shift in his seat in a way that suggests he's listening but pretending not to.

"Sure," I say.

We drive farther, navigating a few more suburban streets as we go deeper into her Spotify playlist. Eventually Lee Ann Womack fills the car. We all lip-synch "I Hope You Dance." I can tell Gianna's calming by the fact that she's once again signaling before turning.

I sink back in my seat and stare out the window. Fenced-in cottage home after cottage home pass like a standing row of dominoes ready to tumble. Ours is an intractably suburban life. Quiet, pedestrian, uncomfortably well-manicured. An invisible yet overwhelming sense of restlessness blankets the neighborhood like dew at first light. Sometimes, I wonder if it's so boring that the people in these houses manufacture drama just to inject spice into their lives. An affair here. A midlife crisis there.

Then my thoughts drift to my parents. To how they've existed in this unpleasant but unobtrusive reality for years now.

Maybe marriages need drama to work. Perhaps white-hot lovers' quarrels are preferable to the thousands of cold stares and shoulders Mom and Dad are enduring. After all, if you're fighting, you're at least talking.

Gianna drives up to this grandiose gate, puts the window down, and flashes the peace sign at the security guard manning the checkpoint. He waves her through. I stare at my surroundings as we crawl down this tree-lined road for about half a mile. The canopy of foliage makes it unnaturally dark, even for a winter afternoon. Amazingly, though, the skies break right as we emerge from under the standing army of pines. Sunlight splinters through wisps of clouds, spilling onto a massive, Mediterranean-style clubhouse that backstops a lush green lawn. It's like we just teleported to spring.

We park, get out, and walk up a wide set of side steps onto a sprawling wooden veranda, Gianna's heels announcing our arrival. It even *feels* warmer here. The sounds of leisure echo all around us. Jazz wafts in from speakers tucked into hidden corners. Golf clubs *pop* balls in the distance. Ice clinks in glasses, metal utensils scrape plates, and a gentle breeze ruffles the flaps of patio umbrellas.

The elderly white guys all wave and greet Gianna by name. Rod and I get mildly curious looks paired with silent sips of drinks as we pass.

"Wait right here, guys, while I go find him," Gianna says. I tense as she walks in and the clubhouse door quietly shuts behind her. The jazz song ends, dying into silence as Rod and I turn around. Everybody's staring at us, even a black-tie waiter in mid-pour. I tug the elbow of Rod's jacket, leaning into his arm.

"Awwwwkward," I whisper.

Rod steps ahead of me, and I have to physically stop my arm from reaching out and yanking the hair pick from his 'fro.

His hand flits up for a wave before going right back down.

"Hey, fellas." Glancing up at the skies, he says, "Nice start to argyle season."

His words are met with stony silence. He steps back to me as they just keep staring. A new jazz song plays—one of the ones you'd hear in a bittersweet 1940s romance, à la *Casablanca*. It's like this for at least thirty seconds, and I just want to slither back to the Tesla.

"RODERICK? Is that you?"

We look left. Two men are climbing the veranda steps that lead to the golf course. The first, with blindingly silver hair and teeth too white to be natural, ascends to the top step before reaching down to help the other. Once he does, he turns and bolts toward us, all smiles.

"Big Sherm!" Rod says as they shake.

Weirdly enough, the guy's tan is so deep and indelible that it almost matches my complexion.

"How you been, my guy?" the man says. His question is punctuated by a laugh that's so fake but well-worn that it's probably become the real deal over time.

"Oh, you know, rippin' and runnin'," Rod says. "This is my friend Kalvin. Kalvin, Mr. Sherman Jefferson Davis. I call him Big Sherm, though."

Big Sherm shakes hands with me, and I suffer a grip that's weathered and tight courtesy of decades of glad-handing and holding nine irons. So tight my fingers buckle, and the rest of my arm follows his pull just to relieve the pressure.

Big Sherm's smile disappears as he looks me dead in the eye: "*Firm* handshake, Kalvin. Always. It shows you mean business."

When he lets go, I cradle my hand to my chest, massaging the joints while muttering "Thanks." I notice the other white guys on the veranda, having found us acceptable, have gone back to their previous business of making idle talk and ignoring us. "How do you know Rod?" I ask.

"He used to bag my groceries at Wegmans."

"Colored or not, he was the best damn bagger at that place!"

I nearly choke on my saliva. We all look at the old guy shuffling toward us, his hunched steps much more belabored than his forerunner. He's older, paler, with wrinkles as crisscrossed and plentiful as pine needles on a forest bed.

Big Sherm chides him, "*Dad!* We don't say that anymore."

"I'm seventy-eight years old," the man grits out. "I fought off the commies in 'Nam and two ex-wives who sued me for alimony. I'll say whatever I damn well please."

"Dad . . ."

The elder holds up a finger. It jabs toward Rod like the needle of a compass. "Hell, I'll do ya one better. The Civil Rights Act got a few things right. One was sending this fine young man our way." His tongue curls around his chapped lips as he sticks out his other hand. Rod shakes it. "Hello, Roderick. You still working at the Wegmans?"

"No, sir, Mr. Davis. You still refusing paper?"

At this, the old guy perks up, a smile squeezing his eyes and showing all his dentures. He hacks out a laugh. "You know what

I always say: Why use paper when you can piss off a liberal? Since they care so much about the environment, they can figure it out."

More hearty laughs dredge up from his chest. He gets about four good ones out before the coughing takes over. Big Sherm puts a hand to his dad's back and ushers Mr. Davis to the nearest seat. When their backs are turned, I hear Rod mutter, "Ol' racist ass."

Big Sherm invites us to sit, and we do because there's nowhere else to go. The waiter brings us happy hour menus, and Big Sherm insists we order an appetizer on him. Rod and I pick the jalapeño poppers when the waiter comes.

When it's Mr. Davis's turn, he says, "I'll have a White Russian. But add a smidgen of extra coffee. Don't wanna make it *too* white. Guess you could call it an Interra—"

"*Dad.*" Out of nowhere, the table lifts and utensils clank. *Did this guy just knee the table?* Mr. Davis sneers at Big Sherm, but Big Sherm's eyes remain locked on the menu.

"Mr. Davis!" someone yells. "Mr. Davis Junior!"

We all look up and it's Gianna. The waiter steps back as Gianna rounds the table, giving both men a hug. She sits between me and Rod.

"Hey there, Gianna."

"Hello, little lady," Mr. Davis echoes.

"Hi, y'all! It's so nice to see both of you." Gianna turns to me. "These two worked with my dad for years on some corporate buyouts." Then she looks across the table. "Kalvin here is one of the smartest people I know. Gives *wonderful* advice. And Rod might be one of the funniest."

Big Sherm nods, pointing right at Rod: "And one of the politest, too. An all-around great guy."

Gianna smiles, and I swear I see Rod's brown cheeks turn rosier. It's like watching Kevin Durant play basketball: Rod's getting assists from every direction.

"Well, this calls for a celebration," Mr. Davis says before coughing again. Covering his mouth, he snaps for the waiter even though he's already here.

"Yes, sir?"

"Drinks for the table," he says.

"Dad, they're in *high school*, nowhere near twenty-one."

Mr. Davis looks right at Rod, deadly serious. "You got hair on your chest?"

"Yessir."

"Good, then you're old enough to drink." The man's focus shifts toward me. "Got hair on your chest?"

I shake my head, to which he raises an eyebrow and asks, "Want some?" He then looks at the waiter and says, "Two whiskey sours for the young fellas and a hot gin toddy for the lady."

Much to Mr. Davis's chagrin, Gianna vetoes the order, beating her hand against the table and declaring, "You're not gonna corrupt us today."

The waiter goes, and we make small talk about school and sports and Gianna's potential college choices for a while until Big Sherm takes the convo in a surprising direction.

"So, Kalvin. What wonderful advice do you give?" he asks.

I freeze up, totally not prepared to answer. First, saying I'm a relationship guru in front of these guys might get me laughed away from the table. But even if it didn't, it's the last thing I'd want to talk about with them.

I'm about to say *Just life advice* when Gianna blurts out "Dating advice."

Big Sherm puts a hand to his chin, the revelation rolling around in his head like a lost marble. Finally he comes out with "Interesting. So you give it to your classmates?"

"Yeah. Just to help them through couples problems. My mom and dad are therapists."

"Oh," he says, nodding.

It's quiet for a while after that. The appetizers come, along with Mr. Davis's drink and Big Sherm's burger.

Rod, Gianna, and I dig in, with Gianna breaking the silence between chews. "How's Sterling?" she asks.

"You didn't talk to her?"

"Haven't got a chance to yet. Why, is something up?"

"No," I say, lowering my voice. I glance across the table and Big Sherm is occupied helping Mr. Davis fiddle with his phone to return a missed call from his physician.

"It's just, there's some things complicating her situation," I add.

She makes an *Oh* face and holds up her hand. "Say no more." She leans in to whisper the next thing: "I'm all about respecting client privacy, so I won't mention it. I will say she's a tough nut to crack but she'll come around."

Roderick shifts beside her. I know I'm gonna get twenty questions on Sterling after we leave here. A wave of guilt hits me just then as I realize how much I've been attempting to keep from both him and Dino. They know I'm doing therapy, but I've managed to keep hidden the fact that Sterling's one of my clients. Yeah, yeah, client privilege and all that. But I think it's more. It's like I'm intentionally keeping a part of myself walled off from my closest friends. And I don't know why.

Mr. Davis gets up and loudly begins cursing into his phone. His son follows, haranguing him with "Will you just calm down for a sec?"

"What's tough about her?" I ask Gianna, biting into another popper.

Gianna looks at me curiously, and I can tell she's weighing the ethics of opening a sliver of her friend's private life to the outside world. After some consideration, she says, "I think it'd be more effective to just show you."

Softly, she grabs my hand and gets up from the table. I shrug at Rod before following her lead. Mr. Davis's yelling seems to get louder the farther we walk away from it. But once we're finally inside and Gianna closes the tall French doors behind us, it stops. I hear but can't see the distant clanging of kitchenware. The room smells faintly of cigars masked by heavy currents of vanilla. The walls are high and oaken and lined with shelves full of hardbacks I'm sure nobody's read in decades. Gianna leads me through that room and then through a sunlit grand ballroom, before turning down a back hallway. She leads me through a couple more until we come across one dotted with waist-high Roman columns that stick out like the spikes of a stegosaurus. Topping each column are busts of nondescript white men or, alternately, rounded glass cases. Gianna tells me the men are country club luminaries. She doesn't have to tell me that the cases are filled with artifacts the club has deemed important. A Civil War Confederate revolver. A signing pen used at the Treaty of Versailles. An Oscar award.

Gianna stops right there, circling the case. "You know whose this is?" she asks. It doesn't take a genius to answer. The name is engraved on a placard right below it. Harold Glistern. *Sterling's dad.*

"He's won like seven of them," she continues. "It was nothing for him to just donate this one."

I look up at her. "Why would he, though?" I ask. I'm having one of those does-not-compute moments wrapping my head around why any Black person would be so gracious to a place like this.

"Her parents are more inclined toward fitting in," she says. "Access. Connections. They see the practical side of it. And they have some super-high expectations for her. Go to Harvard, marry well, carry on the family legacy."

"What's the family legacy?"

"Her mom's a bestselling novelist, and her dad's some bigshot screenplay writer. And they're always making Sterling feel bad for *not* being those things."

"But she's just a teenager."

"Right around the exact same age her parents started showing signs of their genius, according to the family history."

"Why would they put so much pressure on her?"

"Why do parents do anything? To make sure their kids succeed. I don't think they really mean to, but they're just so wrapped up in their own massive success, they don't really consider anything less than that 'worthy.' I mean, Sterling's really good at math and science. Just not *great*. And her parents have been trying to change her good to great for years. Stuff like that can give you self-esteem issues over time. You should talk to her about it sometime."

"Seems a bit heavy for a seven-minute conversation."

"Well, come to the mall tomorrow and talk," she says. "We'll be there around six. I'm helping her try on dresses for the ball."

"Really?"

"Yeah. You and Rod. We could use some male perspectives. Chadwick's mom bought his dad a WaveRunner for his birthday, so they're gonna be testing it out on the lake before Chadwick and Jordan head to the movies in Larchmont. So they're all booked."

"Jesus, sounds . . ."

"Rich? That'd be an understatement," Gianna says, pointing toward a door at the end of the hallway.

"What's that room?"

"The Boston Room," she answers. As in Chadwick Boston. "Chadwick's ancestors are pretty old money. Deep ties to the club. I honestly think that's the major thing he and Sterling bonded over when they first got together."

My brow furrows as I look at her. "The money?"

"The pressure to succeed," she corrects. "It's kinda weird how they come from totally different backgrounds, but in one specific way they're in the exact same boat."

She takes me into the room. Various plaques and framed pictures of Boston men line the walls, but otherwise it looks like just another gentlemen's parlor. She gives me a quick and haphazard history of the family. Ivy League, this. Wall Street, that. I don't know if it's what she intended, but by the time she's done explaining and we're headed back, I feel a little bad for him. Not bad enough to stop moving in on Sterling, but bad enough to feel slightly guilty about it. *Just* slightly. I mean, a connection bonded by a shared sense of privilege sounds pretty weak to me. Sterling and I would share so much more. Better to sever the tie now before they get too invested in each other. Honestly, I'm doing them a favor.

We go back to the table and to Rod, and awkwardly watch Mr. Davis yelling into a phone while Big Sherm shadows him. Then we talk more about *Hamilton*, with Rod and Gianna bonding over favorite songs. It's not long before Mr. Davis yells, "Awww, shit on a stick!" and storms back to the table—which isn't so much "storming" at his age as it is "aggressive shuffling."

Mr. Davis slams his phone on his napkin as he sits. He sets his eyes on me. "You give advice, right? You want some damn advice? Don't get old!"

Big Sherm returns, too, shaking his head. "Dad just got a new doctor. A recent med school grad."

"He's a big dumb oaf is what he is," Mr. Davis grouses. "With those big-ass Dumbo ears. It's unnatural. Kinda like . . ." He points right at Gianna. "You still hanging around that boy, um, what's his name? Gordon? Jurgen?"

"*Jordan*," she corrects, her head angling down to the nearly empty appetizer plate.

"Big dumb oaf."

"Dad!" Big Sherm almost shouts. After reining in his tone, he leans in to whisper-shout. "We don't talk about people like that."

Mr. Davis looks at his son, fire in his eyes. "The boy got drunk last year and *took a piss* right on the seventh hole fairway! Remember that? The Independence Day tournament? A *piss*! Like the damn golf course was his personal urinal. The most disgraceful thing to ever happen in the one-hundred-and-fifteen-year history of this club!"

I'm thinking, *Segregation?* But I don't actually say it. Instead, I lean back to glance at Rod just as he does the same. His eyes are as wide as I know mine are.

"Dad, please."

"Pissin' on the grass like a damn dog! What's he gonna do next, hump the flagstick?"

"*Dad!*"

There's a loud bang again, and the utensils shake. Other tables look our way. I've never actually seen a plant die on the vine, but I imagine it'd look a lot how Gianna does now, her face blooming red as her confidence just withers away into nothingness.

Mr. Davis shuts up after a few more incomprehensible utterances, and after that it's just awkward small talk and skyward glances and silence. We finally leave about ten minutes later, and the first thing Gianna says once she's driven past the gate is "He's gotten better since then."

Sensing her shame, I just say, "We've all done embarrassing things."

Rod quietly starts humming Drake's old classic "Marvins Room" from the back seat as he looks out his fogged-up window. Gianna doesn't catch it, but I do. The lyrics come to me like water through a sieve:

*I'm just sayin' you could do better . . .*

# Eleven

**I spend most** of Saturday on a surreal, emotional Tilt-A-Whirl, yanked back and forth between worrying about Dino and worrying about tonight's dress fitting with Sterling. I nail-bite my way through two MLS soccer matches, check my texts excessively for God only knows what reason, and pop in and out of *ZW3* looking for Dino at least ten times.

None of it helps me feel any less unsettled. Rod finally calls midafternoon and saves me from myself by suggesting we catch a matinee before the big show with Gianna and Sterling. We hit up the newest Fast and Furious offering.

When we exit the theater, I have to squint as my eyes get used to the light. It's a nice day out. Sunny but damp. Humid but breezy. A day better suited for the middle of May than February.

"You think they're running out of ideas?" I ask as people stream past us.

Rod yawns underneath the marquee and then says, "Shoot, that was the best one yet."

We debate the movie as we walk the outdoor strip mall. Going back and forth with him makes me wish Dino were here. She's the biggest movie buff of our trio, and no doubt she'd be chiming in with endless insights about the cinematography and CGI animations. It feels weird just us two, actually. It's like she's a ghost at my shoulder. I think about Rod's suggestion that I apologize. It weighs more heavily on me today, but I'm still not quite there yet. She's at least gotta understand why I said what I said. Why Rosie would be so bad for her. Why River would be a total upgrade.

Rod and I make our way into the main building but stop to look at the directory to find the dress store. It's one level and two hallways away, so we take our time. The closer we get, the more antsy I become. Teeth-grinding. Knuckle-cracking. Hand-in-pocketing. It gets so bad that Rod has to hype me up by the escalators near Macy's.

We walk into Hawt Couture, the high-end dress shop, and I see more colors than I was aware existed. And girls—girls with their moms, girls with their friends, and girls alone, scavenging the racks and riffling through the dresses lining the walls.

No guys, though, except us.

The music is all instrumental, airy and light, like something Susie McNamara's group No Strings Attached would play. One of the workers comes up to us, sporting a smile way too big to have worked for long in retail.

"Hi, guys!" she says. "Valentine's present for the GF? That's soooo Hawt."

"Actually, we're not—" I start.

"Lucky you came this weekend because there's a twenty-percent-off significant-other discount for all rack dresses."

"A what?" Rod asks.

"A significant-other discount. It used to be the boyfriend discount, but we switched to S.O. because it was kinda sexist and gendered, and maybe even a touch homophobic. And Hawt Couture is committed to smashing the patriarchy and looking cute while doing it. Isn't that just awesome?" she asks.

"That's *Hawt*," I answer. "But, um, we're not—"

Rod nudges me, and my mouth snaps shut. Looking toward the back of the store, he says, "We'll get back to you on that discount," as he pulls me away.

"Okay, great!" she says.

When we're out of earshot, I ask, "Why'd you lie to her like that?"

"I'm tryin' to help you out. You don't think Sterling will appreciate twenty percent off?"

"I'm not her significant other."

"And you never *will* be with that attitude."

I see Gianna standing at the entrance of the dressing room checking her phone. I get nervous again, and Rod notices. He wheels to face me, grabbing me by the shoulders.

"I don't know if I'm up to this," I say.

"*Look.* You've already taken the first step."

"I have?"

Rod nods. "You've got the single most important thing of hers right now. The one thing every guy wants."

My eyebrows lift. "What's that?"

"Her *attention*. Now use it, bro."

As much BS as Rod spews, his Rodibles really hit the mark sometimes. I do have Sterling's attention. Not only that, I've earned her respect and gratitude. It's time to make a move. To assert myself as the number one guy in her life, Chadwick and his non-spades playing, Dockers-wearing ass be damned. By the time we leave this mall, I'm determined to put Sterling firmly on the path toward calling it quits.

Rod shouts Gianna out as we approach. She hustles our way, giving us both hugs.

"You guys ready to help Sterling say yes to the dress?"

"Ready," I say. All my nerves come rushing back right then, as I realize she's probably half-naked just beyond that wall. *I am soooo not ready.*

*Okay, wait, no.* I shake the nerves off. *I* am *ready.*

"Why ain't you in there?" Rod asks.

Gianna dons a sheepish grin that quickly sours into a sulk. "Because I'm supposed to go to Jordan's parents' lake house that weekend."

"That's still on?" I ask.

She nods. The word "Unfortunately" slips out as quiet as a field mouse.

I shrug, treating the lack of progress like it's no big deal.

"There's still time," I respond. I say it because it's true. There is. But also because shaming her for inaction would only do harm. Confronting Jordan was a step in and of itself. Too much, too soon could set her back.

"I wish I could just do it," she says.

"Look, Rome wasn't built in a day," I say. "It took time to put up those walls. Your walls will take time, too. Don't be so hard on yourself."

"Thanks, Kalvin. It just feels like my walls are as high as sidewalks."

"And your frustration is valid. Do you realize, though, that your walls were basically nonexistent when we first talked?"

Reluctantly, she nods. "Yes."

"So remember that your progress is equally as valid."

"All right." Gianna peeks beyond the cutout opening dividing the dressing rooms from the rest of the store. She whispers "Sterling" very loudly.

"I'm coming!" Sterling calls out. "Just gotta get this zipper. It's tight."

"Need help?"

"I think I got it," Sterling says.

Gianna turns back to us. "We do so much just for one measly night of partying it's not even funny."

"It's astounding," I reply.

"That's why I'm glad y'all are doing this dress thang today," Rod says. "Y'all on that school grind. Got grades to keep up. Practices. You need to treat yourself every once in a while. Make yourself feel good for a job well done, a life well lived."

She looks right at him, her eyes sparked with earnestness. "That's absolutely right, Rod. You're one of the few men who realize how therapeutic this can be."

Hesitantly at first, but then more forthrightly, Rod reaches for and takes her hand. Gianna giggles at his ever-so-slight tug, and then he twirls her.

"I know you're gonna try on a dress before we leave," he says.

"But I've got nowhere to go," she says.

"Self-care is its own destination," he replies.

Gianna giggles again, but this time it's different. The timbre isn't just amused but playful. Almost flirty.

"Okay, coming," Sterling singsongs. The three of us look toward the fitting room entrance.

She saunters out, and it's like an angel just walked into the room. She's in this flared white dress with metallic gold floral beading at the bodice. Bare skin peeks out of a neck that dives down to her chest, and I have to keep myself from staring.

Sterling shakes her head at Gianna. "Not medieval enough," she says.

"It is soooo medieval!" Gianna replies. "You are soooo ready for a knight to come rescue you."

Sterling looks at Rod: "Whatchu think?"

"Knight bait," Rod says.

She nods and turns to me. Twirling, she asks, "This damsel enough for you?"

"I would lock you in my castle tower," I reply, only realizing how stalkerish that sounds after I've said it.

Sterling studies her dress a while longer, running her hand along the trim before saying, "Yeah, I'm still not feeling it. But thanks, guys."

Gianna sucks in her cheeks as Sterling heads back into the dressing room. Leaning in close, she says, "It's been like this for the last twenty minutes. Too medieval. Not medieval enough. Too dressy. Not dressy enough. It's a freaking *dress!*"

"Is she trying on another?" I ask.

Gianna's back sinks against the wall as she holds up two fingers. Her head droops as her butt hits the floor. Sterling does try on two more dresses, and she hates them both, to our astonishment. There's nothing to hate about them. One gives off Audrey Hepburn vibes, and the other makes her look like the beautiful Greek huntress goddess Diana.

After Sterling changes back into her jeans and T-shirt, we leave the store, Gianna loudly complaining about how Sterling has yet to realize how gorgeous she is. They go back and forth like this as we walk toward the food court, Gianna with the effusive praise and Sterling with the volleys of self-deprecation. I wonder if her deflections relate back to what Gianna said about Sterling's parents yesterday. Could her parents' drive for perfection extend to other areas in their daughter's life? And if Sterling's not internalizing the obvious truth of her beauty or smarts, in what other ways could she be selling herself short?

I get my chance to prod when Gianna pulls Rod into

Sunglass Shack to try on a few pairs of shades she'd been eyeing. "I always thought dress shopping was a mother/daughter type thing," I say.

"That outing would definitely end up with one of us in tears."

"You don't get along with her?"

Sterling takes her time considering the best answer. We pass by a perfume vendor and a massage chair kiosk, its manager leaning against the booth, thumbing through a magazine. A boy and girl shout in the distance, and the perfumier mists a soft floral scent right before a potential patron.

"I love her," Sterling says. "And I know she loves me. But one thing to know about her is she's an author by trade. And sometimes I feel like I'm less my mom's daughter and more a character in one of her stories. She's constantly revising me, always trying to edit me, make me better in some way."

"I would absolutely hate that," I say. "I take it this extends beyond your backyard science experiments."

She nods. "Everything. And it's not like she really means to do it. It's just who she is."

"And who is she?" I ask.

"Wildly talented. Eccentric but not weird. Always getting down on herself."

"About what?"

"You know, it's wild. She's a bestseller who feels totally guilty about not working out every day or not knowing how to cook all that well. And I'm just like, *Mom*, we'll survive. You just be you."

"Like an hourglass."

"Her body?"

I shake my head. "Her mind."

"How so?"

"Never totally fulfilled. Always seeing a part of herself as empty in some way. She can't see that she works just fine, even if there isn't always a perfect balance. Doesn't know that what she's got is exactly enough."

Sterling stops in the middle of the walkway, streams of people angling around her like she's a rock jutting from a stream bed. After I notice she's not beside me, I turn and see this curious smile on her face.

"Kalvin?" she half laughs.

"Yeah?"

"How are you so smart?"

I shrug. "I just listen to my parents a lot, I guess."

"That's where you got the hourglass analogy from?"

"No."

She laughs again. She walks right up to me and cups her palms around my shoulders. I get lost in the deep brown of her eyes as she says, "A word of advice?"

"Shoot."

"Never hide your own intelligence behind theirs."

I nod hesitantly. "I will try."

"You will *do*. And you can start now. *You*, Kalvin, not your parents: What's the best possible advice *you* can give?"

Such a simple question, but I can't think of anything. It's like asking what's the best cloud to pull out of the sky as a keepsake.

There are so many. But also, it never occurred to me where my parents' advice ends and where mine begins.

I shrug. "I dunno."

She shrugs, too, as if to say *Oh well*, and I wonder if she's disappointed I didn't answer.

We pass a few more stores with contented silence as our company. Either we've lost Rod and Gianna, or they've ditched us, but I'm not sweating it. We go to Life in Neon to browse through their novelty T-shirts, and then head to the Apple store to look at the newest iPhone because Sterling needs hers replaced. Finally we double back toward the food court.

There, we get Häagen-Dazs. Sterling, a waffle cone, three scoops of cherry vanilla rising like the Appalachians above the cone. I choose a single scoop of pistachio in a plain cup. She bites into hers, getting ice cream on her nose and top lip. I always had thought of her as beautiful and gorgeous and resplendent, but a new adjective shuffles its way to the fore-front: "adorable."

She licks her lip and wipes her nose and says, "Okay, let's play a game. You're on death row. Your last meal has to come from one of the places in this food court. Which do you choose?"

"Wait, what am I on death row for?" I ask.

"Does it matter?"

"Yes, I'd like to know." I mean, who wouldn't want to know what type of criminals their friends would peg them as?

"Okay. You're, um . . ." Sterling's eyes go skyward, searching for the answer as if it's out in the universe. After a moment, her wide-eyed gaze settles back on me: "You are a serial check forger . . ."

"That's it?"

"Who kills the victims of his check-cashing schemes and buries the bodies in the confetti of the voided checks that you shred."

At this, I squint, raising a finger. I have questions.

"Yes?" she asks.

"Why would you shred an already voided check?"

Her hands slap the rise of her jeans, and she makes a face like *I don't know*. "You tell me. You're the Gregg County Check Slayer."

I eat some ice cream. "Oh, so I've got a nickname now?"

"Don't all the great serial killers have nicknames?"

"Is that your idea of a compliment?" I ask.

"Yeah, of course. You should feel proud."

Taking another bite, I say, "Okay, then. What would *you* be on death row for?"

"Easy. Machete killing all my girlfriends' terrible exes. I'd stalk them on their dates, sneak into their houses, and right when they make that move where they snake the arm around the new girl . . ." She makes the neck-slash motion.

"Gotta love a girl with a plan," I say.

We sit across from each other at one of the tables on the outskirts of the food court. A clique of middle school girls walks by giggling. A woman drags her crying toddler the opposite way.

"So, to my original question," Sterling says. "Which restaurant?"

I look around before settling on Try Thai. "Now you," I say. "Auntie Anne's."

"The pretzel place?"

"I *love* pretzels!" she protests.

"Pretzels are the worst. And besides, Auntie Anne totally Columbused Aunt Jemima's entire brand. The Black community had their famous aunt, and then the whites just had to have theirs."

Sterling's expression gets all serious as she goes into lecture mode: "*First of all*, pretzels are the best. Second, Aunt Jemima was actually a racial stereotype foisted upon us by white profiteers. And lastly, how do you even know Auntie Anne is white?"

"The only seasoning she knows how to use is salt."

Nodding, she says, "I'll give you that."

A line of melted ice cream spills onto the webbing between Sterling's thumb and index finger. Without thinking, she licks it, and I smirk. She pauses, embarrassed. Slowly, taking her hand away, she says, "Sorry, I promise I'm not a dog."

"Glad to hear."

She abruptly rises from her seat and hustles to the Häagen-Dazs booth, coming back with a plastic spoon. She works like a wizened sculptor carving out edges of ice cream from the cone, careful not to touch the places she's already licked. She carefully relocates each spoonful into my cup. By the time she's done, I have twice as much ice cream as I purchased.

"I can't eat it all," she says. "I'll get brain freeze."

"Thanks?" I look at the cherry vanilla and pistachio swirling together. I eat a spoonful.

"How is it?" she asks.

"Fruity. Nutty. Not a bad combination. Like a chaotic mess, but in a good way."

She laughs. "*Chaotic mess.* I like that. Describes my fam to a tee."

"They can't be that bad if they made you," I reply.

"Touché, I guess." She looks around at the passersby before reengaging with me, propping her hand against her chin as she leans into the table. A few strands of curls drift into her face. She uses her cone hand to swipe them away. "So enough about my peeps. Tell me what's up with yours?"

"You wanna know about my family?" I ask.

"Yep. Spill it. Give me the deets."

"There's nothing to talk about," I answer.

"Come on, dude. They can't be perfect."

*Far from it. But I can't tell Sterling that, can I?*

"I never said they were. It's just . . . they're kind of boring."

"Almost everybody's parents are boring. That's way different from what I'm getting at. So you, Kalvin, are telling me your parents don't have fights, arguments, or anything?"

"They don't really fight. They just . . ." I catch myself before stumbling into an admission.

Sterling's head tilts, and I know she caught it, too. They just *what*? How much should I divulge of their situation, now that I've revealed that a situation does, in fact, exist? What's the ethics line here? Where's the boundary between indulging friendly reveals and spilling family secrets?

"Kalvin?"

I snap to, and she's staring at me, waiting. I don't know how long she's been looking like that, but I do know that her eyes are as inviting as I've ever seen them. That my secret, if I choose to divulge it, would be safe with her.

I open my mouth, and the words stall at first. But then they come rushing out like a breached dam. "My parents have been going through a rough patch this past year. Past *several* years, actually. But it'll all be fine because I've got a plan to fix everything."

Her expression is dubious at first, and I wonder how dumb I must sound. I brace for a lecture, a tut-tutting that partitions dreams from reality, fiction from fact. But it never comes. Her face just softens into something far more accommodating.

"My parents separated once," she says. "A few years back."

"They did?"

She nods. "I honestly thought it was my fault. Like I wasn't the daughter they needed me to be."

"And how'd you get over that feeling?"

"I didn't. They just got back together, and I didn't have to deal with it."

"So it was that easy? They just turned the page"—I snap my fingers—"like that?"

Sterling shakes her head. "No, no, *no*. It wasn't easy. You can't just erase the past. The page still has smudges and smears and

185

crinkles where they balled it up and threw it away. But it's *their* page, imperfect as it is. They edited their own story. I stayed out of it. It's the only way."

My assumptions about the lecture were spot-on. Except from her it felt less like a lesson and more like a note slipped onto my desk by the pretty girl in my classroom. Covert but confessional. Even though I've gotten more comfortable talking to Sterling, it's still weird in a way. In my therapy sessions, I'm in control, steering the conversation, doling out pieces of advice like cards at a blackjack table. But with Sterling, I feel like I'm the one on the couch ready to spill my feelings. She gives just as well as she takes. Probably better.

Maybe under a different circumstance I would've taken her words to heart. But not now. I'm so close to Hawaii. To our pu'uhonua. To fixing things. Why give up now?

I nod away the wisdom, and we finish our ice cream, hopscotching from topic to topic like two kids on a playground. That is, until I get the stomach to talk about her and Chadwick.

"So . . . still swimming toward the horizon?" I ask.

The way her eyebrows twitch, I know she knows I'm referring to Chadwick. She dabs her lips with a napkin and says, "Bad news? Yes. Good news? At this rate, I might qualify for the next Olympics."

"Then why try on dresses today?" I ask.

She shrugs. "Hope. Denial, maybe."

"Sounds like a pretty horrible way to live."

"Don't tell my parents that," she mutters.

"Why not?" I ask.

She bites her lower lip, her gaze drifting to the table before lifting slowly to me again, like a sunrise. "They kind of see Chadwick as a golden boy. And don't get me wrong. It's not like they don't think I have options. They're just of the mindset that, if the perfect guy fell right into your lap, why even look elsewhere?"

I stir my spoon into an empty cup, thinking long and hard before speaking again. It makes sense that Sterling's parents are pushing her toward Chadwick. She's expected to be a genius. She's expected to do great things. Marrying an upper-class scion just fits. When she's looking off into the distance, I steal a glance. My heart breaks at the sight of an outsized personality like her shrinking more and more into a caged bird with every conversation. The cage is invisible to most, but all too real to her.

"Do your parents know you two aren't doing well?" I ask.

"It's not like I've told them. But they're not blind. They can see he doesn't come around as often."

I want to say so many things to her, the first being that she can't let her parents live her life. But my words don't come fast enough. Someone beats me to it.

"Sterling?"

I look up and see Chadwick approaching from the side. He looks shocked. Jordan's a little ways behind and they're both holding sodas from the theater.

Sterling eyes him quizzically. "Hey, um . . . I thought you were going to the Larchmont AMC?"

"We got there too late, so we came to this one," Chadwick says.

"And you didn't text?"

He looks right at me as he answers her. "Didn't think I needed to. Why didn't *you* text *me*?"

"Because I've told you for two straight days I'd be here," she says, a sharpness edging into her tone like a hand slicing through a closing elevator.

"With him?" Chadwick asks.

Sterling glances at me, disbelief scribbled all over her face. "Yes. I do have friends outside of our relationship, Chad."

"Like this loser?" Jordan replies as he weasels his way to the table. Sidling up to Chadwick, he adds, "You got a siren, you'd better keep her close, bro. They attract all types, even the ones punching way above their weight."

My hands grip the table. I want to punch him right now. But I can't guarantee that won't get me tossed down an escalator, so I hold it in. Sterling, on the other hand, seems like she's just getting started. She rises from the table, wagging a finger in Jordan's face.

"Might wanna get a handle on who's close to *your* girl, bro," she says.

Jordan blinks, as if the response were a fastball, high and inside. A part of me hopes Rod shows up again with another shovel full of dirt, but I don't see that happening.

"Sterling, why are you with another guy without telling me?" Chadwick asks, his tone more pressing than before.

Calmly, Sterling redirects her attention his way. Gone is the bluntness and the verve, replaced by words that are pillow soft.

"Chad, it's really not what it looks like. If you could—"

"Don't tell me to calm down, Sterl."

"He's just a friend," she responds. "He's been helping me through some stuff."

Chadwick jabs a finger into his chest. "I'm your boyfriend. I should be helping you."

I don't know what comes over me, but it makes words slip out of me like ice through fingertips. "Maybe if you'd paid more attention to her than the random texts you get, you'd see there was an issue to begin with."

I stand, adrenaline pumping through my veins. I'm bouncing a little. I actually feel ready for, even excited about the hell I've just unleashed. Sterling glares at me, her expression an alchemy of anger paired with vague suspicion. But I don't care. I just gave Sterling the perfect setup to pummel him into the pavement. An opportunity for me to be there for her when Chadwick is exposed for the high-class dirt he is.

Still looking at her, Chadwick points to me: "What is he talking about?"

Though she doesn't move, I can see her psychologically shrinking back from a fight. The light sparking out from her eyes like the last spent embers of a firework. She sucks her cheeks in, swallowing any comebacks.

"Sterling."

She looks at him. Smiles weakly. "It's nothing," she says.

Chadwick glares at me before returning his gaze to her. "Good to hear. We're heading out. Gonna hit up Mocha Palace next. You coming?"

She nods, getting out her phone. "Just let me tell Gianna real quick."

"Okay, then. Jordan's car's behind the theater. You two can meet us there."

With that, the two boys go, Jordan holding up the peace sign with his back turned. Switching it to a middle finger when he's sure Chadwick's not looking.

When they're out of sight, Sterling plucks up napkins and gathers her purse, her eyes landing on me once more. She gives me the same weak smile she gave Chadwick, but somehow it's worse, buoyed by an undercurrent of exasperation.

"See you tomorrow?" I ask.

She nods stiffly. "Yep. Tomorrow." The words come out hollow.

"Great," I say.

"Great."

Her long curls whip around as she turns and leaves. I just stand there for a moment, stunned, thinking it through. How could a rapport that started so sweetly end with such a bitter aftertaste?

# Twelve

**I know now** what people mean when they say it's lonely at the top. It seems the more successful my therapy practice has become, the more those closest to me don't want to talk to me. First Dino. Now Sterling.

Not that Sterling and I are actually fighting or anything. But it's been exactly twenty-four hours since she gave me that look before walking off with Chadwick, and I still can't decipher it, no matter how many times I've replayed it in my head. But I know it wasn't good. Of course, I *also* can't figure out why she left the food court with him instead of me. I'd set her up perfectly for the confrontation she initially wanted to have. Why would she pass?

*Apologize, dummy.*

Rod's advice rattles around in my brain.

For some reason, I feel the nagging pull to tell Sterling I'm sorry. But how, exactly? And why? Like the Dino situation, I don't think I actually did anything wrong. I know Sterling seemed upset after the exchange between me, her, and Chadwick, but that's not my fault. I just gave her a clever path to a breakup. It's not my fault she didn't take it.

At least she'll be at tonight's mixer. I know if I can just explain my rationale, she'd absolutely get why I said what I said. He's uncaring and inattentive to her. An absolute jerk face. And not only that, he doesn't *get* her like I do. Could he ever relate over microaggressions or vibe with her to old-school hip-hop? No way.

But I can't complain too much. The irony of a week scarred by personal setbacks is that even though my social life has taken a hit, business couldn't be better. I'm booked through next week. I'm well on my way to getting the $10,466. Hawaii—pu'uhonua—is just an arm's length and plane ride away.

Candy orders are still flat, but it doesn't matter. Therapy is what matters. More and more, people are seeing the shallowness of the whole candygram game and actually making real, lasting changes. All because of me. I'm helping these kids more than concentrated sugar and a nice note ever could.

This morning, I took stock of all my clients last week, and for the first time the ones with non-relationship issues surpassed the ones coming for couples' problems. The Gregg County High student body is changing in a massive way, putting mental health first. It's gratifying to be at the forefront of this movement. After his last session on self-esteem building, Jarron Thomas actually called me the "Pied Piper of Personal Growth." *Me? I mean, I'll take it, though.*

The thought brings a smile to my face as I sit in my room trying to drown out my parents' raised voices beyond my doorway. It's Sunday, so they're not podcasting, but they never fight, so I don't know what's up with them. I play hip-hop from my computer and lay out the black shirt and blue tie I'll be wearing to tonight's mixer.

Then I sit on my bed and put the finishing touches on a candy bouquet I'm gonna give Sterling at the country club. It's not like an apology or anything. Just a truce, a peace offering. A way to say *No hard feelings*. Besides, I might as well make it with all the surplus candy I've got lying around. The bouquet is made of Sterling's faves: mini Snickers and Twix and Almond Joys carefully taped to wires to look like blooms of chocolate. I even used one of those decorative pails you get at craft stores and covered the foam blocks with chunks of fake Easter grass.

I thought about making one to give Dino on Monday. But honestly, why? I didn't do anything wrong. I told her the truth, and truth hurts sometimes. Why be with someone so on the fence about you? Rosie's in college. She's hours away. That's not a bad thing. It's just not *her* thing anymore. Like that group TLC once said: "Don't go chasing waterfalls." Why can't she and Dino see that? They're both searching for things that aren't for them, and as a friend I can't let that slide.

I set the bouquet on my desk by the door and take my shirt off the hanger. Around the third button, I stop, listening to the noise coming from the living room. Either the music got quieter or my parents' voices rose a few decibels, because I can definitely make out words now.

They . . . *are* fighting.

"Did you check in your file cabinets?" Mom asks. "Maybe you put it there."

"Yes, it ain't there!" Dad replies.

"Then where is it?"

"If I knew that, we wouldn't be searching all around the house!"

I feel a weird mix of anger and fear swelling in my chest at this—something less than yelling but far more barbed than normal conversation. I'm angry they're fighting but fearful for what it could mean. Is this the next step in them growing apart? *The last?*

I text Rod to see when his mom's gonna swing by. I check my shirt and tie in the mirror and then pace the room like a captive lion. I park my butt on the bed, get restless, and jump up to pace some more. But nothing I do can ward away the noise. To yell for them to be quiet would be to acknowledge there's an issue, so I don't do that. I suffer through it.

"Every big thing that's come up, you've shrugged it away until it got beyond your control," Mom says.

"LaTonya, it's just a mistake!"

"It's part of a pattern, Deion! Think about it: If those papers you'd misplaced were a business contract instead of a—you know?—would you be reacting so nonchalantly?"

Papers. I whirl around and eye my bookbag tucked into a dark corner of my closet. The papers in there. The ones I took from the mantel. Could they be the same ones Dad thinks he misplaced?

"That's different!" Dad says. "That's our money. Our careers."

"And this is our family!" Mom's voice launches into a shrieking yell, but just as quickly splashes into a fit of soft weeping. I get close to the door, ear pressed against it, tears in my own eyes.

I hear Dad's footsteps shuffling toward her. "Baby, I . . ."

A quiet no backs him away and sucks the air out of me. His footsteps sound louder as they go past my bedroom wall, but not heavy and confident like usual. Deflated. Defeated. A door opens and closes again. The weeping gets louder before quieting as it slinks off in the opposite direction.

I head over to the closet, determined to face up to what I've been avoiding. My hands shake as I extract the envelope. I want to vomit. Deep down I know what's coming. I pull out several papers. It's legalese, words meant for lawyers and signatories and those who've had way more schooling than I have. But I get the part that needs getting. On almost every one of the pages, a phrase pops out that any middle schooler could understand. "Child Joint Custody Agreement."

The news is what I probably knew all along but couldn't bring myself to admit. My parents. My everything for so many years. Just ending it like that. Trashing their marriage as if it were Monday's garbage haul.

*No. No! That can't be.* This isn't possible. Mom and Dad wouldn't take this step without talking to me first. It's a mistake, somehow. But it's right there. In print. I kick my bedpost. Then again. And again. And again until my toes ache.

I hear a car horn outside my window. I stash the papers back in my closet before walking out into an empty hallway. I leave without saying goodbye, with the full knowledge of my parents' impending split crowding my mind.

I'm too late. It was all for nothing. I failed.

It's just Rod and me climbing the steps of the country club deck. I didn't end up inviting Dino because of our fight. As I get closer to the party, volleys of unspoken condemnation beat down my mood. Unlike Friday with Mr. Davis and Big Sherm, the deck is clear of tables. A slight breeze comes and goes like an invited guest. Black-tied waiters stand like chess pieces at equal intervals across the platform. Lights string out from under rooftop rafters in chaotic, crisscrossing ways.

I survey the crowd of students huddled in various cliques that spread out like constellations. A lot more GHS students than I expected belong to the club. I know probably a quarter of them. Thanks to therapy, most know me. I hear several shouts of "Yo, Kal!" and "What up, Kalvin!" and one unfortunate "Shmelley!" from a football player who's already pretty wasted from pregaming.

However, my actual clients don't shout me out. Rather, they give knowing grins before angling their gazes back to the glasses they're nursing. I would smile back, but I'm just not feeling it tonight.

Rod's hand curves around my shoulder.

"Yo, cheer up, bro," he says. "You acting like your future girlfriend ain't just a door and a conversation away."

"I'm trying. It's just . . . family stuff."

"And is your family here?" he asks.

"No."

"So what can you even do about whatever issues y'all got now? Might as well enjoy yourself." He points. "Look, we got free food. Nice weather. These white folks ain't asked us to teach them the Cupid Shuffle or the Griddy."

"They haven't asked *yet*," I reply.

"Right. So I reckon we got a twenty-minute window to just be free, man. Enjoy ourselves."

I take Rod's words to heart. I might as well try to live it up. Besides, if I'm in a sour mood, it'll make connecting with Sterling even harder. It does make it easier that Chadwick left town today, and if Rod's worried about a Jordan appearance, he's not showing it.

I take a glancing look at the crowd, scanning for her. Not seeing her right off the bat relaxes me. I can work off some of these nerves by chitchatting with others. That's exactly what Rod and I do, mingling from constellation to constellation. For us never having been invited to a party like this, everybody's disturbingly friendly. Dino, who has been to these, calls it the Shuck and Thrive phenomenon. It's where rich white people so overwhelmingly outnumber Blacks that they can't help but let their guard down. In this universe, we're a novelty or curiosity rather than a threat. We're the melanated stars of the party.

The last group we amble our way to is doing sing-alongs right in front of the DJ booth. They're singing request after request of rock and folk hits like "Don't Stop Believin'" and "Sweet Caroline," which Rod and I nod and hum along to, but we draw the line at a song called "Chicken Fried." Apparently, it's a Southern classic, but we don't stick around to find out why. Luckily, right as we're excusing ourselves from the group, Gianna and Garrison Charles spill out of the French doorway leading into the clubhouse.

Gianna's hanging off Garrison's shoulder and laughing at something he just said when she spots us across the way. Her face lights up. She shoves a glass filled with brown liquid into Garrison's hand and hustles over as fast as her stilettos can carry her. Halfway to us, she gives up and kicks off the shoes before bolting into a run.

"Roderick!" she yells, her hug knocking him back a step. "Tesla Gang!"

"*Gang gang*," he replies.

They break from their embrace, and I see Gianna's face, dewy and flushed even redder than her hair.

"I'm so glad you could make it! *Ohh*, and I've got some great news, too." She leans in and looks all around as if searching for spies. "So I was headed to the tennis courts yesterday when I saw Mr. Lipton in the main parlor. I realized he'd been day drinking, because he does that a lot now since his wife left him. I start chatting him up about *Hamilton*. Turns out, he's pegged me for Angelica Schuyler, which I already kinda figured. But the big news is, he's down to you and Marcus Tibbs for Aaron Burr."

"*What?*" Rod whisper-shouts.

The DJ's music winds down as he announces the festivities will resume inside the ballroom. Garrison finally catches up. He's holding both their glasses in one hand and Gianna's discarded shoes in the other. I dap him up, whispering, "Is she drunk?"

Garrison shakes his head. "Not a drop of alcohol."

Gianna puts a finger to her chin in mock deep thought. She eyes Rod up and down before asking, "'Pardon me, are you Aaron Burr, sir?'"

I'm about to ask Garrison how he's doing when Rod puts a hand to his heart and raises his head to the sky as he launches into the critically acclaimed "Wait for It." For a second, I'm sure that *Hamilton* star Leslie Odom Jr.'s voice is being piped in from some hidden speaker. I go slack-jawed as Rod waltzes from first verse to second. Garrison gasps. It occurs to me then, in all my life I'd never actually heard Rod sing. Like, *really* sing. Just as amped as Rod is, Gianna jumps into the first chorus like she's on a springboard. And she's pretty awesome, too.

Others stop in their tracks, watching the duet. With the DJ's music gone, Rod and Gianna own the night. Perfect harmony. Perfect expressions. Perfect energy. It's like they exist in their own little universe, with everyone else orbiting them. For one fleeting moment before reality sets in, I can see it. *Them*, together. And to my surprise, they look good that way.

By the last chorus, half the patio's belting out backup vocals. When the song ends, Rod and Gianna clasp hands and jump up and down again, Gianna's bare feet and Rod's dress shoes thudding against the hardwood. Several people whoop and yell.

"You see how good we are?" Gianna says.

Garrison bends his lips to my ear. "Glad Jordan's not here to see this?"

"Wait, why isn't he?" I ask.

"He got banned from all social events last year. Pissed on a putting green or some shit like that. Idiot."

"That seems to be the consensus with him," I reply, thinking back to Mr. Davis's rant.

"That consensus would be accurate."

I nod toward Gianna. "So why's she with him?" I ask.

Garrison makes a face as we stare at the two. Rod and Gianna lock elbows as they head down the steps to the golf course to practice their lines. "Sometimes when we don't know ourselves, we use others to fill in the blanks," Garrison says. After a breath of silence, he adds, "Welp, I guess I should hunt them down. Give *Footloose* over there her heels back."

He starts off. I think about what he said and nod. "Look at you, Mr. Psych Expert. You might just have Gianna pegged."

Garrison pirouettes until he's facing me. He shrugs as he backpedals away. "I learned from the best. Just so you know, Gianna's not the *only* one here who fits that mold."

I squint, training my eyes on him as he disappears down the steps, but then I get it. He's right. *Sterling* fits that mold. Sterling's using her relationship with Chadwick to mask her own insecurities. It's amazing how, to avoid looking at our own flaws, we'll try to patch over the things in our lives that aren't perfect. Sterling has to see this about herself.

I head inside, looking for the main reason I came here in the first place. It's not long before I spot her. She's alone, posted against the far wall of the grand ballroom near the dessert table.

I weave my way through a swell of students, and I'm about forty feet away when Maddie lurches right in front of me. Like Gianna, her face is glowing red. But unlike Gianna, I can definitely smell the alcohol on her breath. It's so strong, and she's so close to me that every word burns my nostrils.

"Well, look what the cat dragged in," she says.

"Get over yourself, Maddie," I say, trying to sidestep her, but she blocks my path.

"Not until I'm over you!" A hiccup trails her words as she pauses to rethink. "Wait, no, not like that."

"Face it. You lost."

"This is just halftime. We've got a looong way to go."

I glance around, taking note of a couple groups of students now watching our confrontation. I lean in and whisper. "Word to the wise. You should stop because you're embarrassing yourself."

"I'm standing up for what's right!" she announces, stomping her left foot on the word "right." Realizing she didn't quite land her point, she tries to correct herself. "No, wait, standing up for what's *left*!" she says, this time stomping her right foot.

My teasing stare is met with a righteous anger that's like wildfire in her eyes.

If I could say one good thing about Maddie, it's that she's always on her game. Always neatly coiffed and perfectly put together. It's jarring to see her lurching into "sloppy drunk" territory. I think I know why she's particularly salty tonight, though. From what I've heard, stu-gov's candy sales have basically dried up. They're even supposed to undertake this massive inventory next week so they can game-plan how to triage and offload their surplus. I beat Maddie once and for all. She took her swing, and she missed. Hopefully by now she's learned that I'm untouchable. I'm on top. I like it here. And I'm not coming down anytime soon.

"Go home and get some sleep," I tell her.

"Don't tell me what to do! Or so help me God, when I'm done with you, you'll be hawking Werther's Originals in an assisted-living facility."

"Goodbye, Maddie."

She tries to block me again. I try another juke, but she hip-checks me. I spin and stagger, nearly losing my balance. She stumbles off to the side. I think about confronting her, getting back in her face and telling her how poor of a sport she's being. But what would it matter? Everybody who's watching can see how thoroughly she's embarrassing herself.

I head to Sterling, who's watching me, having witnessed the whole thing play out. When I get to her, I say hi in an eager way, like a kindergartener introducing himself to a potential friend on a playground. I'm nervous, I can tell. Not nearly as cool as yesterday. Something about our last conversation's already got me off-balance, and I've barely said a word.

Her hello is nice enough, but definitely not anything close to excited. I gulp down the doubt starting to bubble in my stomach.

"Having fun?" I ask.

"Not really."

"What could make it better?"

She raises an eyebrow. "Keisha Illan is here. Want me to introduce you to her? You know, for the ball next weekend?"

"No thanks," I say.

"Porsche Langford?"

"Naw, I think I'm good, actually," I say.

Sterling stares at me for a moment, like she's looking into me, not at me. Her jawline sets. When her look starts to get unnerving, she breaks it with a slow nod. "Mm-hmm."

Cool. I guess. Don't actually know what that was about, but I nod anyway. A new song comes on and people rush to the makeshift dance floor at the center. It gets way louder with this one—orchestra horns paired with hip-hop bass notes. I shoulder up to her and ask, "Wanna go somewhere more quiet?"

Both of her eyebrows flit up in a way I don't think she intended for me to notice. She replies with a short "Sure."

# Thirteen

**We slink out** a side door and wind our way through more empty spaces until we find the same hallway cluttered with the columns and artifacts Gianna showed me Friday. It's quiet once I close the door behind us, but I can still hear the muffled bass and feel it vibrate through the soles of my shoes. Sterling takes off her heels, letting her feet feel the cold floor.

She points. "There's a veranda out that door with a really nice fountain if you wanna go outside."

"Too cold," I reply.

"Okay," she says, nodding. We wander down the hallway a while longer, without the company of words.

I pretend to study the paintings of rich white men lining the walls as she walks three columns ahead of me, going her own way as if I'm not even here. She approaches the Oscar case. Her dad's case. Her steps slowly circle it, like a vulture checking a potential meal for signs of life.

"This is my dad's contribution," she says. I look from the paintings to her and then the case, pretending I don't already know. "His second Oscar. He won it when I was five." Her hands touch the glass encasement. "He took us to LA and everything. Me and him stayed after the ceremony, just the two of us. When he donated it, he said to me, 'Baby girl, one of these days you'll have a case of your own.'"

"Wow. Sounds like he expected great things from you."

"Yep. He'd make it a point to take me to this very spot at least once a year to say it to me. Did that every year from five to twelve."

My steps wander closer. I get one column away and ask, "What happened at twelve?"

She shrugs. "Reality set in. He figured me for the militantly average person I actually was. Not the genius he wanted me to be."

I close the distance between us and grab her hand. She looks up at me, surprised, and I almost drop it because I'm surprised, too. But I manage somehow to power through the words. "You think you're average?" *Why?*

"You think I'm *not*?" she asks.

"Sterling, I— *Your* 'average' is the speed of light, the roar of the ocean, the first day of spring."

She's taken aback, for a moment reduced to a handful of thoughts and blinks. I press on.

"*Your* 'average' is a force of nature. I wish you could see that."

She shakes her head. Slowly at first, but then picking up intensity and resolve. It's like what I've told her isn't just wrong but impossible.

"What if what you all see is a lie? What if my calling is to be unremarkable? What if my parents are right about me? They would know, right? They've known me longer than I've known myself."

"Parents don't know everything," I snap.

She laughs. It's short and cutting in a way I don't think she meant it to be. "This coming from a guy whose parents are literally experts in adulting."

My head shakes in spite of me. All the fear and anger from just hours ago whips around me again. To tell her would be to admit it's happening. Can I do that? Do I want to?

I squeeze her hand. "My parents . . . they're, um . . . my parents are separating." The words come out halting, then tumble out one on top of the other, like they'd been trapped behind a heavy door.

Sterling studies me, her hand tightening around mine. I can't tell if she's shocked that it happened or shocked that I'd hijack the conversation like this, so I desperately throw out more words to explain. My teary eyes go every which way to avoid her stare as I add, "I just found out. Right before I came here. They haven't told me yet, but I saw the custody agreement, and I don't know where I'll be or which school I'll attend or whether the podcast will survive or we'll just go broke, and I just—"

"*Kalvin.*"

I snap back to her. "It's okay," she says. "I mean, it doesn't *seem* okay, but it's gonna be okay."

She's all blurry, but her sympathy could shine through a rainstorm.

*It's gonna be okay.*

God knows I needed to hear that. I needed to hear it from someone who'd been there. From someone who'd seen her parents go to the ledge before backing away. In this moment, Sterling isn't just my crush. She's the girl who gives me hope. She's the one person in this world who gets what this feels like.

My breath grows wild and ragged. Hers is even. I'm jittery. She's steady. Her palm warms mine, and I want that same feeling for every part of me. My eyes close. I step in, drawing my lips near hers.

"*Wuh—*"

I kiss air where there was once a face. Her hand jerks away from mine, leaving me pinching mere particles. My eyes spring open. Her face isn't just horrified. It's cartoonishly horrified.

"What are you doing?" she snaps.

"I was—"

"Are you fucking kidding me?"

Her teeth are out like fangs of a rabid animal. Everything about me just wants to shrivel up and die, and that's *before* she jumps behind the Oscar case to put an obstacle between us. Like I'm some predator! *Jesus, how could I be so stupid?* I want to bang my head against a wall.

"I thought you—"

"I have a boyfriend! *Chadwick!* Remember? A boyfriend whom I love?"

I know I'm wrong to the fifth power, but something about hearing his name sets me off. I look over her shoulder and see the Boston Room, the homage to wealth and privilege and douchebaggery that she *still* somehow wants to attach herself to. Embarrassment and exasperation war in my stomach like two dogs barking and clawing at each other from opposite sides of a fence.

I point past her. "Why him?" I spout.

Confused, she looks back. Seeing nothing but the room, she redirects her glare at me. "*He's* not the problem. You are!"

"No, he *is* the problem!"

Her fists tighten, and I can see she's about to storm off, so I add, "I'm sorry, okay."

She's breathing hard, eyes boring into me. "What I did was presumptuous and disrespectful of your personal space, and I would do *anything* to take that moment back. I know you hate me right now, and you have every right to, but what I did was *nothing* compared to what he's putting you through."

Her arms cross. She straightens but stays.

"And you know it."

"You don't know anything," she replies.

"Well, tell me, then. Because you've been coming into my closet for weeks now, and for the life of me I can't figure why you'd still be with someone who doesn't give you the time, respect, and honesty you deserve."

"I love him, Kalvin! What else is there to know?"

"For one thing, you should know if he loves you back!"

Her hands drop, slapping against her thighs. She shakes her head. "Okay, screw this. We're done here." She starts walking, and she's four columns away before I think to speak again.

"Why don't you confront him?" I ask. My voice is pleading. Not even for me anymore. For *her*. I really can't understand why she'd let herself be walked over like this.

Sterling stops. It's silent for a long while, save for the wisps and vibrations of music bleeding in through the walls. I hear her sniffle.

I tweak my question. "Why didn't you confront him? Yesterday, at the mall."

She turns, looking but not moving. I see a tear line at her cheek.

"That was your chance," I add, my voice softening.

Sniffling again, she wipes her cheek and calmly walks back to me, wagging a finger. She stops, looking me dead in the eyes, every exhalation heavier and angrier than the previous. Her voice breaks as she says, "*No!* That was *your* chance!"

"What?"

"That was *your* chance, Kalvin!"

I shake my head. "I don't understand."

"Oh, bullshit! We both understand perfectly well you were trying to force my hand. Get us to break up so . . . *what?* So you could swoop in? Be my knight in shining armor? Was that your plan this whole time? Was that why you made that completely asinine candy corn analogy last week? To make Chadwick look bad?"

She stops speaking, waiting for an answer. Waiting for me

to say no. Waiting for me to say what I obviously can't. Because it's true.

When I don't answer, she does it for me: "I spent the whole day today hoping I was wrong about you. That I was just being paranoid. And after the conversation about our parents, I'd convinced myself I was. But you betrayed my trust, Kalvin. And you pissed away what might've been a great friendship."

She reaches into the pocket of her dress, pulling out three paper bills. She takes a $10 bill and slaps it onto the case, right above the Oscar. Somehow, seeing the money there makes the situation more painful. It means this wasn't a friendship or even a friendly chat among acquaintances. It was a business transaction.

She turns and walks away, leaving the words "Consider this our last session" to me and the wind.

I have to rest my head on the case to keep from falling over. That's how weak and helpless and utterly nonfunctional I am. But mostly, it's that dazed feeling of a boxer being hit by one too many jabs that's got me wobbly. Long after Sterling's gone, I stagger up and back toward the ballroom, led mostly by sound since I don't know these halls. When I'm in one where the chandeliers are shaking, I know I'm close. The music stops and the DJ announces a slow dance, and it's only when the music gets quieter that I realize I have a headache, too.

A door opens at the end of the hallway, and a rush of cool February air hits me. What really wakes me up is who enters. Rod and Gianna. She's tucked under his shoulder, and they're giggling like best friends sharing a secret in the back of a school bus.

They see me and whoop and yell. Gianna hugs me, and then looks sternly at Rod. "Don't. Go. Anywhere!" she demands. "I've gotta use the little girls' room."

Rod points toward the exit door. "Hey. There's no line on the back nine."

She bursts into knee-slapping laughter, barely getting out, "My boyfriend is so stupid!" as she heads into the ballroom.

Right when the door closes, Rod's fist slams into his hand as he gets all excited. "Yoooo. I gotta tell you about the conversation me and Gianna just had."

He proceeds to tell me. Despite my mood and the fact that my headache is getting worse, I nod politely as Rod spins a narrative about their time out on the golf course, an incredible series of events of the *Gulliver's Travels* mold.

"So. Remember at the mall, right?" he asks. "Well, I was able to convince Gianna to go back to Hawt Couture tomorrow afternoon to try on dresses for herself. So she's literally gonna be standing there modeling all these beautiful dresses right in front of me. And *then* she's all like, 'If I'm showing you mine, you gotta show me yours,' so she's taking me to the Suit Shack afterward to try on tuxes. She said she's got an eye for this. Said she'd have me lookin' svelte. You hear that? *Svelte*, bro! And then after that she—"

I hold up a hand. "Rod, can we please just stop?"

He squints at me. "Bro, what happened? You talked to Sterling already?"

I nod.

"How'd it go?" I begin to turn away, but he grabs both shoulders, twisting my body to face his. "Naw, naw, naw, my boy ain't goin' out like that. You *will* win over Sterling by the ball. Now, you finna march back in there and hit her with the swag attack." His head moves from side to side as he studies my face. "No eye crust. Eyebrows on point. Acne coming back, though. Left cheek. You poppin' 'em?"

"*No*," I protest, pushing his hand away.

Rod straightens. "Good." With a broad hand, he swipes down the chest of my shirt and then pivots, creating a lane for me. "Do your thang."

"I can't do my thang, Rod. It's over." I head to the exit. I figure I can waste time at the golf course until the dance is over. Nobody'll bother me that way.

"Kalvin, you are this close. Lemme just put in a good word with Gianna. Once she tells Sterl Girl how great of a guy you are, she'll come around."

"Don't bother," I mutter.

He bends closer. "What?"

I wheel around to face him, fire and fury in my eyes. I don't see Rod. Instead, I see the one person who's blocking me from my pity party of one. Who's shoving an absolute fantasy down my throat. Who's getting break after break after break with Gianna while I can't even get Sterling to stop looking in Chadwick's direction.

"I *said* 'Don't bother'!" Confusion creases his brow. He couldn't get a clue if it were taped to his forehead. Well, it's high time someone burst his bubble. I jab a finger into his chest as the ballroom door opens a few feet away.

"What's goin' on, Kal?" Rod asks.

"What's going on is you're being finessed. When all's said and done, Gianna's gonna stick with Jordan, and we're both gonna look like suckers."

"Yo! Gianna just called Jordan stupid!"

"But she also called him boyfriend!" I jab his chest over and over, backing him up against a wall. "Why can't you understand she's just stringing you along to get Jordan's attention? She'll never be with you because you're *not* on her level. *Jordan* and *Teslas* and *country clubs* are her level! You will *never* be that. And everybody can see that except you."

He sidesteps me, and my eyes follow. And I see three students to my left, staring at us. Watching me light into my friend. And for *what*, Kal? Because I couldn't stomach being rejected so I'm taking it out on him?

I focus in on him again. Lips set at a tremor, eyes red at the wells. My heart sinks. And it's his turn to jab a finger back at me.

Voice low and on edge, Rod says, "I may not be those things. But I am a great guy. A good dude. If Gianna can't see that, then that's the breaks. But if *you* can't see it? Then why are we friends?"

He pushes open the ballroom door, leaving me on the outs with pretty much everyone.

# *Fourteen*

**All empires fall.** It's the truth.

The Roman Empire. The Song dynasty. The Khans of Mongolia. The ancient Aztecs. The British imperialists. All either wiped from earth or a shell of their former selves. Historians debate the reasons often but usually settle upon some mix of overextension, insolvency, and a loss of unity over time.

All it took for the fall of my empire was a misplaced key.

I'm sitting alone in the back of the cafeteria on Monday, trying not to think too much of a session I'd had earlier that day with Ashlynn Carter. The toughest I've had, honestly. Got me thinking about some things.

To compound that angst, my social life's pretty much in shambles, too. I'm doing my best not to look at Rod and Dino, who are sitting at a table near the bathroom, or Sterling and Chadwick and their crew over by the entrance. That's when the first cancellation comes. I hear a knock at the tabletop and look up from my tray. It's Genevieve Jacobs, one of my standing Tuesday appointments. Right now, she's standing across the table, her face a weird mix of sympathy and resolve.

I do my best to paper over my detached interest with my "office smile."

"Hi, Gen. Is something wrong?"

"I've gotta cancel" is all she says.

I nod, rubbing my closed eyes and the bridge of my nose like a professor after a long lecture. It's this tick I have for when I have to deliver bad news. "You know I have a forty-eight-hour cancellation policy, so you'd still be charged." I really hate doing this. She's a nice girl, easy to work with. But time is money. And money's money.

She waves it off. "It's fine," she says, fishing a ten from her jeans and sliding it across the table. I palm and pocket it. She doesn't move, though, and there's this disquieting quiet between us amid the din of noise in the cafeteria. The kind of shared silence where you know something bad will follow.

"I'll see you next week?" I ask.

"Actually, I think I'm gonna cancel all my sessions," she replies.

"Why would you—"

"Can you just take me off your books, please?"

Hesitantly, I nod again, and it's like the gesture is a starter pistol. She can't get away fast enough.

About five minutes later, I receive a text. Hazel Zhao. She's my Friday intake: Not coming Friday! No need for therapy! All better now!!! Thank you!! XOXO.

I read the text five times before replying, trying to tease out any clues as to why a girl who'd been on my waitlist for two weeks would suddenly get cold feet.

*That's so weird*, I think.

And it just gets weirder. Five more people cancel during the lunch period alone. Afterward, Ronny Spears stops me in the hallway to terminate his sessions, and Paisley Thomas slips me a note during fifth saying she's done, too.

By the beginning of sixth I'm in full-on panic mode, wondering how more than half my clientele slipped away in less than an hour.

I get my answer during seventh period. Mr. Tribblett turns the lights off, and I start taking notes like everybody else when I feel something poke my back. I ignore it but feel it again seconds later. I twist my torso and see Stillman Austin in my periphery. He's staring right at me, the eraser end of a No. 2 pencil pointed in my direction. He leans over his desk so far my cheek feels the heat of his breath.

"So sorry to hear, dude," he whispers.

"Hear what?"

"About your parents."

*About my parents?* I twist my body even more to face him. I squint at him. "What about my parents?"

He squints right back at me. "How do you not know?"

"Know what?"

Stillman's eyes abruptly return to his notes as a grating voice rings out from the front of the class: "Mr. Shmelton. Mr. Austin."

I turn around in my desk, mumbling, "Sorry, Mr. Tribblett."

I spend the next minute or so furiously catching up on

drawing different covalent bonds in my notebook while trying to figure out what Stillman could possibly be talking about. That's when I hear something to my right. I look over, and Stillman's sliding his phone onto my desk. The screen is unlocked. I take it. The whispered words "This was posted on GCH Confidential gossip app today" float into my ear. At first, I'm confused. The post just looks like a scanned PDF document. It's anonymous. I read the caption first: **The "expert" is living a lie!** followed by the hashtags #busted and #fraudalert. I scroll past the letterhead of the document and see what everybody else has surely seen by now. My heart shatters as I read the first few lines:

THE PARTIES OF DEION SHMELTON AND LATONYA SHMELTON AGREE TO ENTER INTO THE FOLLOWING ORDER REGARD- ING CHILD CUSTODY AND VISITATION:

**I. CHILD CUSTODY AND VISITATION**

1. The parents shall share JOINT LEGAL CUS- TODY of the minor child, Kalvin Shmelton.

A. The parents shall share in the responsibility to make decisions regarding the health, education, and wel- fare of the child . . .

It goes on.

I skip to the bottom and see their signatures. My throat tightens. My notes blur before my eyes. I want to rip them up like confetti and scatter the papers out the second-floor window. I want to curse Stillman for even giving me his phone. But mostly, I just want to know why he has this. Why this info would be at school anyway.

I hand the phone back. My voice weak and brittle, I ask to be excused. I spend the next five minutes pacing the stairwell at the far end of the science hallway, shying teary eyes from the few people who pass me. When I can't stand this any longer, I head to the bathroom, crying softly in a stall and then palm-wiping my cheeks in a mirror. The pain of it all crowds my face. I stare at myself, hollowed-out and wan.

I shake my head. Slap my hand against the porcelain of the sink.

I pull up the GCH Confidential app on my own phone, staring at the post as I wonder who could've done this. How could they even have accessed this document? The answer to both questions comes with a single word.

Maddie. Somehow she must've gotten her hands on the envelope. But how? Those papers have been with me the whole time.

Have they?

I think back to last Wednesday, Zoe Mortgenson knocking on the Candyland door. Me scrambling to collect the papers. *Did I get them all?*

*But even if I didn't, how could Maddie have accessed them?*

Oh no. My heartbeat quickens against my chest as I shove my hand in my pocket, desperately rooting around until I touch metal. I pull out my keychain and hold two silver keys side by side. I can literally feel the blood drain from my face as the obvious comes into view: They don't match. Mr. Perkins told me to try *both* keys that day he gave me the new ones. I only tried *one* key on Friday, but not the other.

I storm out of the bathroom and sprint to the C wing, my legs churning like engine pistons. Once I stop and the adrenaline wears thin, fatigue and dread turn my calves and thighs to lead. I press forward. The class doors are all closed, with dialogue of a movie sifting out of one, and a teacher droning on about IT networking setup in another. I head to the closet door.

When I open it, I barrel toward the spot where I tossed the envelope a few days ago and watched as all the papers scattered about. I thought I had picked up all the papers, but what if I didn't? I get on all fours, dropping my head to the concrete to look into the tight space beneath the bottom shelves. I don't see any papers. I nearly hit my head when I hear a voice behind me.

"Missing something?" *Maddie.*

I don't even have to turn around to know.

"I almost ignored it, you know. Getting a wrong key."

I hear footsteps, and then her grating words again. "Chalked it up as a simple mistake by a churlish cad of a teacher."

My fists clench as she continues.

"But after last night's mixer, I got to thinking. What if it wasn't simply gross incompetence but genuine serendipity? So this morning I checked. And lo and behold . . ."

Slowly, I get up, turning to face her. Gone is the syrupy slur and unsteady walk of the weekend mixer. Now, she wears that smug smile of hers like a favorite piece of jewelry. The key and the paper hang precariously from pinched fingers at her chest. My mind flashes back to the hallway on Friday. Perkins's *Yo, Mad dog.* Maddie's glare.

I watch as she paces the room. The image of her strutting etches itself into my mind like a leaf print in freshly poured concrete.

"After I got in, I got curious," she says. "Took my time. Browsed the shelves. I mean, why not? Who wouldn't window-shop Shangri-La? It took me a while, but I found your weakness. A single piece of paper gathering dust under a shelf."

"Maddie, can you—"

"Walcott, Walcott, and Brown," she announces, her voice rising against mine. "They're divorce lawyers. I know that because my dad, who's also a lawyer, happens to know *Jonas* Walcott, one of the partners."

"Give it to me!" I demand.

"Oh. *Sure, gladly,*" she says. She marches right over and hands me the paper. "You'll need this more than me. I assume you have the rest of the agreement, so be sure to read the section about holidays and special visits carefully. I'm sure you'll want to have a say in whose house you'll be ringing in the new year and such."

The paper drops from my hand to the floor. I don't even know why I asked for it. The damage is done.

"You think this will sink me?" I ask.

"Oh, I *know* it will. Face it. Your credibility is shot, primarily because it's just an extension of your parents'. And if your parents can't mend their own relationship, then why should kids expect you to mend theirs? Especially since all your relationship advice comes from them. And they clearly don't know what they're talking about."

She continues her lap, folding her arms as she aimlessly casts her words toward the ceiling: "I assure you that whatever preconceptions you have of me, I'm quite a reasonable person. Unlike some people in this room, I actually have principles."

My stare zeroes in on her as I grit out, "This is what I get for being better at business?"

"No. It's what you get for not staying in your lane, Kal." Although spoken with a smile, her words have all the sharpness and bite of a knife to the throat.

I let my eyes close to this nightmare. I hear her stepping around me, smell the sweet, breezy mist of her perfume. I sigh and say, "And my lane would be?"

"Your therapy business seemed quite the rave. And although I'd trust you to give me advice as much as I'd trust a snake in Eden, other teens, oddly enough, find you perspicacious."

I don't want to give her the satisfaction of asking what that word means, so I just assume it's a good thing.

I walk up to her, half blocking her way. "Why would you take it away from them, then? If they find it so perspa . . . perispa . . ."

"*Perspicacious*, keep up!"

"Yeah. Whatever. Why'd you sabotage it?"

"Because *you* sabotaged stu-gov's candygram sales! You've been doing it for two years now, and *finally—Friday!*—it happened! We hit zero. *Zero*, Kal. Do you know what 'zero' means?"

I wave her question away. "It means you use stu-gov's rainy-day fund to cover the deficit, big deal."

"The fund is empty," she says, and I hear the slightest crack in her voice.

This catches me off guard.

She explains: "A little over a year ago, a few rogue stu-gov officers made two ill-timed and legally dubious investments in crypto. When the market tanked, we lost nearly all our savings. And ever since admins found out, they've had us on a much tighter financial leash. No new fundraising schemes. No project overruns. No bailouts from on high. We booked our vendors in September, thinking we could easily make up the difference with increased candy sales. But then *you* came along with your business and screwed us even further. So I repeat: Do you know what 'zero' means?"

I watch as she comes close to me, so red in the face it looks like she's a lit match near a leaky gas line. "It means we can't cover all our costs of the ball this week. It means prom funding gets dicey. It means I . . ."

She stops right there, and I catch the surprise in her red-rimmed eyes. What was she going to say? *I failed. I let the school down. I underachieved for the first time in my life.*

She swivels away from me, and I hear her sniffle. She wipes a sleeve across her face. Within seconds, though, she's turned back, stepping up to me until we're nose to nose.

"It means if I lose, we both do," she says.

She walks past me and leaves the closet.

At that moment, I feel the same righteous anger of a toddler whose parents just swiped their toy because it's bedtime. But another feeling drifts into my consciousness. As weightless and insignificant as this morning's snow flurry, but it's there. I feel pity.

For some odd reason, I pity her.

I spend the remainder of the period in there thinking about why. But I can't put my finger on it.

*Why do I pity someone whom I have every right to hate?*

With Dino, Sterling, and Rod, even though I was saying what I thought was best to them, I can see their beef. My tone, my approach, the timing. All those things could've been off. But with Maddie? There was absolutely no justification in the world for how she treated me. And yet, I almost don't want to be mad at her.

Maybe that's the therapist in me. Accommodating to a fault.

Correction: maybe that's the *former* therapist in me. Two more people cancel their sessions by the time I walk out to the parking lot after final bell. At this rate, I'll be at zero by morning.

As I stand next to Sterling's parking spot, I get another text from that Forsyth number, even more pressing than the previous texts: Please, can we talk? Will pay double!!!

I look at it a long time as I bounce on the balls of my feet, the nerves and the cold making me unsettled and active.

I'm almost tempted to take the client, considering my client list is suddenly empty, but I conclude it'd just be way too much of a hassle. I ignore it, jam my phone in my pocket, and wait for Sterling.

I don't wait long.

I spot her from a distance, fumbling to get the keys from her purse as she dispenses goodbyes to some seniors streaming out into the lot. The moment she sees me at her Prius, she huffs. I just stand there, mouth half-open, taking a step back as she unlocks her door. I guess I should've thought this through. Somehow, I assumed just being here would be a Grand Act in and of itself. Like the endings of all those teen movies where the guy waits outside for the girl. But all she says is "Move."

I get palpitations as she sits in her car and starts the ignition. I knock at her window right as she puts her hand on the wheel. At first she does nothing, just stares straight ahead as cars move past to exit the lot.

"Please," I say, knocking again.

She closes her eyes and pushes a button. I hear the loud whir of her window coming down. "What?" she says.

"Can you please tell me how I was wrong?" I ask. "Aside from the kiss, I mean."

She opens her eyes, looking dead at me: "Really?"

Even I know that wasn't the best start to a mea culpa. I take a deep breath and begin my backtrack: "Okay, okay. I know what I did. But can you blame me? So yeah, maybe I overstepped my boundaries and took advantage of my situation, but you're *you*! You're gorgeous and witty and intelligent, and you deserve the best from anyone who has the privilege of coming into contact with you. Chadwick wasn't giving you that. You said yourself you had trouble trusting him. That's why you confided in me, remember?"

"*Of course* I remember!"

"So why be with him?" I ask.

"Because it's my *choice*, Kal! Nobody else's."

She turns forward again and starts to put the window up. My breathing stops and I get all panicky thinking she could be driving out of my life for good. At the last possible moment, I jam my hand into the window, feeling the pinch at my fingers just above the knuckles. Her Prius accelerates out of the spot and my body lurches with the car, just barely keeping up. We've gone a good ten feet before she realizes I'm stuck. The Prius abruptly stops, shock covering Sterling's face as she puts the window back down.

I try shaking out the pain but also I'm trying not to show how bad it hurts. When she asks if I'm okay, there's this weird moment where a tear forms in my eye and my voice dive-bombs lower to say, "I'm fine."

With the shock worn off, Sterling stiffly nods. A car honks behind us, and we both realize she's in the exit lane of the parking lot. I see she's about to drive off again, so I scramble for any words that might keep her.

Bending low and getting into her space, I ask, "But why choose the wrong thing?"

She turns to me again, her face pinched. She shakes her head. "You just don't get it, do you?"

"Get what?"

"That people have to live their own lives! Make their own mistakes."

This actually draws the anger out of me. She couldn't be more off base with this one. I think about my psychologist parents, whom people flock to for direction. How much strain they must feel bearing the emotional burdens of others.

I think about myself, how I've felt that same weight for the past month. Jabbing a finger into my chest, I say, "If *anyone* gets that, I do! People come to me with their problems, their issues, their *mistakes* every day! I try to help people cope with them!"

"You try to *fix* them! With Dino. With me. With your parents! But people don't grow that way. They don't *live* that way. You never let those closest to you just live." Suddenly, something changes in her expression. She takes a deep breath. It's like she realizes she's getting too worked up. I follow her lead, relaxing my body. Much more calmly, she says, "I've thought a lot lately about why I am the way I am. How something, probably stemming from my parents, has me a little fucked up inside. I'm going to do something about it. Not sure what yet, but *something*. And it won't be for them, or for Chadwick, or for you, but for *me*."

"That's awesome," I say. "But why are you telling me this?"

"Because I think you should do some introspection, too."

Two more cars honk, and I step back at the noise. Sterling takes the opportunity and puts up the window. When it's all the way to the top, she looks at me. Even through the quickly fogging glass I can see the earnestness in her expression.

The glass barrier muffles her words, but I get the message loud and clear: "Let people live," she says.

She drives off. I stand and watch as her taillights blur into a line of many more.

The next day, only Avery shows up for her standing Tuesday appointment. Although she's still game for therapy and actually spends the last two minutes encouraging me, I feel like driftwood the whole session, aimlessly carried by the tide of apathy. When it's over, I don't return to study hall or busy myself with inventory or do anything, really. I just sit in Candyland, thinking about how thoroughly I've messed up just about everything I had going for me. I'm mentally replaying the Kiss That Never Was for at least the tenth time when I hear knocking. I jump up from the stool, lunging for the door as if it's the one-in-a-million chance that Sterling's come to tell me she forgives me. I pull the handle, hoping. When I see who it is, I stagger backward, surprised.

Chadwick wedges his foot into the door first before the rest of his body, as if he thinks I might try to push him back out. But I don't. I let him in. He's sporting his usual catamaran-chic attire. Sperrys, khaki shorts, peach button-down shirt with sleeves rolled up just below the elbows.

As Chadwick slowly circles the room—circles *me*—I fully expect a beatdown, a threatening message, or string of curses as long as the Nile. But weirdly, I'm not nervous at all. More numb than anything. Maybe it's because everything I expect him to do, I've deserved for quite some time. He pushes and displaces pieces of equipment, exposing candy bags. Several times, he looks curiously at the shelves and menacingly at me, as if he's not quite sure whether to commit violence or ask for a menu. By his third lap around, I realize he came in here with no plan. Just a white-hot desire to *do something* about his current situation.

*But what to do?* I don't think either of us know.

After a while, I get impatient. Whatever happens, it needs to go ahead and happen. Hesitantly, I ask, "You wanna sit down?"

"No," he snaps.

His response annoys me. Oh, so he *can* speak. He just didn't want to speak first. That's whack. If he's gonna storm into my closet, the least he can do is initiate the conversation.

"Well, then, what do you want?"

His steps quicken, and suddenly he's bumping into my shoulder, his breath crashing into my neck. "I want to know why."

I catch my balance. In a fit of anger, I shove my forearm into his chest to get him out of my space. He rears his arms back for a push. I brace but it never comes. I square up to him. His cheeks are rose-colored. It's almost like there's smoke emanating from his head. He's as heated as I've ever seen him, but still not willing to fight for Sterling.

My resolve firms as I point a finger right at him. "You want to know why I liked a girl you couldn't seem to find the time of day for?"

"I want to know why you moved in on my girlfriend."

"Because you left the door wide open." I flinch as his fist

slams into his palm. He brings both hands up to his mouth as if he's biting a knuckle sandwich. It's like he wants to explode but isn't sure how. Oddly, though, I feel like if he does, the unfortunate victim would be a shelf post or a candy bag or a piece of sound equipment. Not me. And even more oddly, now that the threat is gone, I feel like I want to actually talk to him.

I make a noticeable production of sighing and dropping my shoulders. And then I say, "It's not that you've got anything to worry about. I made my move this weekend. She slammed that door right back in my face."

Something changes in him with that reveal. The muscles along his jawline relax, and it's like the fire blinks out of his eyes. A long silence trails my words. Then, slowly, the tension leaves Chadwick's body. He moves past me, and I hear the drag of wooden legs against concrete as he sits on the stool. I slink toward the back shelf, my back finding a post, my body sliding down to the concrete.

"She rejected you?" he asks, not quite believing it.

I nod.

He looks up at the ceiling, smiling. The laugh accompanying it is short and quiet and not insulting in the least. Like he's laughing not at me but at a memory. "You know," he says, "Sterling rejected me three times before she finally agreed to be my girlfriend."

I squint. It's my turn not to believe. The way I'd envisioned it, Chadwick just drove up to Sterling one day in his douche-class Mercedes and the rest was history. But I guess that was a dumbass assumption, in retrospect. Sterling's way smarter than that. No way she'd be impressed by a fancy car or lots of connections or money.

"What finally changed her mind?" I ask.

"I got in a fight with my dad one day," he replies. "Over golf, of all things."

"Golf?"

"Yeah. I wanted to do this whole junior lifeguard training camp. You know, pick up a skill, learn how to do some good in the world, hang out at the pool with friends all summer. But Dad insisted I spend time out on the links to get face time with people who could help shape my future."

"But how old . . ."

"Ninth grade," Chadwick says, wryly shaking his head.

My arms hug my knees as I lean into the conversation. It's weird how when listening to him—really hearing his story—I still think he's a prick, but maybe slightly less of one? Like, Diet Prick, perhaps? Somewhere, underneath the thin layer of bronzer and through the thick fog of Axe Body Spray, there's an actual personality. I'm sure of it. A real human, with real thoughts, worries, and emotions. I can finally start to see why Sterling fell for him in the first place.

"So you called Sterling up after that and spilled your feelings?" I ask.

Again, he shakes his head. "The argument was at a country club our families both belong to. She was there for an event and caught the tail end of our fight. After Dad stormed out, she came and asked if there was anything she could do, and we talked about things for a while, and we just . . . kept talking."

I nod. Sounds like a very Sterling thing to do. I think of how inviting she is to talk to. How open she's been. How it seemed at times she was my therapist, pushing me to do better, to think deeper. My eyes keep trained on my knees as I say my next words. Words that could dash any hopes of ever being with Sterling. But I know it needs to be said. And it's the right thing to do.

"Sterling initially came to me because she was suspicious you were hiding something from her." I peek up for the quickest of glimpses, and he seems startled at the revelation. But the moment is infinitesimally brief, like a reaction to a pinprick.

He says nothing, so I continue.

"But despite that, she wanted to see it through. To strengthen what you two had."

"She did?" he asks.

"Yeah, because that's the kind of person she is. Determined. Hopeful. Loyal."

"True," he says.

"She's one hundred percent for you, dude. But are you the same for her?"

Chadwick's mouth barely opens, and the "What?" that comes out is little more than a whisper. I honestly didn't mean to say it in an accusatory way, but how else can you really ask that question?

I don't respond to his question. I simply get up and touch his shoulder as I walk to the exit. I grab the handle and open the door as he stands and faces me. "Sterling deserves the world," I say. "Whatever you do, don't make her wait for it."

# Fifteen

**Apparently, the only** thing that can bring my family together these days is a total stranger. I'm watching them sitting on the couch, awkwardly shifting beside each other as if nothing about this scenario fits. The reporter stands before them, waiting for the duo to settle, fingering the spiral edge of his notebook as he studies the living room decor.

The guy is here for *Breaking the Mold*, a popular podcast that features trailblazers in the tech world. All three decided to conduct the interview in the living room to create a more homey atmosphere, so the guy's fancy microphones and ring lights flank my parents.

As one of the first and most popular couples therapy duos in the podcast world, Mom and Dad have achieved near universal recognition in the psychology field. But that hasn't come without its problems. Mom actually didn't want to start the podcast. But she relented and she was great at it. Still is, actually. *Both* are. And together, they're a spectacle to watch, an aurora borealis of interpersonal dynamics. I've seen them drive callers to cackling laughs and cathartic sobs in the same breath.

However, even after they hit it big, Mom's discomfort only grew. In podcast world, they were great. When the microphone was on, so were they. But in the real world, it seemed like Mom was fading into the background of the marriage. Becoming an extra in her own show. I could see it when we'd host guests and have dinner parties. Dad's loud exhortations and Mom's tired smiles. Dad gathering friends around the living room to regale them with stories or waylay them with life advice. Mom feigning headaches and heading to bed early.

The show didn't *create* the distance in their relationship. Unfortunately that dubious honor belongs to me. But the show definitely never helped fix it, either. There's a new phrase I'd recently read in some article about "quiet quitting." Never going above and beyond in a job you don't think appreciates you. Although she shows up every day, I get the feeling Mom quiet quit the podcast years ago. It seems both might be doing the same for the marriage.

It's Wednesday. Two days since I found out about the custody agreement, and I haven't confronted them yet. Every time I want to, I lose my nerve. I dread what they might say. As long as there's no answer, this remains a problem to be solved. The matrimonial equivalent of a really tough algebra equation. Raise 560 more dollars, add a guilt trip or two, carry the one, and voilà.

I'm pretending to be in my room studying while watching them from a tight angle in a dark hallway. I at once have the best and worst view of their crumbling relationship. Mom tries to get comfortable next to Dad, her arm brushing against his. Abruptly, she gets up, not to shift but to stand.

"Are you sure you don't want anything to drink?" she asks the reporter. "Tea? Soda?"

The guy nods. "I'll take water," he says. I assume it's because it's the third time she's asked and not because he actually wants it.

Mom disappears, and that's when Dad decides he'd like to do some interviewing.

He leans toward the guy, squinting at the name tag attached to the lanyard around his neck. "So how long you been at this job, . . . Fritz . . . Hollis?"

"Two years," he responds.

"You like it?"

"It's a start. Long hours but good benefits."

"Just remember: you can kill time there, but don't let it kill you. Ah-*HA-HAAA!*" Dad slaps his knee.

Fritz smiles in an unsure way—like he doesn't know if he should be amused or mildly insulted by Dad's joke. I'm honestly not sure, either. Usually I suffer through Dad's wisecracks in a grin-and-bear-it kind of way. But today they're just plain annoying. How can anybody laugh when things are looking so bleak?

"You got a wife, Fritz?" Dad asks.

"Fiancée," he replies.

"She like your hours?"

"She, um . . ."

"Because if she ain't down with it, y'all in a world of hurtin' even before y'all begin. You know what they say: happy wife, happy life."

I look up at the ceiling. The words grate on me. *Happy wife, happy life, huh?* Things don't look too happy from my POV.

"Sounds like you two are having a blast without me." I crane my neck to look back at Mom as she returns, putting a glass of ice water on the coffee table in front of Fritz.

Fritz ignores the water, instead starting his recording equipment. Then he clicks his tongue and lightly slaps his notebook against the table. "So let's get started, shall we?"

The first half of the interview goes well enough, with Fritz asking softball questions about Mom and Dad's daily routines, biggest misconceptions about fame, and weirdest call-ins. He asks them about being "celebrity parents," balancing work with raising a child. Mom answers with her trademark modesty. They're imperfect. Human. Fallible.

My parents' faults are absolutely invisible during the interview, though. Throughout, Mom and Dad show flashes of the rapport that made their podcasts so breezily casual. They even get Fritz laughing and joking at a few points, quizzing him on his fiancée's expectations for kids and the boundaries he needs to set with his future in-laws. For a few minutes, it's like *he's* on the therapy couch, wading through the minefield of marriage before he even sets foot there.

It's when Mom gets a question about art imitating life that things start to go sideways.

"Keeping a successful podcast fresh is one thing. With the

pressure and busy schedules, how do you also manage to keep your marriage fresh and healthy?"

Dead silence sweeps out the ease of conversation present just seconds ago. I glance at Mom. It's like her mouth cranked halfway open before a bolt slipped in her jaw and it got stuck. Dad tries to jump in, but his words stall out, too.

"Our marriage is, um . . ."

The reporter cryptically adds, "*Is* it healthy?"

Mom and Dad turn to stone. The reporter takes advantage of the lull, cautiously reaching into his bag. He retrieves a single printed document and stretches it out toward Mom. She takes it. She looks confused.

Dad sees the look on Mom's face and leans in as she shows him the paper. The reporter clears his throat, announcing, "This is a printout of an impending divorce agreement that was recently leaked online. It'd just come to our attention a few hours ago, but apparently it was first published Monday. I've since gotten two sources close to you to confirm your marital strife. Is there any validity to this?"

I'm speechless. Angry, stunned, and absolutely robbed of the ability to verbalize my thoughts.

Then the rapid-fire questions come, each one like a bullet piercing the family shield:

"What's the true status of your marriage? Would a potential divorce impact *Right the 'Ship*'s marketability? Will you shift focus now from relationship advice to co-parenting advice?"

"Please stop," my mom whispers.

237

"Ma'am, your audience would like to—"

"Sir, please . . ."

"I'm sorry, but it's obvious your marriage is—"

"*Private*," Mom snaps, finally looking up at him. "Our personal life is nobody's business."

The reporter looks down at his notepad. He knows he's got something. We all do.

"Doesn't your fandom deserve to know the whole story?" he asks.

"Our fandom has endured this long without it," she responds. "They'll be okay."

"So no comment at all?"

Dad sinks back into the couch. The look he gives Mom is brief but damning, as if throwing up the deflection was the wrong move. Mom does the same to him.

I see them both languishing as the reporter scribbles in his notepad. These two people who are magnitudes more confident than me, humbled by a novice reporter's interview. The stunned feeling wears thin, and some sentiment between embarrassment and resentment takes its place, curdling my stomach and making my fists clench. I feel a marrow-deep urge to speak up for them, to protect them. *Them* as a unit. *Them* as an idea. *Them* as a pleasant memory I want so desperately to be a reality. I step out of the shadows and into the room.

"They're working it out, but their marriage is fine!" I snap.

All three look at me. "*Kalvin*," Mom says sharply.

The reporter seems taken aback. He sputters out with "You're the son, I assume? Do you have a comment?"

"I already gave you my comment. So put that in your podcast, asshole!"

"KALVIN!" Mom yells.

"Son, you'd better watch it!"

I glare at Dad. "Why are you two jumping on my case when he's trying to trash your marriage and take down your business!"

"Kalvin, you need to ca—" Dad says.

"And why aren't you giving him a straight answer!" My words come with spit. I hear my voice going up in register as declarations become desperate questions. "You two are gonna be fine, aren't you? You didn't tell me yet because you're working through things, right? I'm not gonna have to pack a bag one day and be whisked to someone's crosstown rental, am I?" They say nothing. My voice cracks: "Am I?"

Again, silence. They're both just sitting there, looking like *Who is this boy?*

My eyes travel to our family picture on the mantel a ways behind Fritz's shoulder as my insides get all queasy. I wasn't prepared for this today. It's half a week too early. I don't technically have all the money. But it feels like my only opportunity is quickly shrinking from my grasp like a low tide.

I storm past Fritz toward the fireplace, stopping right as the heat hits my thighs. I grab the picture, taking a moment to really let the imagery sear itself into my mind. I hear the stiff

239

wind bending tree leaves in the distance. Waves crashing against rocks, before smoothly sliding back out to sea. I taste the ocean mist, heavy with salt and spray. I smell the sea in all its tang. I feel sand between my toes as we stand at a cliff's edge.

I feel our love for each other, fitting gently around me like a lei.

*Pu'uhonua.*

I take the picture over to them. Dad's mildly shocked when I put it in his hands. Mom leans into him, touching the frame as I speak.

"I wanted to give this to you on Valentine's Day. Not the picture, but the gift behind it."

Mom looks up at me, empty-handed as I am. "What gift, Kalvin?"

"A trip back to Hawaii. Lanai, to be more specific. Remember that place? The little cliffside village where we just stood, looking at the ocean, wondering how life could get any better?" Even speaking out loud about it brings a smile to my face.

"Kalvin, this is—"

"Now, Mom, before you say anything, I'm paying. I've priced out the cost and everything. I've saved almost ten thousand dollars so far! All socked away in my room. You guys don't have to worry about a thing."

Mom ignores me, instead rising from the couch and turning her attention to Fritz. "Sir, I think our interview is over."

She puts a hand to his back, forcing the issue. Confusion sweeps across his face. "I just have a few more questions."

"You need to go," she says firmly.

"Can we schedule something by phone?"

"Just *go*," she replies, escorting him out of the living room.

I look back at Dad as I hear the door shut. If anything, my sales pitch takes on a more pressing tone: "Dad, I know you've been wanting to get back to traveling regularly. This could be our start."

"Kalvin . . ."

"And this could really help fix things for you two. Consider it a down payment on the rest of our lives together."

"*Kalvin*." Dad and I both watch as Mom storms back in.

"*What?*" All my muscles are wound up. I'm bursting with anger. "*What exactly is your plan?*"

"Kalvin, calm down!" Mom yells. The sound jars me. She's never yelled at me before, but right now she looks like a skinny Hulk with a ponytail, so I'm not surprised. But I'm not calming. In fact, I get angrier that she wants me to.

"How can I calm down? Better question: Why are *you* so calm?" I shout right back.

Dad's hand grips my shoulder.

I wriggle away, parroting their famous slogan: "'Even in the roughest of seas, you can still right the 'ship!' Remember that? Or was it just a bullshit catchphrase used to build your brand?"

"Kalvin Jarius Shmelton!" My dad's booming voice freezes me. The energy it takes me to bay and fume and vent my rage flows back into my core. I feel like a detonator, just itching to explode.

"Tell me I'm wrong!" I say. "Tell me you're not calling it quits."

The silence is my answer. Mom puts trembling hands to her mouth. The crow's-feet deepen at her eyes as a pitiful sound slips past the gate of her lips. I watch as a tear slides down her cheek.

"Mom?"

She doesn't—or can't—say anything, so I turn to Dad, my voice wrenching from angry to achy with a pain I've never felt.

"*Dad?*"

He shakes his head as I say, "I can fix this. My plan can fix this! We'll go to Hawaii and everything will be fine!"

Their silence is too much to bear.

"This is how we are!" I snatch the picture from Dad's hand and smash it to the ground. "*Broken!*" Glass shatters at my feet. "Why won't you help me put us back together?"

*Broken.*

I want to say so much more, but sobs overwhelm my ability to speak, so I break down, double over, drop to a knee. Footsteps rush behind and I feel Mom's arms wrap around my back. The too-tight kind of hug moms give when you're badly injured or woefully ill.

I think I'm both.

And I know it's over.

# Sixteen

**I storm into** my room and spend the next two hours drowning in tears and my pillows until I drift to sleep. Sometime afterward, Mom and Dad walk in with a plated tray and wake me up with the smell of chicken pesto pasta, my favorite. Although they mean well, it's like one of those death row last-meal situations, a culinary symbol of the termination of their marriage.

I groggily but greedily eat up because I'm starved, and they wait patiently, Mom at bedside, Dad at the foot of it. When I'm done, they prod me about what happened out there, and I show them the custody papers I found on the mantel. Their faces crater at the revelation. Dad looks especially devastated. He silently curses himself for having left them there as Mom whispers "Oh baby" and strokes my duvet-covered thigh. By happenstance is the last way they wanted me to find out. As parents must do, they add a dash of anger to my pity party since I did go through their private stuff, but I can tell their hearts are not in it.

I apologize for my outburst, and I mean it. But they

correctly sense there's more to my remorse than just that particular moment. Dad puts his hand on mine.

"Son, you know there's nothing you could've done, right?"

I don't say anything because I don't know. Everything in me says if I only could've just told them about Hawaii a day earlier, studied a little bit harder, been a little bit less of a hardship . . . then maybe.

"I'm also sorry I couldn't be better at this," I say.

"At what?" Dad asks.

"At being a good son. Not being such a burden."

It's like Mom can see these very thoughts weighing me down, because she jumps in with "You were the best son a family ever could've hoped for. And guess what?"

"What?"

"You *still* are." She leans in closer, willing me to raise my eyes from the covers to meet her own. "Listen. Your father and I are separating. But it's because of us, not you. And that'll never change the fact that you'll always be our son. The best outcome of our marriage and best part of each of our lives."

Hearing that jars me. It's like the moment you go from just barely awake to actually awake. I know parents say that kind of stuff to their kids all the time, but to hear it in that moment of doubt hits differently. My heart really feels like it's swelling right now, in the best of ways.

"And we're sorry," Dad adds. His eyes have taken on a glass-like quality, so I know this is hard for him to say. It's my turn to touch his hand. He smiles, and his voice cracks through it. "So sorry we didn't communicate what was going on. That we made you feel responsible for our problems. But know this: you were *never* the problem."

I think about his last declaration a long time before speaking. I don't actually *know* this. Right now, at least. But I think I'm getting there. And it helps for him to say it.

I nod. "Thanks, Dad," I say.

I look at both of them. Really look at them. I take note of how tired they are. Not just the late-night kind of tired but the exhaustion that stems from a long journey. They've carried so much all these years. Their own problems and those of countless others, as well. I wonder how long they'd been holding on to their fraying rope of a marriage. How long they'd been going through the motions for an audience of thousands and of one. What a grim catharsis it must've been to realize it was over. I feel sad for them yet again, but deeper now. I don't understand it all, but I understand it more.

Mom asks to see the lockbox with the money, and I pull it from underneath my bed. Both riffle through the bills, thoroughly impressed, and mildly disturbed.

They ask me how I got it, and I tell them. Once they're assured none of it's been obtained by illicit means, they neatly pack all the bills back in. Mom places the box back in my lap.

"You spend this money on yourself. You earned it," she says.

"Spend it on what?" I ask, genuinely wanting to know.

"Doing what teens do best. Making questionable decisions," Dad answers. He follows that up with his trademark ah-*HA-HAAA!* This time, Mom and I laugh with him.

I'm not the most rebellious kid, so Mom and Dad aren't used to the whole "grounding" thing. I suffer through the obligatory lecture on etiquette and "keeping family things family." I tear up again as they explain the custody agreement in detail, but their assurances make it seem that while it'll suck, maybe it won't *completely, absolutely, totally* suck. They even lessen my worries about the family finances by saying they'll keep the podcast going, just with a new focus on co-parenting and life after divorce.

When that's all done, they literally have to huddle outside my door and speak in hushed whispers before marching back in, finger-wagging and sternly saying, "Just so we know you've learned your lesson, double chores for a month."

They leave me overwhelmingly sad but with a glimmer of contentment about the situation. A glimmer as faint, but as promising and prevailing, as splinters of first light at dawn. Never once did either of them hint at any animosity, and even their body language suggested they were more relaxed around each other tonight than they had been in quite some time. And even though they leave me wallowing in an ocean of what-ifs, the blame doesn't weigh quite as heavy. The catastrophe doesn't seem quite so catastrophic.

After they're gone, I play some Madden football on the PlayStation and attempt and fail to do homework. And then I feel a burning need to talk. To not be alone. To have someone else not carry my burden necessarily but just to know that it's there.

I can think of exactly one person to talk to. The person who hasn't returned my texts or calls for the past week: Dino.

For the first time, I am overwhelmed with a desperate ache to apologize. Not just to explain. To truly, genuinely apologize for what I said.

Also, I just miss talking to her. Dino has this way about her that makes terrible things seem less terrible, and the good seem great. She's like leaven to dough, but instead of making bread rise, she raises my spirits.

I text her again. She doesn't respond. I know she isn't busy with homework or anything because she never does it past eight p.m. So that leaves two options: she's ignoring me or she's talking to Rosie.

I'm still miffed as to why Rosie's back in the picture. In breaking up with Dino, she probably did them both a favor. Why retie a knot that's been undone?

But I realize now that's not a question for me to answer. It's for them.

I forgo texting again and call. She doesn't pick up. Then I get an idea. I get up from my bed and sit in my swivel chair, grabbing the game controller and turning on *ZombieWorld*. I enter our open world and see she's logged in, too. Now, I just have to find her. I spend the next fifteen minutes sending my Utahraptor through all sorts of hell, literally. To be honest, it's a nice distraction. A way to get away from the hell I've made my actual life.

When I enter into the Underworld level, I battle it out with the undead husk of a Giganotosaurus. It's a boss-level monster, and I have to climb the lava cliffs a few times to snipe it, but eventually I get it to its knees. I drop down and creep up to it. When I'm sure it's dead, I—

The camera view shakes and all of a sudden my raptor's shrieking inside the mouth of *another* undead Giganotosaurus. My M16 goes flying. The dinosaur drops me with my life bar at 8 percent. I can't even get up, I'm so weak. The Giganotosaurus growls over me and rears back with a guttural roar for all of Hades to hear.

Then, just before it lunges to eat me, the screen goes white. Light mushrooms out and sucks back into a finite point as the dinosaur explodes. I stagger up, but another explosion knocks me off my feet again. Rolling over, I see the shattered bone and ghostly green entrails of the first undead dinosaur I encountered.

I look around, but nobody else is anywhere in sight. Static comes into my headphones, then a voice: "Always keep an eye out for the second one. They hunt in packs."

"Dino?" I say.

"Yep. It me."

"Where are you?"

"Out by the abandoned Mall of America in the Elysian Fields."

"There's an abandoned mall in the Underworld?"

"Yeah. These games just get more realistic every year, don't they?" she says.

I scale a lava cliff and sprint across the burning meadows until I see the mall. I go inside and pass the food court and then walk all the way over to the Macy's before calling out for her again.

"I'm over by the bombed-out Panera Bread," she says.

I run as fast as my raptor legs can take me. When I get there, Dino's Spinosaurus is leaning against a brick pillar slurping up a smoothie. She holds it out. "Want some? It's Caribbean Passion. It'll help your life bar."

I take it and drink until my life's above 50 percent before handing it back.

She nods toward a chair. "Sit."

I manage to navigate around the outdoor railing but make a mess of the actual sitting, my tail knocking over several chairs and a shade umbrella as I squeeze my butt into a seat. Dino leans her rocket launcher against the pillar and sits, much more easily even though she's four times as big.

"Thanks for saving me from the Undead Giganotos back there," I say.

She waves it off. "Don't mention it."

"How'd you even get the launcher to shoot that far?"

"After I defeated the Hellhound Army, I got satellite-guided missile capabilities."

"Well," I say, "even so, you didn't have to save me. And I'm sure after how I'd treated you, you didn't want to."

"Of course I wanted to. That's what friends do," she says. "They help each other out."

A wave of shame hits me just then. It was so easy for Dino to support me at the drop of a hat. Why couldn't I have supported Dino like that? I feel like I've been so caught up in Sterling and my plan and being a therapist, I've forgotten how to be a decent friend. And what good am I if I'm no good to those who matter most?

We sit awkwardly in silence for just a moment, until I ask another question. "So what you been up to?"

"Just thinking about some things."

"Rosie?"

"Maybe."

I tent my tiny raptor hands as I lean into the table. I feel like letting all my pent-up regrets spill out of me. My atonement is a dam that's about to break. "Dino, I'm so sorry about what I said. You have every right to make your own choice about your love life without being insulted."

She nods. "Thank you, Kal. I really appreciate that."

"So you're not mad at me?"

"Oh, I'm *still* very mad at you. And you will pay."

"So . . . you're plotting revenge on me?"

"No, you're actually gonna pay. Gas tax goes up to seven dollars per every two weeks."

"Seven dollars?"

"What?" she says. "Fuel cost is rising, and they *just* installed a toll on the one-fifty-seven. These potholes aren't gonna fix themselves, ya know."

"Okay, fine," I say. "And just to be clear, I really am sorry for being an asshole."

"Don't beat yourself up about it," she says.

I feel embarrassed to ask, but I have to make sure we're good. "Car ride tomorrow?" While taking the bus the past couple days has been okay, nothing beats riding in a vehicle with working heat.

"I suppose. One condition, though. You ride shotgun. No upcharge. Rod's banished to back seat again."

"Why? Wait, Rod splurged for front seat?"

She shakes her head. "I waived the fee. I guess I just needed the company while you were gone. But for the past few days he's been practicing his expressions in the rearview while belting out songs for *Hamilton*, and it's driving me absolutely up a wall. It got so bad yesterday, I considered challenging him to a duel."

"Wait, you knew Rod could sing?"

"Psshhh, yeah. You didn't?"

Not until last weekend. But I should have, much earlier. That fact pricks me with guilt. I guess you never truly know the real cool stuff about a person unless you ask. And I probably never asked because I doubted Rod could be extraordinary at anything. I feel a gut-punch level of shame about this. Rod's not only an extraordinary singer and friend. He's an extraordinary person. And now he's not around for me to tell him just that.

"So how's things going with you?" Dino asks.

"Not great. Maddie Trout outed my parents' separation to the school's gossip app, and my clients are canceling because my credibility's ruined."

She sits in rapt attention as I explain the tragedy that was this past week, guiding her through my disastrous encounters with Rod and Sterling. All leading up to Maddie's revenge. When I'm done, all she can ask is "So it's for real?"

My raptor nods. "You didn't see the GCH Confidential post?"

Dino's Spinosaurus shakes its head. "I hate that app. Deleted it like a year ago. The only drama I've heard lately is some noise about how somebody from stu-gov was mad because they were struggling to pay for a DJ for the ball. But that was it . . . Wait, how'd Maddie get ahold of that info?"

"It's a long story."

"Really?"

"Actually, no. It's a very short story. She was mistakenly given a key to the storage room and found the custody agreement in there."

I go into detail about the showdown with my nemesis, and Dino asks questions and offers observations like a curious med school student. When she asks, "So was it scanned in color or grayscale?" I get suspicious.

"You almost sound in awe of it," I say.

"*No!* Not at all," she replies.

My raptor bats an eyebrow in her direction.

"I mean, she's like a toxic person. *Nobody* likes a toxic person! We. Hate. Toxic people! *Blech!*"

I don't necessarily believe her. After all, Dino has spoken favorably about slashing Rosie's tires. It's no secret that she holds a special place in her heart for revenge fantasies. If I caught her and Maddie together comparing notes, it wouldn't surprise me at all.

After studying her for a while, I say, "*Good.*"

"Yep. *Good.*" Dino slurps her smoothie as a ghostly wind stirs the litter around us. Out of the blue, she demurely adds, "I just maybe admire her commitment to toxicity. A lot of stick–to–itiveness there. You can't teach that."

I don't know exactly what to say to that, so I just leave it be.

The ensuing lull in conversation gives me a chance to reflect on all I'd lost, or almost lost, this past week, and how I saw none of it coming. No wonder my clients left me. They should have. My life's been a mess of my own making.

Suddenly looking up, I ask, "Dino, am I a bad person?"

She doesn't hesitate to answer. "You're a *person*, Kal. Don't be so hard on yourself."

It's the simplest insight imaginable, but it hits my core. I've been thinking of myself as a therapist, an entrepreneur, a savant, and a savior this whole last month. Rarely have I thought of myself as just a regular person. Rarely have I embraced the freedom that comes with fallibility.

"Thanks," I say.

"You're welcome," she says absently.

"Sterling said I should just let people live their lives."

"And she's right. People don't grow if they can't learn from their mistakes. And they can't learn from their mistakes unless they're allowed to make them."

Makes perfect sense. I see this with my clients every day. Mistake after mistake after mistake. But I can't live their lives for them. Their lives can't, and shouldn't, revolve around what I think is best, because then it wouldn't be theirs. Therapy only gives them tools to grow. Whether clients use those tools has to be up to them.

Just then, thoughts of my parents overwhelm me. How broken they must feel. How scary the future must seem to them. But how—unsure as it may be—it's better than what they've been living through. In all my lashing out and lamenting today, never once did it cross my mind to consider how they were handling the breakup of their marriage. This realization makes me beyond sad. I thought I was done crying, but the emotions and tears from just hours ago come stampeding back.

"Dino?" I say. I snivel and snort into my headset microphone in a way that totally gives away the ache inside me.

"You okay?" she asks.

I sputter out with "I was soooo wrong about soooo many things."

She simply says, "Yeah, sure. You did some wrong things, but for the right reasons."

I think of Sterling and of Rod, and I know that's not totally true. "I'm not so sure," I say.

Conversation slows again, but that's okay. It's that comfortable silence among friends. My raptor rises to pick up a few loose items of trash. A Sephora bag. Two drink cups. One of those triangular pizza boxes. I don't know how big on conservation Hades is, but I put the items in the recycling bin anyway.

I sit back down, eyes traveling up as I watch a murder of Murder Crows track along bloodred skies. When she thinks my raptor isn't paying attention, Dino's Spinosaurus looks around before gazing over my shoulder. I catch it and get what's happening. I think of a roundabout way to ask her about it.

"Why're you still at the mall anyway?" I ask. "Seems like you've cleared out the Cambions and Necromorphs."

"I was just . . ." After a moment's pause, she comes out with it. "I was waiting for somebody."

There's no need to ask who, but it's obvious she's been waiting for a while. I spot the cinema marquee behind her.

"So, you two were gonna catch a movie or something?"

"Kal. It's a video game. You can't watch a movie during a video game."

*But you can order pizza by the slice, apparently.*

Dino's Spinosaurus abruptly stands, chucking the smoothie into the trash can and walking off. I give chase as she heads toward the Urban Outfitters with the collapsed roof. We hear the far-off screams of Nightwailers and the nearby gurgle of water, but otherwise all of Hades is engulfed in a peaceful silence. The

Spinosaurus sits at the lip of a massive water fountain lit with red and blue light and shimmering with copper pennies at the base. I sit next to her.

The rush of water reminds me of something. Some*one*, rather.

"So River's gone, huh?" I ask.

Dino's Spinosaurus nods. "Yeah. But honestly, I'm okay with that."

"You two seemed so good on paper, though," I say.

"Yeah. On paper. She's really interesting and smart and down-to-earth. And we had some great discussions. But she's just not for me."

Hesitantly, I ask, "And Rosie is?" Not in a trolling way. In a genuinely curious, wanting-to-understand way.

During the ensuing silence, I take stock of the emptiness that surrounds us. The fact that if I weren't here right now, Dino would be, still waiting. *Just* waiting, for God knows how long. When Dino finally speaks up, she doesn't actually answer the question.

"We were just gonna take a stroll, ya know. Just hang out. Like old times."

I nod. "That's cool. And she'll be here soon," I reassure her.

She doesn't respond.

I keep her company for the next ten minutes or so as she tells me about the next boss we'll face and we talk Marvel spin-offs and splash fountain water at each other. Rosie's Nomingia dinosaur eventually shows up, and she offers a hasty apology and stumbles through a semi-coherent excuse. Dino accepts, of course, and I gracefully excuse myself from the conversation. I head for the abandoned parking lot but look back as I pass a Cheesecake Factory overtaken by thistle and weeds. I watch them, holding hands by the fountain, both dinosaurs looking cheery.

While I'm still unsure about their future, I can honestly say I'm here for Dino *now*.

# Seventeen

**Right before midnight,** I wake up to a text from Dino. I have to blink myself to full awareness to make sure I'm reading it correctly:

> Emergency. Keep quiet. Meet me outside in 10.
> Wear all black.

Obviously I start to freak, and when she doesn't respond to my multiple texts to clarify what's happening, I shift into full-blown panic mode. I kick off my tangle of covers and tumble out of bed. I throw on sweatpants and a hoodie and light-foot my way out of my bedroom and to the front door. It's not lost on me that the very first time I'm grounded is also my first time sneaking out of the house. The sadness of the day still anchors my spirit, but I'm weirdly revived by the prospect of late-night shenanigans.

I slink through the front door and hustle down the drive-way, exhaling clouds at my lips as I wait for Dino's Hyundai. For about two minutes, I stand on the curb of the cul-de-sac, arms crossed to guard against the winter wind. I hear her car before I see it because the headlights are off, giving this night a true *Mission: Impossible* vibe. When she arrives, I try to open the passenger seat, but it's locked. Dino nods toward the back, so I jump in there. She's accelerating before I can even get the car door closed.

"Could you hold on until I at least get my whole body in the car?" I ask.

"My bad, bro," she says. "I'd forgotten you had impossibly long giraffe legs."

Latching my seat belt, I ask where we're going, but "Just out visiting" is all she says. I check my phone. "Why would you possibly want to visit someone at eleven fifty-eight p.m.?"

"Okay, could we stop with the twenty questions?" she asks.

"That was *three*."

On a hunch, I get out my phone and check Instagram. I get the answer there. Rosie, or @ItsThePrettiestRose8, posted a food-porn pic of Sopa Azteca and beef empanadas a few hours ago, captioned with "Not feeling so hot, but the fam's got me covered." *She's back at home.*

"Midnight rendezvous with the ex?" I ask.

Headlights shine into the vehicle, and I see her peeking into the rearview. She's wearing a hoodie along with her trademark ball cap pulled low over her brow. "I wouldn't exactly say that."

"So what are we doing?"

"You'll see."

We ride for a while as the silhouettes of houses scroll by

us and suburban streetlights cast us in a ghostly glow. It's cold out, so the edges of Dino's windows still hint of fog, and it takes a while for the car to get toasty. We avoid talking about my parents, and even Rosie, as we make our way through empty streets. Mostly, conversation alternates between upcoming *ZW3* mods and new movies in theaters like *Star Fleet 7* and *A Third Second Chance*. In all this talk, I realize we're taking an absolutely roundabout path to Rosie's, if that's where we're going. No turning left onto Magnolia or cutting through Jernigan Park. In fact, from the few times I've been around her neighborhood, we don't seem to be headed there at all.

Recognition sparks in my eyes as we turn a corner crowded with a stately Victorian hemmed in by a picket fence. I know where we are now. It's not Rosie's neighborhood. It's Rod's.

Before I can say anything, we're pulling up beside his house. Hedges rustle, and Rod pops out, crouched and jogging toward the car. He ducks into the back seat, only realizing I'm there after shutting the door. His look is one of sheer contempt, and he opens his mouth to voice it, but Dino cuts him off.

"What's going on with you two?" she asks.

"Ain't nothing going on," Rod says, letting his body sink into his seat.

"Obviously there is something because I've never seen you so pissed, Rod. Now spill it."

Rod doesn't speak, and there's at least thirty seconds of awkward silence before Dino huffs and takes off. For the next two minutes, only the revving and decelerating of the engine and the whir of the heater fill the car. Several times, Dino looks back into the rearview, eyes like lasers, but she says nothing.

Whether it's from the guilt that's been building up or that nuclear stare, I feel the urge to pipe up. "Rod, I'm sorry. I shouldn't have said what I said." Rod doesn't reply to or even acknowledge my admission, so I press on: "You're one of the kindest and coolest people I know, and Gianna would be lucky to have you."

Still nothing. He just gets out his phone. I search for Dino's eyes in the rearview, wondering what, if anything, I should say next. Her gaze is fleeting and expressionless, as if to tell me I'm on my own.

I look over at him. "What else can I say?"

"A lot" is all he says. He shifts his body away from me, huddling against his window.

With that road closed, I get out my phone, too. I see a text. Same Forsyth number. I think to ignore it again, but something stops me. I text back and jam the phone into my pocket.

Turning my attention to Dino, I ask, "How'd the chat with Rosie go?"

We slow to a stop at a red light. Seconds tick by. The moment neon green filters into the car, we accelerate again. "Really well, actually," Dino says. "We laughed and caught up and totally connected on a lot of levels."

"That's good."

"She said to tell you hey." Her voice catches on the last word in the way of a hangnail hooked on a piece of fabric: brief but noticeable.

"She did?" I ask.

"Yeah." The car comes to rest at a stop sign. An SUV makes a right onto the street we're on, casting light into the car. Dino's eyes are glossy, eyelids damp at the edges. She sniffles and continues: "She said you still owe her a Twix for losing that bet you made on the Final Fantasy side quests."

I think I know what's coming, and it's all I can do to smile at the memory even though every muscle in my face is grappling for a frown.

"Tell her it was best two out of three," I say.

"Kal?"

"Yeah?"

I brace for the news. Rod perks up, too, glancing at me before peering into the front. I feel a lot of things right then. Hurt. Angry. Immensely sad. But I don't feel vindicated. There's absolutely no impulse to trot out a finger-wagging *I told you so*, and for that I'm grateful.

"I broke it off with Rosie," she says.

I'd already preloaded *I'm so sorry that happened to you* in my mind, so it takes a moment to reorient my brain to the revelation. "You what?"

"I said I just couldn't go through this with her again."

We pull over to a shoulder, and I get out of the car as Dino starts bawling. I cram myself into the passenger's side. Rod gets out, too, opening and kneeling at Dino's door as she spills her guts and more tears than I've ever seen her cry.

We both know what Rosie meant to her and the strength it must've taken Dino to break it off. She's the only one of us who's had the experience of long-term commitment. Of dreaming of a future with someone else in it. Of love. And although the idea of these things coming from teenagers sounds quaint and naive to most people, we know it's real.

I listen not as a therapist or a judge, but as a friend. No expectations. No words, really. Just a shoulder to cry on. When she's done grieving, she lands in that weird place where she feels worse for wear but, also, better. And thanks to Rod and me, she doesn't feel alone.

Both of us return to the back seat, and we continue our trek to Rosie's. When we get there, we park across the street. The lights are off in her home. It's a small, nondescript one-story cottage house with dogwood trees dotting the lawn. A plain concrete path leads to the front door. Honeysuckle hedges stripped of leaves by winter round the house like a threadbare skirt.

At the beginning of the drive, I'd assumed we were on some kind of revenge mission and had resolved myself to only participate if it didn't involve committing a felony. However, the fact that Dino broke it off with Rosie doesn't gibe with the revenge narrative, so I ask why we're here. Dino doesn't answer. She just gets out and heads to the trunk, opening it, pulling out a backpack, and gently closing it. She returns to her seat and cuts the ignition. She pushes a button on her phone and the melody to Olivia Rodrigo's "drivers license" begins playing. Rod and I glance at each other, confused.

Rod asks again: "Dino, what are we doing here?"

"We're—" She smacks her head. "It's stupid. Let's just go."

She grabs at her keys again.

"You need closure, don't you?" I ask.

Her hand freezes.

"You ended it, but it doesn't feel over yet."

"Am I dumb?" she asks, voice high-pitched and whiny.

"You're a *person*," I answer, parroting what she'd said to me earlier. "You need what you need. Now tell us what that is."

After giving it some thought, she turns the song volume to no more than a background hum. Then she reaches into the backpack and pulls out a candle, a lighter, and a long, tapered wrought iron holder.

"Rosie's always had this thing for the royal family, especially Princess Diana," she explains. "Consequently, one of her favorite songs is Elton John's 'Candle in the Wind.' He performed it at her funeral."

"So you're using this candle to symbolize the 'death' of your relationship."

Dino nods, and I get it, but I kind of . . . *don't?*

I think that's okay, though. The only people who do have to get it are Dino and Rosie. I nod as well. "Okay, let's do this."

We all get out of the car and dash across the street. Rod stops at the sidewalk to keep lookout, while Dino and I sprint to Rosie's front landing. I nearly trip over a garden hose, it's so dark. Dino crawls behind a hedge and peeks into the nearest window to make sure nobody's stirring, and we both crouch. She sets the holder down and twists the candle in tight. She'd given me the lighter, but after sparking the flame I stop, the fire no more than an inch from the wick.

"*Hurry*," Dino whispers, looking at the door.

I shake my head. "You do the honors."

She takes the lighter from me, closing her eyes and moving her lips as if miming a prayer. She opens them with new resolve. She lights the candle and we run.

All three of us basically throw ourselves into the Accent. Dino cranks the engine, staying in park, and we watch with a quiet satisfaction at our mission completed. A single candle at the doorstep of a former love. A symbol of once-blazing love slowly burning itself out.

About ten seconds in, all of us arrive at the same realization.

I ask the uncomfortable question: "How's Rosie gonna know it's there?"

After thinking it over, Dino starts honking the horn. Ten, fifteen times maybe. Rod and I slouch low in our seats, covering our faces with our hoodies. To our amazement, the lights still don't turn on.

"Are they deaf?" Rod asks.

"No," Dino says. "It's a loud neighborhood. Maybe they're used to hearing car horns."

"At half past midnight?" I blurt out.

Dino turns around in her seat and looks dead at me. "Kalvin, you'll have to go knock."

My heart jumps. "Me?"

"Yes! Her mom and dad will have a much harder time recognizing you if they see you."

"What about Rod?"

"He's too slow!"

*Dammit.* All the pressure of the night shifts on me. The short path suddenly seems never ending. I get out, ducking behind the trunk as a car passes. When it's all clear, I run. I'm at the door before I can even think about it, rapid-fire knocking and pivoting to jet back. It's all done within fifteen seconds, and I'm back in the car huffing. I sink damn near into the floor, just knowing I've been caught.

Rod and Dino keep watch for me. The car's still parked, but I can hear Dino's foot revving the gas.

"Are they out?" I whisper.

They both say no.

Rod and Dino huddle across the center console as I raise my head, peeking out the window. How could an entire family sleep that deeply?

"Are they even here?" Rod asks.

"Yes!" Dino answers, her voice frantic. "I can see their car."

"You sure it's their car?"

"It's in their driveway, Rod!"

They're damn near yelling at one another, but I'm quietly struck by a new crisis unfolding right before my eyes. I guess we should've known not to put the candle in the wind next to a line of dried honeysuckle bushes. But *should've known* and *teens* go about as well together as *fire* and *teens*, or *after-midnight antics* and *teens*.

Dino and Rod turn just as the fire from the candle tipped by the wind eats through the first shrub and latches on to a second. Dino literally falls out of the car and into the street, stumbling up as she yells, "FIRE FIRE FIRE!"

She runs into their yard, waving her hands.

Rod spills out of his side, rounding the trunk and hustling toward her, yelling, "We gotta go!"

"FIRE FIRE FIRE!" she yells. "ROSIEEEEEE!"

He has to physically pull her back as the fire claws at a third shrub, growing so large it begins to reach the brick framing.

I get out, sprinting back to the house, despite knowing I'm dead if someone catches me. I grab the thing I spotted when I first snuck up here: a garden hose tucked next to the landing. I turn it on and point as a light flicks on.

"ROSIEEEEEE!"

I douse the first bush with a jet stream. The front door swings open. Not wanting them to see me, I panic. I point the nozzle at the entrance, spraying water into the house. They scream and I throw an *Ahhhhhh!!* right back at 'em. The stream sends whoever it was flailing back.

"Dino, we gotta go!" I hear Rod yell, but Dino's not having it. If anything, she becomes even more hysterical as the flames reach the fourth bush, just a few feet away from the window to a darkened room.

"That's Rosie's grandma's bedroom!" she shouts.

Oh shit! As calmly but firmly as possible, I shout, "Mrs. Ortiz! There's a fire outside your window! You have to leave!"

"She can't speak English!" Dino yells. She manages to free herself from Rod and tearfully runs to the window, knocking forcefully.

"¡Abuela! ¡Abuela! ¡Sal, por favor! ¡Tu casa está en fuego! ¡Apurarse!"

Grandma's light switches on, and I hear yelling from behind the house. I drop the garden hose and run toward Dino. Rod and I both have to drag her to the Hyundai. Sirens flare in the distance as we tear off into the street. I look back and see Rosie and her family fighting to get to the hose, dousing the flames to nothing more than ash and steam. Dino pulls off a perfect, skid-marked L-turn before fishtailing onto a narrow side street.

We're three blocks from the house when we feel safe enough to stop looking back for cops and breathe again. Shortly after the breathing comes the laughter—uproarious, belly-cramping, tear-inducing laughter. Dino even has to pull over, and I have to take off my seat belt we're laughing so hard. I'm crunched over when Rod spills onto my back, squishing me.

"Dude, get off me!" I chuckle.

"I'm sorry!" He giggles. "But did you really spray somebody to keep them inside a house that was about to catch on fire?"

He gets off, and I sit back up, leaning against my door, breathless. "I . . ." Deep breath. "Couldn't let 'em . . ." Deep breath. "See me . . ." A last fusillade of laughter punctuates my explanation.

"You wild for that, bro," Rod says, leaning against his side. We're both smiling ear to ear, and for the first time tonight I can sense that even though he's justifiably mad at me, eventually we'll work it out.

I sniff the shoulder of my hoodie. I smell like smoke. The whole car does. Dino leans her head back against her headrest as the sunroof whirs open. She looks straight up as drizzle spritzes her face. Dino lets out a sigh so relaxed I feel the stress leaving my own body. Then she says, "I feel like I'm in a John Green novel. But make it Black, ya know?"

"*Jaquan* Green." I giggle.

Dino starts to drive off again, and I put down my window, stretching my head and neck out as the wind whips at my face, beating my hands against the rooftop, whooping to the star-flecked skies. A day that began as a catastrophe doesn't really feel like it anymore. Sure, we almost burned down a house, and I'm now a product of a broken home, but I've got my friends, my health, and my peace of mind. And for the moment, that's exactly what I need.

The night doesn't end here. At least not for me. We pull up to the front of our school ten minutes later, at about 12:40.

As Dino slows to the roundabout, she says, "You sure about this?"

Her face is a marriage of skepticism and frustration. I refused to tell them who I'm meeting or what it's about. Only that it isn't anyone they know.

"Yeah," I say. "Just make sure you're back in half an hour to pick me up."

"Where we gonna go for half an hour?" she asks.

I shrug. "I dunno. The McDonald's on Harrington is open till one, I think."

She sticks her hand out. "You got McDonald's money?"

I dig into the pockets of my sweats, pulling out a $10 bill. I hand it to Dino. She looks surprised. "Wow. You actually *do* have McDonald's money."

"Thirty minutes," I say, getting out. Dino peels out of the driveway. I turn toward the entrance, and the person I'm meeting is right there. She's sitting on a bench underneath the canopied walkway. She's stock-still, her head bending over the glow of her cell phone. Light shines down on her in a way that makes her look like an exhibit at a museum.

I walk over, her head barely lifting as my footsteps go from padding asphalt to crunching the mulch that lines the walkway. Her grin is easily dimpled but insincere. Her Stanford sweater is too large to be anything other than a hand-me-down from Dad or big bro. She's got her brown hair messily clipped and gathered behind her head, like she just woke up and came to meet me.

She scoots over, and I sit beside her. There's no going inside tonight. It's locked. But I'd rather not go in anyway.

"Hey," I say.

"Hey."

"Glad to put a face to all the texts." She nods but doesn't say anything. I put my hand in front of her. "Kalvin."

We shake. "Nice to meet you. Grace."

I watch as candle flies flutter above me, letting silence do its work as she thinks about what she'll say. At first, she just fidgets with her phone before laying it on the bench space beside her. Her pale skin is red at the cheeks—from the cold or something else, I have no idea.

I ask "How'd you get my number?" to break the silence.

She tells me a cousin goes here. "He knew I was having some issues." The quiet floats in with a breeze. I breathe into my hands. She hugs her arms. We wait for nothing. Finally she says, "I was beginning to think you'd never get back to me."

"For a while, I thought that, too."

"Bet you're wondering why I'd come all the way from Forsyth High."

I nod. "It had definitely crossed my mind."

"It's just, my situation involves someone at this school, and I was hoping you'd have some insight since you go here."

"Palace intrigue isn't really my thing," I say.

Her eyes pinch closed, and I read the regret on her face. "Not, like, gossip or anything. Just . . ."

I wave off her words. "You don't have to explain anything to me. Just tell me about your situation."

Her hands tent over her mouth and nose, and her deep exhalation clouds the air in front of us. She startles as one of those muscle cars revs on a nearby street but refocuses once the noise fades into the small hours of morning.

"Okay, there's this guy I've known for a long time. Since

elementary school. Well, we were always very close. Even dating for some of it. Then he moved away in seventh grade. But a few months ago, we reconnected by chance, and we were thinking maybe we could get back together."

"But the guy has a girlfriend now," I add.

Grace gives me a look riddled with curiosity bordering on outright suspicion. "How did you know?"

"Because I know the guy. It's Chadwick."

To abate her confusion, I explain. I really didn't know at first, but something about her persistent texting got me wondering who this person could be. Her number started to congeal in my mind, and before long I thought I'd recognized it from some other situation. When she texted tonight, it came to me. Sterling had showed me the message sent to Chadwick's phone when she first came to the closet. The numbers were the same. Grace's text was the catalyst for Sterling's distrust. If Grace had never texted, I may never have had that chance encounter with Sterling.

I'm honestly not mad or disgusted or even mildly put off at all this going on behind Sterling's back. Maybe I'm tired. Maybe that little button inside of me that says to be self-righteously judgmental has been pushed so much lately that it's broken. But looking at Grace, I don't see a villain or temptress or "the other woman." I see a teenager, as confused as the rest of us, trying to make the best of her reality. A wave of sympathy crashes over me.

"I've never done something like this," she says. "And I feel so bad for wanting to be with him. It's just so hard knowing a person you have such great chemistry with is unavailable." Her tone makes clear her words are more of a plea for understanding than a declaration of truth.

"You feel like you're soul mates?" I ask.

She thinks long and hard before answering: "We've never used that word. And honestly, I don't know if teens are mature enough to have that sort of thing, but—"

Her words end there. However, the *But*— tells me all I need to hear.

"And Chadwick feels the same way?"

She nods, wiping a tear from her eye. "He says the girl he's with now is wonderful, and I know she doesn't deserve any of this, but the heart wants what it wants, right?"

"The heart isn't the only thing that matters," I respond, and she nods.

"I know it's stupid, and not a day goes by that I don't think I'm totally stupid for putting myself through this. But I don't wanna be one of those people looking back on life with regrets."

I gaze out into the dark, trying to picture Sterling. What would she say if she knew this conversation was taking place? Would she be heartbroken? Happy? Both?

"So do you think I should go for it?" she asks.

"Sounds like you've already made your choice," I mutter. "That is, if Chadwick's truly on board."

"Yeah . . . I guess so," she confesses.

I tilt my neck till I'm looking at her again, willing her eyes to meet mine. "So tell me: Why are you really here?"

Her eyes hold the look of a toddler caught with snacks before dinner.

I go on: "Grace, anybody could've given you that advice. You didn't come just for that, did you?"

Slowly, Grace resets her expression, fragile resolve overtaking the embarrassment. "Can you tell me about her?" she asks.

The question catches me by surprise. Why would anyone want to know details about the person they're pulling the rug out from under? Besides that, the ethics of me saying anything are a minefield. Sterling was a past client. Up until a week ago, I thought she could be something more.

The therapist and the friend in me want to shut down this whole line of questioning. But the empath—the person who came to an empty school to meet a stranger in the dead of night—sees something bigger at play. Grace wants to resolve her own inner conflict over this. She wants to reconcile what she's about to do with who she is.

I think about what Mom and Dad used to say to listeners at times like this.

*We're not here to tell stories. We're here to tell the truth.*

That's exactly what I do. I tell her the truth about Sterling. How she has a silver tongue, a heart of gold, and a smile worth diamonds. How she wouldn't hesitate to buy you a free Gatorade with loose change just because, or spend a day volunteering since helping people is her thing. How she loves spades and loves Snickers even more. And how despite all that, she's maddeningly insecure in a way that's confusing to everyone but herself.

I honestly don't mean to make Grace cry. But by the time I'm done painting Sterling, Grace is painting the concrete with her tears.

"She seems great," Grace snivels.

"She is," I agree. I put a hand to her knee. "But you seem pretty okay yourself. And you're right. The heart wants what it wants."

She leans into me as I give her a side hug. We talk for a few more minutes about other things—school life at Forsyth High, school life at Gregg County, anything but relationships—and then Dino texts to say she and Rod are coming back.

I escort Grace to her car, a blue Mazda sedan sitting lonely in the lot. When she cranks the ignition, she puts down the window to say goodbye.

"You know, it's a great thing you're doing," she says.

"*Was* a great thing," I answer. The words surprise her. She doesn't know exactly how to respond, and I don't know exactly how to explain that she'll be my very last client.

Instead, we just say our goodbyes. I stand and watch as she pulls out of the lot.

Before Dino returns, I get out my phone and call in a favor.

# Eighteen

**That afternoon, I** find myself hopelessly lost in the valley of *meh*. I spend an unhealthy amount of time plotting ways to give my candy stash away. I know I'm done with therapy, but I think I'm done with candy sales, too. Maybe I'll throw the bags from a second-story window or lay a pile out in front of the parking lot right before dismissal. Whatever it is, it's gotta be quick and easy. I'm done putting energy into this. Done.

"Kalvin?"

My eyes spring open, and I see Mr. Tribblett, my seventh-period teacher. He's sitting at his desk and staring at me through thin-rimmed glasses. I stumble through an apology as I pack up and scurry out. Dread in my steps, I head to the opposite end of the hallway and shut myself in the storage closet. The place I'd been avoiding all day.

I pull my candy bags from the shelves and do one last inventory. It feels surreal counting the Snickers and Starbursts and Peppermint Patties. Actually it's surreal just being in here. This was my headquarters, my entrepreneurial hub. This was the place

I cut my teeth and surely rotted many others. After today, I don't plan on ever coming back.

I walk over to the "Candyland" sign posted on the back shelf. Pulling it down, I run my fingers across the rough cardboard and mutter, "You win, Maddie."

I hear knocking. I ignore it. After about three seconds, it stops. I go back to the candy pile, cocooning myself among the bags. I slide my palms down my face as the finality of the day sinks in. It's over. Maybe I won't even give the candy away. Maybe I'll just haul it out back and it'll be food for dumpster-diving raccoons by evening. That sounds easier.

In a fit of frustration, I grab a bag of Jolly Ranchers and sling it across the room. It explodes as it hits the shelf, sending individual reds and greens and purples skittering everywhere.

I hear another knock. *What?*

"Could you please just go away?" I say.

A syrupy sweet voice floats into the room. "Kalvin?"

I pause. "Sterling?"

"Can I come—"

We're already making eye contact before she can finish the question. She blushes at my eagerness, and I get really self-conscious, shrinking back as she walks in.

Neither of us speak for a moment. She seems at a loss for words, and I don't know what I could possibly say to make things better. I busy myself arranging items on the electronics shelf, pretending I'm not sneaking glances her way as she paces the room, head downcast. Suddenly, she freezes, her head popping up.

"Listen," she says, "I just wanted to say I'm so sorry about what happened to you earlier this week. Having your family's issues put on blast like that is just raw."

"It's . . ." My first instinct is to say *It's okay*, but I know it's not. So I just say, "It's whatever."

"When I see her next, I'm gonna give that privileged little bitch a piece of my mind."

I stop counting, turning around to square myself to her. I don't tell her my anger at Maddie has dulled significantly since our confrontation. I just say, "I thought you were friends."

"'Acquaintances' is a better term," Sterling says. "She's more Garrison and Avery's friend than mine."

"Does Gianna like her?" I ask out of sheer curiosity.

Sterling's head shakes, and she has to brush a few curls away from her face. "They don't really get along. Ever since Maddie's mom caught them vaping two years ago and Maddie tried to put it all on G, it's been quite the rocky relationship."

Intrigued, I plant myself on the shelf, ignoring the fact that an edge is digging into my back. "Why do you all hang out so much, then?"

"Expectations, I guess. Somehow, it's expected that the rich kids should float through high school in harmonious serenity. No fighting. No friction. Just positive energy."

The way Sterling says it with raised eyebrows and a Sharpied smile signals she knows the expectation is bullshit. But that doesn't mean it's not potent. I think back to when we first met.

How I'd assumed her life was picture-perfect. How I couldn't have been more wrong.

The conversation dies out again. Awkwardly, I get up and go back to pushing around equipment.

After a moment she says, "Well . . . that's all I wanted to say." I see her wave from my periphery.

"Thanks."

"Well, bye."

I tense up, not knowing what to say that'll make things right. Should I make one more stop on my apology tour, or is it too late for that? Why couldn't I swallow my pride on Monday? Why'd I have to be the expert? Why couldn't I just be Kalvin?

Several Jolly Ranchers crunch underfoot as Sterling walks toward the door. She's well beyond the threshold when I whip around and spout, "I know where your name comes from!"

Her footsteps stop and then start again. Her shadow precedes her, creeping back inside. Her expression, shaded by the doorframe, is one of vague curiosity.

"'Sterling.' It's an anagram of your last name, 'Glistern.'"

She slow-walks back into the room, a soft smile edging into her cheeks. "I asked how you got the name a couple weeks back, and you told me to figure it out. And I did. I skipped fourth period that day."

"Just to figure out my name?" she asks.

"Yes. And because I had an English quiz I'd forgotten to study for. But that was secondary."

She laughs. "Sure it was."

"It's true!"

She nods slowly, beaming. "Well, congrats, Kalvin. You and Gianna are the only two people here who know that. Rarefied air."

Pride wells up from somewhere deep within, but I do my best not to show it. "Why did they do that?" I ask.

"My parents? They're, uh, word people all right. And I'm more of a math person."

"You're a person," I reply.

She nods again. I stand straight, walking to the other side. "Be that as it may, they don't really consider my interests a worthy pursuit."

"Why not?" I ask.

"They think mathematics is—how would they phrase it?—not aesthetically significant."

"Are they serious? There's tons of beauty in math. The golden ratio. Sacred geometry. *Harmony.*"

Sterling gives off a sad little laugh. "Try telling them that."

I make my way back to the shelf, fitting my butt in between a subwoofer and a computer monitor. "Can you sit for a sec?" I ask.

More Jolly Ranchers crunch as she drags the stool to the center and sits. She lets her bookbag and purse straps slide from her shoulder, both making a thud as they hit the floor.

"Candy?" I ask.

"Sure, I'll take a piece."

I go for the Snickers, but instead of handing her a piece, I grab a few bags. Her face wrenches into heightened levels of shock with each unopened bag I shovel into her lap.

Finally, at bag number six, she says, "Whoa, whoa, whoa," letting them all fall. "What are you doing?"

"Getting rid of them. They're useless to me now."

"Why?"

"I quit selling."

"Again. Why?"

I gaze at the pile while explaining that trying to make other people happy has left me drained and exhausted. Somehow, the explanation morphs into a lament on my screwups with Dino and Rod and then a swashbuckling tale of our weekend misadventure at Rosie's. Every once in a while, I catch her watching me. She sits there, lips pressed tight but face brimming with sympathy and interest. When I'm done, she goes, "Quite the roller coaster. Maybe you and I should trade places so you can process on the couch for once."

I shake my head. "I am officially retired from therapy."

"Why? Because Maddie sabotaged you? You're doing a great thing."

*Am I?* All I see looking back is an inescapable path of damaged relationships. I might as well have been a tornado.

"Not that great when you really look," I say.

"No, Kalvin. This is all Maddie's doing. I can help you get your clients back."

"It's all *me*," I say. The admission feels like a weight lifting from my shoulders. "I need to work on myself for a while, before working to help others."

"Dude, half the school is committed to some form of wellness because of you. Can't you see that?"

"I see that those closest to me were hurt the most."

"But you'll work past that. Dino and you are cool now. You and Rod are kinda sorta speaking again." I wince, shaking my head at that. "And your parents are still amicable," she says. "Who's left?"

I look at her. My eyes say everything my lips can't. I know she knows the answer. But instead of speaking it, she just nods.

"I'm sorry," I blurt out, without even thinking.

She waves me off. "Kalvin, you're beyond forgiven. You shot your shot. It's what most of us would've done."

"No, not for that."

"For what, then?" she asks.

"I think I held you on a pedestal for a long time," I say. "You deserve to be just a regular person."

"Yeah . . . regular," she says. Her head tilts down and away from me in a way that signifies she's not totally comfortable with the topic. I decide to change the subject.

"I actually am taking a turn on the couch," I say.

"Like, real therapy?"

"Yep. Starting next week."

At this revelation, her body does a full swivel on the stool as her eyes follow me. A look of amusement mixed with awe sweeps across her face. I can't help but stare at her lips, slightly parted—the way lines appear at her brow like how sands shift at the beach. My back can't handle the shelf anymore, so I stand, wandering any which way. As I get close to her, her scent hits me. Vanilla and hints of some kind of flower.

She looks up at the ceiling and thinks long and hard before asking, "Can I make a confession?"

"Shoot."

"Beginning next week, I'm on the couch, too. It's my way of working on those unresolved issues I was talking to you about. Issues you helped me resurface—in a good way."

"*Really?*"

"Really," she says. "I've come to realize that while my parents meant well, the expectations they had for me did quite a number on my psyche. So I talked to them about it, and how I wanted to try therapy, and they were surprisingly receptive."

Shrugging, I say, "Well, the couch is a good place to be."

"Yep. Dr. Kimberly Hallard. She seems nice. We're doing something called . . . CBT?"

"Cognitive behavioral therapy. Me too, actually."

She lifts an eyebrow. "Oh, you down with CBT?"

I grin. "Yeah, you know me."

She stands, arms lifted. I face her, lifting mine as well.

"You down with CBT?"

"Yeah, you know me!"

"You down with CBT?"

"Yeah, you know me!"

"Who down with CBT?"

"Every last homie!"

We both laugh at our tweaked and repurposed Naughty By Nature lyrics. Another *Black* thing. Another *Us* thing.

Then she rises from her chair and picks up the Snickers bags. She puts all except one back on the shelf. She cradles the other tightly across her chest. She simply says, "My fee."

"Fee for what?" I ask.

"Preventing you from being a dumbass and giving away thousands of pieces of candy."

I shoot her the same, slightly amused but mostly exasperated look my parents would give me when I'd make some overly optimistic declaration like *I'll do my project before school tomorrow* or *The Panthers could actually win it all this year.*

"It's either that or throw it away, Sterling."

"Okay, well *fine.* Give it, then. But at least do something special." Her lips suck in as she draws a deep breath. I think she's genuinely annoyed. She demands I promise not to trash any, lest she rain down the fires of hell on me.

"Okay, okay!"

She points. "I will smite you, Kalvin Shmelton."

I step toward her. She backs away, waving her finger right at me like it's a wand. "Consider yourself smited? Smitled? *Smote!* You've been smoted."

I slap my hands against my waist. A laugh spills out from my lips, half of it born of amusement, half of incredulity. I look into Sterling's eyes, full of hope and wonder. At that moment, I

284

feel like I'm the rational adult *tsk*ing away a child's dream, even though I know she has at least a year on me.

"You know, you should actually apologize for that." She's trying to maintain a poker face, but she's half smirking as she says it.

"For what?"

"Apologize to all the candy lovers everywhere for thinking about trashing your stash."

"You know what, screw it," I say.

I get on my knees and give her the praying hands treatment.

"You are not being serious right now," she responds.

"Oh, you want serious?" I get up again and rummage through my stash. Bringing out a blue Ring Pop, I return, lowering myself again. Her mouth shoots open as I get on bended knee.

"You are so extra."

"Want me to hit up Susie McNamara and No Strings Attached, too?" I ask. "Hire them out to play? Give your ego a soundtrack?"

"*My* ego?" she says, crossing her arms. "I didn't ask for this!"

"But you are worth it . . . ," I reply. "As a friend."

Surprisingly, I don't get all twitchy with nerves or read deeper into the situation than it is. Yes, I'm still crushing hard, and yes the embarrassment of the weekend is still fresh on my mind, but it's more than that. I feel comfortable around her because she's cool to be around. We're cool together.

"Sterling, I'm truly sorry for how everything played out."

She pretends to whimper as I place the "ring" on her finger, fanning her face with her free hand. As I get up, she licks her ring.

"Such a sweet apology," she says. "Figuratively and literally." She licks again and says, "Okay, lie down. I wanna try something."

I can't help but be nervous. It's not every day your gorgeous, slightly off-the-wall crush commands you to lie down. My skin tingles as my neck touches cold concrete, and I have to blink away the light directly above me.

"Okay, now, close your eyes," she says. I make a *WTF* face but she volleys right back with a *Big auntie who don't play games* face, and I relent. I hear the splitting open of plastic bags, then the rustling of hands touching wrappers.

"It's winter," she continues. "Your alarm goes off. You wake up, peeling off layers of blankets and staggering to the window despite the unbearable cold. You look outside. What do you see?"

"The mailbox?"

"*Snow*, Kalvin. You see snow."

"Ooooookaaaay?"

"So what do you do?" she asks.

"I go back to bed."

"You go outside. And once outside, you . . ."

"Play?" I squeak out, more afraid of her wrath than I probably should be.

"Correct! And what do you do while you play?"

"Have snowball fights. Build a snow fort. Make snow angels."

"Ding ding ding!"

My body feels the weird sensation that accompanies getting buried under a hundred pieces of candy at once. Then another hundred. Then another. I open my eyes to see her pouring bag after bag after bag right on top of me.

"What's this!"

"What's it look like? You're going to make a candy angel."

As the candy piles up on my chest and legs and torso, the weight of it gets heavier, but in a good way, like massages people sometimes get with those stones. I enjoy the feeling of candy washing over me. The sheer innocence and utter ridiculousness of the moment is almost cleansing.

"Where do you come up with this stuff?" I ask.

"I dunno," she says right before scores of Reese's Cups pelt my face. She picks one up from a middle shelf on the far wall, unwraps it, and pops it into her mouth.

"Oh, so it's like that, huh?" I say.

"Like what?"

"Just take one and not offer me any."

"Sorry," she says. She grabs another and slides it between my slightly parted lips.

She pours God knows how many more bags on top of me until I'm basically covered. The wrappers of various candies tickle my temples. When she's done, empty candy bags are everywhere. She takes a step back to admire her work. I spread and contract my arms and legs to clear my space, making a reasonable facsimile of a "candy angel." I hear a click and notice the phone at her side.

My eyebrows raise. "You just took a picture of me?"

"For blackmail purposes."

I gasp. "Why?"

"You never know."

I reach out a hand. "Okay, fine. You've had your fun. Now let me up."

When she reaches down to help, I pull. She laughs as I drag her down with me. The weight gets that much heavier as we lie there, chin to chin, separated only by a crushed layer of candy.

"Woooow, Kal! Smooth move. I think we were about an inch from busting our foreheads together."

"Well, that would've been your fault because you do have a big forehead."

I feel the sting of her slap to my shoulder. Then she rolls off me and we both lie there, staring up at the ceiling in the cramped closet. I imagine we're on a cloud because that's exactly how I'm feeling right now. We both stare up at the ceiling.

"When I was a kid, I used to go out into my backyard and just lie like this in the grass," Sterling says. "I'd literally see if I could count each individual grass blade I could feel touching me."

"You and your numbers."

"Always."

I turn my head so I'm looking at her, and for an instance I'm taken aback by the contemplative look she wears so well. I've never seen her quite like this: not happy, not sad, just letting her mind untether itself from the world and roam free.

"Did you used to make snow angels as a child?" I ask.

"All the time," she says. "I was born in Minnesota, so snow was basically a six-month thing."

"What about now?"

"Whenever it snows, I'll play. Sometimes I'll go out with my kid sister. Mostly, though, it's for the nostalgia."

"Ever done it with Chadwick?"

"He would *never*," she says.

"Why say it like that?" I ask. The question isn't meant to troll at all. I'm actually genuinely curious.

"He takes himself very seriously."

"Sounds like it."

She shifts a little, and her hand brushes against mine. The touch shocks me, sending a shiver through my spine and setting all my nerves on fire. The way she looks at me then, her eyes deep and penetrative and a touch unsettled, I know she felt it, too. She wants this just like I do. I can't imagine why anyone wouldn't.

Our hands interlock, drawn together like magnets. I gulp, waiting. She bites her lip. I move my head in closer but something stops me. The same thing that pulls her hand away from mine.

Her throat clears. "Yeah, Chadwick. Serious."

Chadwick. The guy who wants someone else. I could tell her about the conversation with Grace. Destroy whatever faith Sterling has in him. I could break client-therapist confidentiality with a stranger and cement something real with the girl of my dreams.

But I don't. I don't tell, and I don't know if I'm right or wrong in keeping quiet. I don't know if a client's privacy should outweigh a friend's confidence. I just know that I'll wait for her, as long as it takes for her to figure herself out. I'll let time do its thing. And if it takes forever, I'll still consider it time well spent.

We shift our bodies back to staring at the ceiling. Chocolate perfumes the air and I feel wrappers scratch my skin.

"How 'bout you?" she asks. "Did you play in the snow a lot?"

I shake my head. "No siblings to play with. Not much snow, anyway."

"Your parents didn't go out with you? Back when things were better between them?"

"Yeah," I say. "They did. At first, at least."

"Did y'all do a lot of things together?"

I'm silent for a long time before answering. "No." The word comes out all wrong, tinny and off-key. I can't put my finger on why, exactly.

"Oh," she says. And then: "You know, I'm here, if you ever need to talk."

For the first time when talking about them, I feel no urgent desire to push back on the invitation. No burning impulse to bar the door against things I don't want to hear or say. I suppose, if I had a therapist, they'd say that's growth.

"Oh," she says again, and I look at her. She's staring at the back shelf. "Where's the sign?" she asks.

"I took it down."

"In the trash?"

I point to where I dropped it, and she shifts her body to crawl over. After digging for several seconds, she dredges it up from the depths. She grabs a marker from a bottom shelf. I hear it squeak against cardboard as she scribbles. She hangs it back up, and I read it:

CANDYLAND

POP. ~~1~~ 2

MAYORS KALVIN SHMELTON

+

**STERLING GLISTERN**

# Nineteen

**It's Saturday. The** night of the ball. My shirt collar rubs uncomfortably against my neck because it's as big as a windsail. It's itchy, annoying, and it makes me feel claustrophobic. Every other minute I hook my finger into it just to give my neck some breathing room.

I do it again as Dino and I enter the school. She grabs my elbow, yanking my arm down.

"Dude, stop. It's not that bad," she says.

"Easy for you to say. You've got it made."

"You see this beehive on my head, right?"

There's not really a beehive on Dino's head. It's a towering "queen's wig" that makes her one of the tallest people in the room. We're both dressed in the royal finery. I'm the "hot Black duke" from the hit Netflix show *Bridgerton*, the gossipy melodrama detailing the English Regency era. She's Queen Elizabeth I, complete with embroidered dress, wig, and queenly wave. When she picked me up, Dino openly mused as to whether I was hot enough for people to make the connection. So in true Dino fashion, she taped a sign on my back that reads "Hot duke from *Bridgerton*."

"Is it on straight?" she asks, squaring up to me. We pause in front of the double-doored gym entrance as I place my hands on her wig.

"You're good."

Students stream past us, similarly accoutered and haber-dashed. King Arthur sits with Merlin at the ticket table. Joan of Arc and Shakespeare attend the door. It's obvious all the students came festive and ready. What's not so obvious is whether the festival is ready for us. I check my phone and it's 8:05. The ball officially started at eight. There's no music, just the low murmur of students greeting one another and barking directions before snapping group pictures. There are no decorations, aside from the massive "Knights and Knaves" banner swooping over the gym entrance.

"You really think they ran out of money?" Dino asks.

"I guess so," I say.

Dino slides her ticket onto the table. Merlin puts it in the lockbox and wand-waves her through.

"And to think," she says. "All because of your little therapy biz bleeding candy sales dry. Guess you really are the knave tonight, huh?"

"What's a knave again?" I ask.

"A rogue. A trickster. An all-around low-down dishonest man."

Handing Arthur my ticket, I shoot Dino a look. "Gee, thanks . . ."

"Only in Maddie's eyes," she says as we both walk inside.

The gymnasium is flecked with so many purple and red

strobe lights it feels like we're trapped in a lava lamp. Not many people are here yet, but the few that have arrived are sitting in groups on the bleachers or raiding the hors d'oeuvres tables.

I keep a lookout for Sterling, but I don't see her. An idle question grows in the back of my mind like a shadow at dusk: How will I react when she shows up with Chadwick? Seeing my dream girl dressed like royalty on the shoulder of her knight in shining armor. Mentally I've prepared myself for the reality, but you can't predict exactly how these things go. I could be cool about it, which would be the best-case scenario. Worst case, I spontaneously self-immolate and Dino spreads my ashes from a rowboat in Lake Junaluska.

I will myself not to think about it by looking around some more. I see Maddie at the far side, where the gym runs into a curtained-off stage apron. Since this is our auxiliary gym, it doubles as the school auditorium. It's where a DJ would be, but only Maddie stands there now, arms folded and looking quite distressed as she speaks into her cell phone. For the fleetest of moments, a sense of pity pricks me somewhere on the inside. Nobody's fretting a ball with no music yet, but if it lasts much longer, all eyes will be on her, and *not* in a good way.

Before I can point her out to Dino, someone else demands my attention.

"Kalvin!"

I turn around and see Gianna waving as she enters. Her showing up is a surprise in and of itself. But the biggest shock is who she's with. Rod's arm is hooked around hers. He's obviously a colonial, with waistcoat, tricorne hat, and stockings that go up to the knees. She's got this sleek royal dress and ribboned hair.

They come up to us, Gianna hugging Dino. As they release their embrace, Dino sizes her up: "Girl, you are looking beautiful! Who are you?"

"Mary, Queen of Scots! Note the red hair! It just fits."

"Girl, you are *rocking it*!"

"And you are?" Gianna asks.

"Queen Elizabeth."

Gianna audibly gasps, covering her mouth. "And what a gorgeous queen you are. I would absolutely die to be you right now!"

"Technically, you already did. I had you beheaded."

They carry on their conversation as Rod and I stand idle. I smile weakly. He doesn't. When I go in for a bro hug like we always do, he holds out his hand in a manner way too formal for friends:

"Kalvin," he says.

We shake. The jovial moment we shared in Dino's car at Rosie's was only that. A moment. Rod was back to ignoring me the very next day.

"Rod. Aaron Burr, I see."

"Who are you?"

"The duke from *Bridgerton*."

"The hot duke!" Gianna says, butting in to hug me. "You look amazing!"

"You too! But I thought you weren't coming. Didn't you have—"

"Psssh . . . the thing with Jordan's parents? We had it out about that and about the pissy way he's been treating people, and I just finally broke up with him! Can you believe that?"

*No, I honestly can't.* Not that I didn't believe it'd eventually happen, but just not so soon.

"Well . . . congratulations?"

"Yes! We should toast," she says. "To the punch bowl!"

"To the punch bowl!" Rod and Dino parrot. Dino attempts to hook my arm to come along with, but I pull away, gazing in the opposite direction.

"I'll catch up with y'all," I mutter.

"Suit yourself."

I head the other way, toward the exit near the stage, the one I just saw Maddie walk through. When I get into the hallway, it's empty, but I do hear the echoey clack of heels somewhere in the distance. I follow the sound. It takes me through several more turns and hallways, and I wind up across the hall from the storage closet where it all started. The stu-gov closet.

She's got the door closed, and my hand freezes before it touches the handle. My heart beats faster, and my body tenses. I think maybe I shouldn't go in. Maybe I should just live and let live.

But then I hear muffled crying coming from inside that legit shocks me. Nobody would call Maddie outwardly emotional, so it's surprising to hear this. Gently, I turn the handle and crack the door open. I peek in and see her facing the back shelf.

It's almost completely bare—just a few empty candy bags

sitting on a middle row. The whole room looks totally different now. To think, stu-gov's near monopoly existed and thrived here a year ago, and now it's like it never was.

The door creaks as I step inside. Even though her back is turned, Maddie doesn't startle. It's like she knew I was following her.

"Come to gloat?" she says.

"Why would I do that?" I ask.

She motions toward the barren stu-gov shelves. "Because you clearly got the last laugh."

"What's there to laugh about?"

She spins to face me. "I come here yesterday and our candy's all gone. You're saying you had nothing to do with this?"

"No, that's not—I mean, I did have something to do with it, but not the way you think."

She huffs, wheeling around again as new tears form in her eyes. I step farther inside. It feels spacious and drafty. No candy bags where there were plenty just days ago, before I spirited off with their supply.

"Yes, Maddie, I was mad at you. And yes, I did take stu-gov's candy. Perkins had accidently given me your spare key, so I got it all. But I—"

"Don't! You masterminded this, just like you planned out how to ruin our candy sales. But guess what? Sometimes things we plan have unintended consequences. *You're* the reason we don't have money for decorations or a DJ, and our music's gonna have to be piped in from the intercom."

I march over to Maddie, stopping at her shoulder. "I quit selling candy," I say.

Her mouth opens, but no words come. Maybe it's because she finally realizes I'm not the villain she's made me out to be. "And what's happening tonight isn't my fault or my responsibility."

"Then whose fault is it?" she asks.

"Nobody's! What I've had to learn the hard way is that people make their own choices. And for the past month, people have been choosing to actually face their issues instead of burying them under a mountain of sugar. If that puts me out of business, then so be it."

"That's easy for you to say. I'm sure therapy is going gangbusters for you. Meanwhile, this ball—my disaster of a ball!—will be the thing I'm known for. The thing everybody'll point to when they say I'm a failure."

Her words grab me somewhere deep. She just admitted what she couldn't earlier this week. Her biggest fear. The thing that keeps her up at night. The reason she so severely lashed out when she saw her success was threatened.

"We all fail at things," I say. "That doesn't make us failures. It makes us human."

I put a hand in my pocket and pull out an envelope, handing it to her. She opens it, pulling out twelve $100 bills.

"For stu-gov. I priced it out. The candy I took from your closet. It came out to eleven hundred dollars, and I added interest."

I back off, my steps taking me to the center of the room. I

298

turn to go when she quietly asks, "Why are you doing this?"

"Because I owe you the money."

Maddie shakes her head. "Not that. Why are you being so nice? I outed your parents' divorce and you're acting like you're not even angry."

"Maddie, the person I've been angriest with lately is myself."

"Why?"

"Plenty of reasons." Describing them all to her would take the duration of the ball, so I leave it at that.

She nods. "But I am sorry."

"There's no need for apologies."

"Yes. There is," she says. "I did a terrible thing. And there's no excuse for it."

I don't respond because she's 100 percent correct. It was terrible. But also because it showed me the truth that my parents were hiding and that I was denying, despite it being right in front of me. She simply forced my eyes open.

"Come on," I say.

"What? Back to the ball?"

"It'll be fun."

"Don't know how much fun a dance can be without a DJ."

"Could you just come?" I ask.

Reluctantly, she steps toward me. I leave, and she follows. Our walk back is slow and at the mercy of an uncomfortable silence. When we get close, I hear the washed-out melodies coming from an intercom system that's hooked to stereo speakers in the gym.

"Could you stop the music?"

She eyes me, confused. She doesn't challenge me on it, though. "Yeah, let me text Lauryn. She's manning it from the main office. But why?"

"Just do it."

She gets out her phone. About a minute later, we walk into the gym just as the sound dies down. A few dozen more people have arrived, and I feel Maddie's embarrassment metastasizing with each bewildered glance cast our way. I do a quick panorama looking for Sterling, but I still don't see her.

Maddie leans into me. "What exactly is the endgame here?"

I don't answer. Instead, I break away from her, heading to the center of the gym to get a better view. Once there, I look around for Susie McNamara. I spot her with friends at a far section of the bleachers.

I wave and she sees me. I point to the stage and she gives a thumbs-up. She pulls out her phone to text and starts walking down the steps. By the time she's near the stage, three other students have reached the apron, too, two of them dragging folding chairs. They grab their instrument cases at the base of the stage and sit down.

By this time, No Strings Attached is drawing the attention of others in the room. They pull out their instruments; Susie with her flute, two seniors with clarinets, and a sophomore holding a sax. Susie clears her throat as the audience gets quiet. The saxophonist dons a white fedora with a thick black band. He puts the saxophone to his lips and begins with a long bass note as a warm-up before launching into a riff I immediately recognize. I start nodding to the Michael Jackson classic "Smooth Criminal."

Maddie looks around as spectators stand still, intrigued but unmoved. She leans into me. "I don't care how good they are. Four woodwinds isn't gonna carry a whole gym," she mumbles.

"Just wait," I say.

The flute and clarinets join as the song hurtles toward a chorus. By the time it gets there, the stage curtains fling open to reveal a full orchestra. Strings, percussion, and brass all flawlessly join the melody. People swarm to the dance floor like moths to a flame, pleasantly surprised at what they think was a well-planned party starter rather than a last-minute Hail Mary pass. More than a few people detour to swing by us on their way, each giving thumbs-up or shout-outs to Maddie. She's speechless through the whole procession, her face looking like she's about to be hit by a semitruck. I'm politely smiling through it. I know plenty of folks who'd question why I went all out to help someone who probably didn't deserve it. The answer is, I didn't. I went all out so that *everybody* could have a great night, deserving or not. Besides, why put a litmus test on who "deserves" to be happy?

I lean back into her, shouting above the noise: "Maddie, are you okay?"

She snaps out of her stupor and gives me the biggest, warmest hug, melting any remnants of ill will between us away. "*Ahhhhhh!!!* Thank you!" she says.

"You're welcome."

"Look, you have to tell people you coordinated this."

"I'm good," I say, and honestly I am.

"I insist." When I refuse again, she says, "You at least have to say something later tonight. If not about this, then about therapy. Get the word out." I know she won't take no for an answer, so I agree.

The song dies down, transitioning into another one, heavy on drums. I watch as Maddie triumphantly strolls into the arms of friends huddled on the dance floor. Someone taps me on the shoulder, and I turn and see Susie, the flutist. She has her hand out. I pull out a second envelope and give her the very last of eighty-seven $100 bills that I'd handed to each member of the full orchestra before the dance.

"Thanks for the favor," I say.

Susie stretches the Benjamin in front of her face. "Trust. The pleasure's all mine."

She walks away with almost the last of the $9,906. When all is said and done, I have $6 left. McDonald's money, as Dino might say. I can't help but wonder how this night could have gone down had I not come up just short of my goal. Would I have started booking reservations and squandered hundreds or even thousands on vacation deposits? Would I have spent my hard-earned money funding a fantasy? I'll never know, I guess.

The one silver lining of that heartbreaking heart-to-heart was my parents telling me to "Go be a teen." I can't think of a more "teen" thing than a high school dance, so I'm glad I could help everyone blow off their stress and do the "teen" thing, if just for one night.

# Twenty

**I'm getting nervous.** I've been here ninety minutes and still no Sterling. I know I shouldn't be bothered by this, but I am. It's like waiting for an eclipse. It could either be the most stunning thing you've seen or a massive letdown. But either way, the anticipation is a killer. On top of that, Maddie never told me when she wanted me to speak, so every time she walks toward the stage my heart jumps. I don't even know what to say. Maddie assumes since I have good interpersonal skills that I'm also a good public speaker, but that's the opposite of the truth.

I spend time doing the head-nod thing at the cusp of the dance floor, and then Keisha Illan asks me to dance, so I do the head-nod/hip-thrust/air-finger-point combo on the floor for a couple fast songs. Then I make my way over to the dessert table, where Dino's hoarding lemon squares. I sidle up to her and stare out at the dance floor. The full orchestra has been an amazing hit. They've played everything from Panic! At the Disco to Olivia Rodrigo's latest to old-school Mariah Carey. Since all the songs are instrumental, a wild thing is happening where students are just looking up the lyrics on their phones and doing crowd-sourced karaoke at the top of their lungs, which everybody seems to be getting a kick out of. Right now, half the crowd's laughing while the other half's belting lyrics to Post Malone's "Better Now." Dino and I sing along, too. I put my lips to her ear after the chorus.

"Why aren't you dancing?" I ask, speaking louder than normal over the tumult.

She takes a bite of a lemon square. "I'm not feeling completely festive after what happened with Rosie."

"Do you need to leave?" I ask.

Shaking her head, she says, "I think it's probably good for me to be around happy people right now."

We watch for a time, and then another question comes to me. "Do you miss going to things like this? With Rosie?"

"Yeah. It honestly is kind of surreal being alone. But I guess you can't find a new dance partner if you're still tangled up with an old one."

"True."

"And besides, dancing alone awhile can have its rewards."

I nod at this. Of all the surprises from doing therapy, the biggest by far were the breakups. Or more specifically, the reactions to those breakups. From Kayleigh Davis and Todd Goldstein a couple weeks ago to Gianna today, and many more in between. Of course they were sad, but a clear sense of relief underlaid the misery, like people were breaking free of something. It's the same sense I got talking to my parents. That somehow, the divorce might be liberating. A balloon untethered, just drifting up and away.

I wonder if I'll have to wait a long time for Sterling, just like I am tonight. If I'm so "tangled up" with her, I'm forgetting there are plenty of other great dancers.

Dino points toward the floor, and I look. Rod and Gianna are absolutely living it up, swaying and twisting and existing in their own world. Gianna's hair flings so wildly that half of it looks like it's on Rod's shoulder. Rod's long since lost his colonial hat, and neat cornrows tamp down what was just days ago a 'fro as big as a folding fan.

"I did not see that coming," I say.

"Maybe it's because you weren't looking hard enough."

I glance at Dino. She reads my baffled look and explains.

"I've known Gianna since middle school. She has *always* had a thing for funny, kindhearted types. If anything, *Jordan* was the exception to her rule. His looks gave him a massive edge with her. Probably blinded her to some things."

I don't remember who all Gianna dated in the past, but Dino's profile does make sense in a roundabout way. Gianna only got really popular the summer after eighth grade, when puberty did its whole swan routine on her. Before that, I'd always taken her to be kind of a free spirit, doing what she wanted to do. So I guess it is weird that she got sucked into that black hole of a relationship with Jordan.

Dino nudges my shoulder: "Speaking of which . . ."

I look toward the entrance to our right. Jordan's standing

there, sweaty, dressed formally but not at all like a royal. Tie loose around his neck and tuxedo shirt tucked out, like he just came from another party. He's got this flushed glaze on his face, too, like someone who's been hitting the bottle pretty hard tonight. He's scouring the dance floor, obviously looking for Gianna, who's blissfully unaware of his presence.

I don't know what gets into me, but I break away from Dino and march right over until I'm in front of him.

"Jordan, you need to leave!"

Without even looking at me, he shoves my head aside like I'm a gnat. I stumble sideways, catch myself, and then move right back into his way.

"*Move*, Shmelley," he says.

"Not until you promise not to bother them," I reply.

He glares at me, caught by something I let slip. "*Them?*" His glare returns to the floor, the searching look in his eyes even more urgent. Suddenly, a bright red light flicks on behind his irises. He sees the two.

Jordan careens toward Rod and Gianna like a meteor. I'm right behind him, reaching for but failing to grab any strip of fabric to slow him down. He pushes his way in, past the outer edges of the crowd, until the rest of it voluntarily splits to make way. A clarinet goes off-key, and soon after, the rest of the instruments crash into silence. Rod and Gianna stop dancing far too late to notice him charging their way, and Rod gets the worst of his arrival. Seeing Jordan push him is like seeing a bowling ball strike a pin. Rod goes sailing back, stumbling to his butt at the edge of the floor.

I look around for any chaperones, but they're nowhere in sight. Probably taking a smoke break. I turn back to Jordan and yell "Hey!" but he doesn't listen. Every bit of his attention is on Gianna.

"How could you do this to me?" he shouts.

I expect her to cower, but surprisingly she yells right back. "What? Are you embarrassed I refused to go to your parents' dumbass party and listen to their dumbass friends talk about how rich they all are? You think that's my idea of fun?"

"I think you should support your man every once in a while!"

"I've been supporting you for a *whole year* now! And for what? Bragging rights?" She points a finger into his chest. He swats it away. "Let me break the bad news to everybody: Gregg County High's All-American isn't all that much to brag about."

Jordan gets flustered at the gasps and hushed giggles behind him. He almost turns to shut them up, but he thinks better. Instead, he refocuses on a target he'd assumed would be much easier: his ex-girlfriend.

"You went behind my back, and for *him*?" he says, motioning toward Rod.

Dino and two guys are just now helping Rod up, and he looks shell-shocked.

Gianna steps into Jordan's space, wild eyes bearing down on him. She hand-waves a shredded curtain of hair from her face as she speaks: "I went with the person who actually gives a damn about what I'm feeling and what I want! Who doesn't just treat me like I'm arm candy!"

"You were lucky to have me!"

"I'm lucky to be done with you!"

They stare each other down. Both look like tinderboxes ready for a spark to blow. Someone says, "Gianna, it's not worth the fight," and she seems to agree. She sinks back from her tip-toes and spins away. Unfortunately Jordan isn't quite done. Her mouth wrenches in pain as he grabs her wrist. Right then, Rod storms onto the scene, shoving Jordan nearly as hard as he'd got-ten earlier. Gianna jerks her arm away as Jordan staggers. Rod stands his ground as Jordan tries to rush him. Two soccer guys struggle to hold Jordan back.

Adrenaline sends my nerves into overdrive. Jordan's yell-ing and slurring and cursing in new and nonsensical ways, and Rod has seconds before the pummeling of his life. I've got to help him. My first impulse is to run up and tackle Jordan while he's hampered. But I think of something better. Rod looks around, and I catch his eye right before I turn. I hurry away from the dance floor, wondering if he's thinking I'm abandon-ing him. I hustle to the center refreshments table and shakily grab the bowl brimming with red punch and ice. My arms tremble holding it. Several cups of liquid slosh out as I wobble back, staining my cuffs and wetting the floor. I come up to the side of Jordan, just as he's twisting away from our teammates' grips. It's right when he's freed himself that he sees me. The anger consuming his face turns to drunken confusion.

"Why don't you cool off, bro?" I yell, lunging for him.

Most of it gets onto Jordan's face and chest. Some of it,

unfortunately, gets on those nearest him. But to them, at least judging from their faces, it's well worth the laugh at his expense.

Jordan staggers back, shocked into temporary sobriety.

"What did you do?" he yells.

I freeze, seeing his shock quickly build into rage. In concocting this plan, I'd failed to account for the obvious: that next he'd come for me. I ball up my fists, ready to do any damage I can when I see Rod walking up behind him. He crouches, grabs a handful of ice, and drops it right down into Jordan's pants.

Jordan wheels around in the clumsiest of ways, losing his footing on the slippery floor and falling like a circus clown. Eventually, he gets upright and makes all kinds of feints toward charging me and Rod, but concerned friends and his own unsteadiness convince him otherwise. He heads toward the doors to applause from a fed-up crowd. Gianna hugs Rod and plants a kiss on his cheek.

Two chaperones barrel into the main entry, surely having just heard the tail end of the tumult. Both yell at Jordan while escorting him out to make sure he leaves, threatening at least twice to call the cops if he doesn't. The lights come on, and the dance pauses for five minutes as students marshal any napkins and paper towels they can find, along with those huge janitor mops and brooms from behind the stage. We make quick work of cleaning, and the orchestra kicks up again with "Better Now."

Rod comes over as I crouch and scour the hardwood for any loose ice chips. He taps my shoulder. I stand to his height, noticing the deadly serious look on his face.

"Jordan's gonna be a problem come Monday," he says.

"Yep. Majorly."

He puts a fist right in front of my waist. "Nothing we can't handle together, though."

"Right," I say, smiling.

I dap him up, and he's lifting and bear-hugging me before I know it. I'm just inches off the ground, but somehow I'm still in the clouds.

# Twenty-One

**I'm in the** middle of scarfing down my fifth pizza roll when I feel a tug at my elbow.

"You're up next" is all Maddie says.

I'd been feeling good up until that moment. Jordan had been vanquished, and Rod and I had made up. I'd assumed Sterling wasn't gonna show, so most of my nerves had frittered away. And everyone looked to be having a great time.

All in all, I'd call that a success. The speech is the last hurdle to what I'd chalk up as a good night. Unfortunately I've had zero time to prepare and nothing really to say. Maddie points me toward the stage, and I begin a slow walk around the dance floor. The lectern that holds the microphone is on the stage apron, right in front of where the orchestra conductor is waving his baton like some fantasy movie wizard. I climb a set of four steps and stand to the side as they furiously play a song I don't recognize.

I raise a hand to my brow before peering out into the crowd. The strobing purples and reds disorient me, and I nearly stumble back and get swallowed by the mass of curtains behind me. The song ends and a new, slower one begins. Once I regain my bearings, I look out again. It's not my intention, but I end up counting the people I spot who were on my client roster.

There's Jarron Thomas, who came to me three weeks ago with no more self-confidence than could fit in a Dixie cup. Here he is now, happily dancing with Kaitlyn Lu, the first girl he'd ever asked out.

There's Reese Liggatt, the girl who'd practically sealed herself off from the world after a particularly traumatic best friend breakup last fall. She's here now, with a *new* friend, quietly observing from a top bleacher. And that's enough.

There are the Carmichael twins, Ginny and Gretchen, arm in arm as they sing Green Day's "Good Riddance (Time of Your Life)" like it's "Auld Lang Syne" at New Year's. A far cry from when they were bickering about having the same boy crush, the same mutual friends, and the same frustrating inability to extricate themselves from each other's shadow.

There's Avery, Garrison, and Gianna. The codependent, the skeptic, and the pleaser. Also the *Firsts*—my Firsts. The ones who didn't quit on me even when things got bad. They're still working through their issues, and I'm as proud of them tonight as I was that very first day they showed up with bags of candy.

And then there's the person I'm proudest of seeing, primarily because I *didn't*. Ashlynn Carter came to me knowing she'd been depressed for some time. Flagging school grades, looming college apps, and the recent death of her mother had proven a perfect storm of fear and loathing and anxiety. Too much for any kid to bear. She'd never actually said the word "suicide," but expressing an indifference to "being here" was more than enough. At the end of our intake, when she asked how I could help her, I got out my laptop and googled "Licensed Psychologists in Gregg County." I canceled my other appointments that day and skipped all of third period so we could see who might be the best fit for her. Afterward, I walked with her to a school guidance counselor's office, and together they talked and contacted her dad to let him know.

Ashlynn came by yesterday to thank me, saying she wasn't out of the woods but could at least see light filtering in through the leaves. Her words "made my eyeballs sweat," as Dad would say. She never offered to pay. I never would've accepted it anyway. I know it's not about me, but she taught me more about how to really help someone during that encounter than all my other sessions combined.

Looking out at them, I get the greedy kind of goose bumps— the ones that aren't just content with consuming my arms but make a meal of my entire body. They give me both the language and the courage to speak. If these people were brave enough to seek help, I can surely find the mettle needed to advocate for them and so many others.

I don't know exactly what I taught or gave them all. I doubt I ever will. But I do know what they gave me. A place to go. A refuge in a trying time. A pu'uhonua. And for that, I'll forever be grateful.

The song dies, and Maddie rushes up to introduce me.

Because I insisted she leave it out, she doesn't mention my financial contribution to the night. But she does point and smile and say, "This guy is more of a hero than most of us know."

I hear applause and get bashful. I push through it as I walk to the lectern. The crowd gets settled and silent, save for a couple whoops, one person yelling "Kalvin!" and another shouting "Candyman!" toward the back.

*Candy Guy*, I correct, if only in my mind.

I position the microphone until it's about three inches from my lips. Then I clear my throat, fully expecting to flinch at the feedback because that's always how it goes in the movies. I'm surprised and slightly knocked off-kilter when there's none.

I take a deep breath and begin.

"Hi, guys. I'm Kalvin." I wave, and there are sprouts of laughter. I nervously chuckle but continue: "As you've learned over the past few weeks, I'm much more of a listener than a talker. So it was a shock when I got asked to speak tonight. And in the interest of keeping the party going and sparing me the embarrassment, I'm gonna keep this short. . . ."

A door creaks at the opposite end of the gym, and a wedge of light appears against a dark wall lined with conference championship banners. I crane my neck and squint to see what the crowd can't.

A guy and a girl slip in and at first pin themselves to the back wall like paintings. Light finds its way to them, showing their faces. My heart sinks. It's Sterling and Chadwick. I lose my train of thought. "But if I, um . . ."

The crowd stares at me. I grip the microphone tighter. A lump gathers in my throat, choking out any words. I don't know what to say. I have *nothing* to say to this.

There's another noise. I look out again. Sterling and Chadwick are inching toward the edge of the crowd. Sterling looks back, then Chadwick, as another girl slinks into the gym, careful to guide the door so that it shuts more quietly than it opened.

*Grace.*

My lips open again, but no sound comes, because I'm not even trying to speak anymore. I'm just shocked at what's happening. Slowly, Grace walks closer. Sterling nods at Chadwick. His nod in return is barely perceptible but still there. He goes to Grace and takes her hand. And my heart explodes as Sterling comes to me.

I can't quite make out the color of her dress in the darkness, but I see parts of it shimmer like a peaceful lake with each step she takes into the crowd. She weaves her way through, her movements as easy as silk or a summer breeze, and when she gets closer to the front, I notice another shimmer. This one, at her cheeks.

*Has she been crying?*

I can't stop looking at her. The smile she gives me is a marriage of happy and sad, grieving and grateful.

Someone coughs, and I realize I've stopped speaking for God knows how long. I put my lips back in front of the mic.

"If I were to ask you *How are you?* right now, most of you would say *I'm fine.* It's our default answer. We say it all the time.

I do it, too. It's what we're conditioned to say. But that answer, a lot of times, is a way to short-circuit the truth. That we're not fine but just don't want to think about how 'not fine' we are. Or maybe we're not really feeling at all, because we've never been taught how."

The audience is attentive. My knees get wobbly thinking that there are hundreds of people out there. I glance at Sterling. Her nod grounds me, steadies me. I push on.

"The 'fine' in *I'm fine* is what my parents would call an 'enough' word. It says just enough to keep people from prodding. Think about it: If you really felt *good*, you'd say *I feel good*. But 'fine' is like saying I feel good *enough*. Good enough to survive. Good enough to get by. Good enough to not need help. And we do that because from the beginning of our founding, American society has obsessed over rugged individualism and self-reliance. We're not supposed to need others to achieve accolades or health or happiness. And if we need others, there's something wrong with us. And we don't talk about how messed up that is, especially when it comes to us teens . . ."

Somebody shouts "Preach!"

My breathing quickens, spurred on by anger. *Righteous* anger. Not for me. For all of us. My words come quicker, too, and surprisingly more fluid.

"Many of us are in the best physical health we'll ever be in. But our mental health too often languishes. Society tells us we should be living the teen movie dream: first crushes and kisses, great parties and sports glory. College visits and hard-earned graduation. It glosses right over the not-so-great things. Depression. Anxiety. Trauma. They affect us all, but we don't talk about those things. We're encouraged to keep them to ourselves. To sugarcoat our suffering. To be *fine*, even if we're not. And that makes us scared. Scared that if we *do* talk that means we're weak. We're abnormal. We're somehow deserving of our pain."

I scan the audience again and see all those faces that brought me here. Reese and Gianna and Jarron and Ashlynn. But more than that, I see everybody else. Every nameless, anonymous person who needs this message, too. I grip the arm of the microphone tight, my words coming out slow and unsure, but still ringing clear:

"Even though I don't like talking, I'd make this speech every day if I could. Because I know for all the kids I've counseled, ten times as many are hurting in silence. So please hear me out." I shake my head. "You're not weak."

I keep shaking it. "You're not abnormal. You're not deserving of pain. You're human."

My eyes find Sterling as my throat starts to ache. Her eyes are closed, but she's nodding at my words, like she's found in them an oasis in the desert. I recall the conversations we had. How so many times during our talks, I felt like I'd found the same.

My voice breaks as I conclude: "Somebody once asked me what's the best advice I could possibly give. I didn't have an answer at the time, but I do now: *Get help*. Get help, get help, get help."

I take my hand from the mic and bolt stage right. I'm well

behind the curtains before the first wave of applause bleeds into my ears. The sound warms me, as well as the pats to the back by a few members of the orchestra. I'm glad my classmates liked it, but I sincerely *hope* they heard it.

The music cranks up again, and I creep back to the curtains, peeking out. I make sure the crowd is lost in the music before sneaking off the stage. I navigate the perimeter of the gym, my head at a slight downward tilt to avoid any eye contact. It's not until I'm back at the table with the pizza rolls that I look up. When I do, Dino, Rod, and Maddie are right there, smiling. I look for Sterling, but I don't see her.

Each takes turns hugging me, congratulating me on my speech.

"We need an encore!" Dino yells.

"Not gonna happen," I say.

Dino lets out an exaggerated sigh. "Well, I'd settle for a toast, if you hadn't given Jordan a bath with all the punch."

"Do you hear anyone complaining?" I ask.

Dino crosses her arms.

Maddie makes a C out of a raised hand as if she's holding a cup. "Well, imaginary toast it is, then!"

I jump in with "Not just for me. For everyone."

"Fine," she says. "To Kalvin, the hero of the night!"

Rod and I raise our pretend glasses, clinking it to hers. Rod says, "To Maddie, who put on a helluva ball."

Then me: "To Rod, living the teen movie dream as we speak!"

We all look at Dino. Her arms are still crossed, her lips pursed and twisted to one side.

Maddie glances at us quizzically, so Rod offers an explanation: "Snubbed Dino tends not to play well with others."

"I do too!" Dino snaps.

"You have a history of this," he replies.

"Since when?" she asks.

"Since third grade, when you punched Jimmy Mattingly for not picking you in red rover!"

"Kara Walters had the twiggiest arms *by far*! Everybody could see that! Why pick her before me?"

Dino stops and turns to me, and I get a sense of déjà vu, once again called upon as the arbiter of another one of her and Rod's disputes. Just like a month ago in the cafeteria. Just like in her car over the "Black Aaron Burr" saga.

Just like old times.

I shrug. "Geraldine, you do have a bit of a problem."

As Dino releases a stream of curses, Maddie looks at me aghast. "Geraldine?"

I nod. "Hence, the artful but still somewhat regrettable 'Dino.'"

"Why doesn't she just go by her middle name?" Maddie asks.

Rod and I look at each other and burst out laughing. Dino goes silent, narrowing her eyes at each of us. Rod manages to eke out an answer between peals of stomach-cramping laughter. "Her . . . it's just . . . her middle name's . . . *Hattie*!"

Rod eventually has to sit on the hardwood, he's laughing so hard. Dino points threateningly at him. "Screw you!"

Maddie looks at her as if she'd just lost a favored pet. Both sympathy and pity swirl in her voice as she says, "Those names. Together. *How?*"

Dino's hands slap her waist. "I know, right? It's like my parents' lifelong dream for me was to be a sharecropper's wife!"

I double over at that, and it takes two full minutes and two false starts for me and Rod to regain our composure. So long that Dino has time to get angrier, get over it, and get a plate for more desserts. We finally settle, and when Gianna appears, pulling Rod to the dance floor, I look for Sterling again. I still don't see her. But when I feel a tap at my shoulder, I know who it is.

I turn, and we hug in a way that's as warm as a banked fire in winter.

"Hi," Sterling says.

"Hi."

Sterling looks at Dino. "So how'd you end up with such a compassionate and insightful friend?" she asks.

Dino stuffs half a lemon square in her mouth and shrugs. Chewing, she mutters, "It takes a village."

Maddie cups her hands over her face and whimpers, "Oh, you guys are gonna make me cry! Just sooo wholesome! I'm so sorry I ever even believed you'd have started that rumor last year."

"What rumor?" Sterling asks.

"That stu-gov's suckers were pre-licked."

Dino gasps, nearly choking on her lemon square. Her eyes bulge, and I hit her back three times just to make sure she spits it all out into her napkin. We wait as she coughs herself back to normal and then looks right at Maddie. "You thought *Kalvin* started that rumor?" Dino says hoarsely, then shakes her head. "Girl, *I* started that rumor!"

"*You* started that rumor?" I shout.

"Are you serious?" Maddie says.

"Yeah, *yeah*! Because I thought you were trying to move in on my girlfriend at the time, Rosie, when you two were pulling those all-nighters for your newscast stuff, but it turns out you weren't, and I found out like a month later that you were actually straight anyway because you started going out with Bryson Tomlin. But honestly, it still feels justified because you were annoying AF last year."

I'm absolutely stunned. All the grief Maddie had been giving me this whole year was because of Dino's subterfuge. So much could've been prevented had Dino not been willing to burn it all down à la that meme with the girl who's smiling at the camera as a house blazes in the background.

Dino turns to me, grinning sheepishly. "My bad, Kal! Who'd have thought that would've come back to haunt you. Small world, though, huh?"

I don't respond. Scratch that. My blank face is its own response.

"Wait, you think I'm *straight*?" Maddie blurts, catching all of us off guard.

Cautiously Dino asks, "You aren't?"

"I'm bi."

It takes a second for the implication to click with the

two, as if they're checking back over a completed math problem before declaring it solved. However, Sterling and I get it immediately. She grabs my hand, gently squeezing. I squeeze back. Our thin smiles are somehow both unassuming and all-knowing.

Dino nods toward the center of the gym. "Do you . . . wanna dance?"

"Sure."

Maddie takes her hand, and they walk out together.

I watch as they disappear into the crowd, thinking they'll either kill each other or start a world-renowned crime syndicate together. Maybe both. I'm not mad about it, though. I guess I'll enjoy the ride.

Sterling pulls me to the floor. We make our way to the center, and I feel the pinprick of regret that our first dance came so late. But she looks wildly happy, despite the tear stains still faintly showing. That next hour is unbridled and weightless, as if our feet are always moving but never touching the ground. We slow dance to ballads and shout and jump along to angsty teen tracks. We grind without inhibition to the sexier tracks, like our bodies are fused together. And we even expertly execute the silly dances like the Kid 'n Play Kick Step as hordes of white folks stare at us like we've just invented the wheel.

Somehow, during that time, we manage to catch up. I tell her about how Maddie and I brokered a truce and how the orchestra came to be. She weaves in the narrative of how she and Chadwick broke up earlier that night. How she was sad but also happy. How he was the same.

The strings float into the last song. I recognize it. Taylor Swift's "Wildest Dreams." Curiously the percussion, brass, and woodwinds sections rise from their seats, grabbing their instrument cases as if they're no longer needed. The movement is a momentary distraction, though.

I turn back to Sterling, leaning in and whispering, "I'm sorry."

"Sorry for what?" she asks.

"You didn't get your dream ball."

"How so?"

"You and Chadwick."

She cups my shoulders, and I round my hands behind her waist for a last slow dance. Her look is as sincere as I've ever seen it. I lose myself for a moment in her eyes, deep brown flecked with gold at the edges. Her words pull me back. "Dreams change, Kal. And realities."

*Dreams change.*

I think about the "dream" I started out with a month ago: that I'd compel my parents to their Happily Ever After. The plan failed miserably. It needed to. And I'm still coming to grips with that. But if their Happily Ever After happens to be apart from each other, who am I to judge or interfere?

*And realities.*

I think back to when Sterling and I had our *sweet*-cute last month: the shy candy pusher cornered in a closet with a girl way out of his league. Who'd have thought we'd end up here together? On the same page but in our own unique stories. We are our own puʻuhonua.

I bite my lip before adding, "And people, too."

Two messed-up people in a crowd of hundreds more. But getting less messed up once we realize others are just like us, in different ways. Once we know that we're not alone.

Sterling shrugs as I glance at the movement around us. "Besides, I got nearly everything." She runs a hand down the waistline of her gown. "Finally found a great dress. Royalty theme. A freaking full symphony orchestra. All that's missing is the candy."

"You sure about that?"

The question catches her off guard and she stops dancing. "What? You gonna give a signal or something and candy's gonna fall from the rafters?" Her incredulous look turns vaguely suspicious for just a moment as she considers if that could be within the realm of possibility.

I glance up. She does, too. All we see is rafters. No candy.

"Sounds kind of cliché, if you ask me."

"Kinda," she replies, still looking.

"Besides, seems hazardous, too."

"Oh, definitely," she says, her eyes still up.

"Are you paranoid?" I ask.

"Maybe. Are you acting a little weird right now?"

"I dunno," I answer. "Maybe I'm just really good at reading a room. You know, that's a skill therapists tend to have, right?"

Her chin lowers. Lines come to her brow as she squints at me. She mouths *What*— as her neck turns and she scans the gym. She realizes what's happening when the first mini Snickers rains down from a high arc like a meteorite, hitting the arm of the person next to us.

"Oh my God," she mutters. I look around and see what she sees. The non-strings orchestra players line the sideline. Their instrument cases are open but they're filled with candy. All my stash plus what I "purchased" from stu-gov. They look wildly thrilled to be lobbing candy at the dance floor, and we have to hold our hands over our heads to shield ourselves from the bombardment.

We crouch as mini Twix and Starbursts and M&M'S bags pelt our shoulders and backs.

"Did you do this?!" she asks, laughing.

"I thought you might appreciate it!"

She bear-crawls toward me for what begins as a hug but what ends as her squealing and hanging on for dear life while I cover her from what feels like confectionery artillery fire. Everybody's screaming and shouting and diving for candy in the most chaotic and joyful of ways.

When it's over, the last riffs of "Wildest Dreams" are still playing. We both stand as others around us corral and pocket as much candy as they can. I hand her a single fun-sized Snickers. Her absolute favorite. The candy that started it all. She gets the significance. Her eyes pinch shut as she holds it up between us.

She clamps her mouth tight with a hand as a tear beads down her cheek. She's shaky.

"Funny that this is how the party ends," I say.

Her eyes spring open and she sniffles. She shakes her head. "No," she says, her voice cracking. "The party is just beginning."

We kiss, and it's the sweetest moment of either of our lives.

# Acknowledgments

There are so, so many.

To my wife, my best friend. The person who gave me every avenue available and every word of encouragement under the sun. This story couldn't have made it to this point in the universe without you. I will keep this short because showing the ways I'm truly grateful would take up an entire book, itself.

To Mom and Dad.

Mom: I remember the very evening, decades ago, when you told me I could be a good writer. I started that night. And look at the blaze your spark created. I'm forever thankful for that, and the countless other "Mom things" you've done to help me along the way.

Dad: I aspire to write positive, uplifting stories that center positive, uplifting people. Nobody in my life embodies that more than you. Thank you.

London and Channing. My two effervescent bundles of energy and laughter. I hope you'll read this one day. I hope this will make you a tenth as proud as you make me every day. I'm glad to be your father.

To my sisters. Shannon, the best storyteller I know. I've been listening for years, learning how to weave tales out of precise emotions and piquant words. Heather, the funniest of us all. You taught me that wit is one of the greatest weapons in a person's arsenal.

To the grandmothers. I'm sad neither of you could be here to see this. But somehow, I know you can see this. And I want to say thank you for all you've done for those who came after you.

To "Mama Gaskin." Your willingness to help and unfailing positivity has meant the world to me and Ashly and our endeavors. We are forever grateful.

To the extended family (especially the Aunts). Thank you for always having my back. I know you've believed in me ever since I was a young boy. And believe me . . . it made a difference.

To the good bosses. Thanks. To the good teachers. Thanks, as well.

To Drs. Gold, Pearce, and Keaton-Jackson. You weren't just "good" to me but great. I regard my years at NC Central as two of the hardest, most fulfilling, proudest years of my life. Eagle pride!

To Stacy and Phil. Two of the most loyal friends and hype men a guy could ever have. I can guarantee I wouldn't be in the place I'm in today if not for you. Phil: I absolutely know you would've enjoyed this book, and that makes me smile.

To the Fellas' Night crew. Your companionship and conversations were top-notch. I'll remember some of those nights for decades to come.

New Visions Writers' Group. You welcomed me, a young writer, to develop a curriculum and impart what little knowledge I had all those years ago. You saw something in me when there wasn't all that much to see. What a confidence booster that is for an upstart.

To Jumata Emill and Kim Johnson. My OG CPs. You will always be the first "fans" of my work, and I'm so glad you've helped me sharpen my craft as iron sharpens iron. I look forward to seeing you both on our respective tours.

To Alyssa Miele. LOL. I was *not* prepared for a seventeen-page critique of a manuscript I'd considered close to perfect! But that's why you're the expert, the editor extraordinaire. I'm glad you loved this story, and I'm so appreciative you've squeezed every bit of potential out of it. Hopefully our shared love of good prose and great candy will carry us far.

To Jon Cobb. Somehow, five years ago you got me and my jokes and my characters and my ambitious story arcs and expansive plans for the future. I'm so glad we've been able to work and synergize together through countless nos and some absolutely world-changing yesses. Thank you for your wisdom, your positive-but-firm critiques, your care and concern, and so much more. Here's hoping for decades of more great news to come.

Thank you, God. Thank you.